A WIFE FOR SILAS

THE DARK LIFE OF SILAS
BOOK ONE

TORI SULLIVAN

AUTHOR'S NOTE

Dear reader,

Let me preface this by saying: **THIS BOOK IS NOT A ROMANCE**. This book is a dark er0tic horror that has heavy dark romance themes, but it does **NOT** end in an HEA.

The triggers are listed below. Please read responsibly and proceed with caution.

-Tori

TRIGGERS

- Non-con
- Graphic violence
- On page sexual assault
- Murder

- Mental illness depiction (sociopath/psychopath)
- Foster child abuse (flashback)
- Brief mention of child trafficking
- Domestic violence

PROLOGUE
SILAS

I ground my teeth as I flipped through the multiple files of women presented to me.

"I pay these fucks a shit ton of money and they've yet to find what I'm actually looking for," I muttered.

My driver and right-hand man, Donovan, glanced at me in the rear view mirror.

"You ever think you might just be picky as hell when it comes to the woman you want?" he teased. "I mean, you can always do things the normal way and try to—"

"Dating is out," I interrupted, finishing his thought. "I don't need love; I just need a stand-in wife to give me an heir."

"And then?"

I shrugged. "Kill her, sell her, break her, use her. Depends on her actions, though."

Dating wasn't ideal for the kind of life I led. On the outside, I was a respectable man in society. I owned several hotels and casinos, donated large sums of money to good causes around the city, and donated the new wing to our children's hospital.

Silas Arnett, the generous savior and smart business man, they'd say. But that was all a mask for the dirty shit I did behind the shiny exterior, the dark underbelly of Arnett Enterprises that I strived to keep secret.

Dating the normal way left too many liabilities in the event that my "wife" wanted to extort me out of money or blackmail me. All it would take was one scorned woman wanting revenge to send my entire empire burning to the ground as well as putting me behind bars for the rest of my life.

And I couldn't fucking have that.

Because of that, I was Palmetto Beach's most elusive bachelor, one women dreamed to be with but never had the chance to. If they knew the dark, depraved fuckery they'd be subjected to while in a relationship with me, they'd realize they were better off not being on my radar.

I flipped through the files once more, just to be sure there weren't any hidden gems I'd skipped. I'd contracted my top two trafficking guys, Jalen and Tommy, to scout potential victims for me with a certain criteria:

-*Easy to grab*
-*Someone no one would miss*
-*Clean bill of health*
-*Somone who could pass as belonging in my elite circle*
-*Someone young enough to bear my heir*

But none of the women in these Manila folders on my lap fit my entire list. I'd yet to find a woman that ticked off all of my boxes. If they were easy to grab, then there wasn't a guarantee that no one would report them as missing. If they weren't on anyone's radar, they were either strung out on drugs, not young enough, or didn't have a clean bill of health. There was always something wrong with every single girl they presented to me, and I was close to putting a bullet in both of them for fucking wasting both my time and my money.

"Patience, man. If you're wanting to find the perfect woman, you're gonna need patience," Donny continued.

I shook my head. I wasn't looking for a woman who was already perfect; no woman would be exactly what I needed her to be. I just needed the perfect canvas to create the perfect woman that would fit into my life. Sure, any woman I came across would kill themselves to share my bed, but they only knew Silas Arnett the billionaire, business tycoon, and philanthropist.

They didn't know Silas the human trafficker, the tormentor, the killer, the sociopath.

"Time isn't on my side, Donny. You know that," I finally said. "Having a kid out of wedlock or without an active mother would only cause headlines, and I don't need more people than necessary in my business."

My phone vibrated in the breast pocket of my jacket. I lifted an eyebrow when I saw the text preview from Harold, my best friend and business partner.

Harold: I think I found the solution to your problem. Call me when you get a chance.

A small grin settled on my lips as I exited the text thread and called him. Harold was just as protective over our businesses—both legal and not—so if he had a potential woman he thought would work for me, I knew it was something he'd already researched a great deal before bringing it up to me.

"*I think that's the fastest you've called me whenever I tell you to get back to me,*" Harold mused upon answering.

My gaze moved to the car window to watch the scenery moving past outside.

"You've peaked my curiosity, and right on time, too. I was looking at the girls Jalen and Tommy found and I'm not impressed." A frown settled on my lips as I looked down at the file still open on my lap. "One of the women has a picture that I'm ninety-eight percent sure is a fucking mugshot."

Harold's chuckle filled the line. "*That bad, huh?*"

"Very, which is why I'm interested in your solution." I flipped the folder closed and put the stack on the seat next to me. "Talk to me."

"*We've had an incident this morning where we've had to fire an administrative assistant,*" he started. "*There'd been reports that she'd been embezzling money out of the business accounts whenever she was given a card to make business purchases. After I completed the investigation to determine if the claims were true, I officially fired her today.*"

I rolled my eyes. "Let me get this straight; you think a fucking thief is the solution to my problem? If that's the case, I should just settle for one of these drug addicts on my lap," I stated, my voice tight.

"*Let me finish before you get your dick in a twist,*" Harold said on a sigh. "*She's perfect because she's checked off all your boxes. She's young enough to have kids, aged out of the foster system so she has no family, and she would look like a believ-*"

able option for your wife. You'd have to get your doctor to check her out to confirm her bill of health, but I already have the perfect way to grab her."

I pinched the bridge of my nose and closed my eyes, forcing myself not to become irritated until I heard his entire plan. "And what's that, Harold?"

"I already had her arrested before she tried to run off," he said.

"How the——"

"I've already made the proper phone calls to have her processed as inmates usually are. She'll get an inmate number and all that, but she'll be brought to you by Chief Ansley instead of going to jail. The judge will come visit you as well to accept her guilty plea and sentence her without trial. It'll be on record that she's in prison, so as far as the free world is concerned, she's in jail for a few years."

I let his words settle into my mind, nodding my head as I processed everything. The idea was genius, really. It would take some work having to create another identity for her so that those who weren't in my pocket didn't ask too many questions, but it was the perfect scenario.

Had I snatched up a random woman, there would always be that chance that she'd run off or try to escape. With this woman, there was nowhere to go. If she escaped me, there was no life for her in the outside world when she was supposed to be in prison. It would make my job a hell of a lot easier. She'd only have two choices: submit and become my wife or go back to prison where I'd have her killed.

"*You still there?*" Harold asked, shattering my musings.

"Yeah, I'm here. I was just thinking on what you said."

"*So, what do you think? Am I a fucking genius or am I a fucking genius?*"

I smiled and nodded, though he couldn't see that. "You know you're a fucking genius, Harold."

"*See? I told you this would be a good solution. You shouldn't doubt your best friend.*"

"You know it takes me a little bit to see your whole vision, but I never doubt you."

"*Then act like it instead of nearly biting my head off when you don't like something I've said,*" he teased. "*Anyway, where are you headed? I need to let the transporters know when to expect you.*"

Donovan pulled up to the headquarters building of Arnett Enterprises, slowing to a stop in front of the entrance. "I just got to the office. I have a few things I have to handle before heading home for the evening."

"*Should I tell them to hold her until you're ready for her?*"

Donovan got out of the car and walked around, opening the back door for me. I held up a hand and shook my head when he looked at me with a raised brow. He nodded his understanding and closed the door again, blanketing me in privacy once more.

"No. Go ahead and have them take her to my place. I'll make the appropriate calls to everyone to have them prepare her for my arrival. I'm sure processing and all that takes time, yes?"

"*It can take however long you'd like it to. I've requested that our guys be the ones to handle her. Chief Ansley guaranteed me that he would be the one spearheading her processing.*"

"Good. Remind me to make a transfer to his account to thank him for his urgency in this matter," I said.

"*Already handled.*"

"Are you at the headquarters?" I asked, lightly knocking on the window to alert Donovan.

"*Yeah, I'm still here. Stop by my office on your way in to grab the file on this woman,*" he said.

I got out of the car when Donovan opened the door, stepping onto the sidewalk. "Perfect. See you in five then."

"*See you then, brother,*" he said and hung up.

"What's got you grinning like a Cheshire cat?" Donovan asked with a grin of his own, closing the door when I stepped away from the car.

"My search is finally over," I said. I glanced around at the passing people on the sidewalk, being sure to choose my words carefully. "Harold was telling me about a situation that happened that deemed someone as the perfect fit for what I need."

"And if it's got you grinning like that, I can only assume that it's just what you're looking for."

"Seems like it so far. I'll fill you in on it later, though." I headed toward the glass doors of the building. "I should be ready to head home in about three hours. I'll call you if I finish before then."

He nodded. "You got it," he said and strolled around the car to the driver's side, disappearing inside.

Everyone greeted me when I entered the building, the blonde receptionist, Lynne, smiling at me when I passed her.

"Good afternoon, Mr. Arnett," she said, her voice bubbly and inviting. She was the granddaughter of one of the executives here, one we knew could keep her mouth shut about certain things.

Harold and I made it a point to only have people we could trust work for any of our companies. Everyone that worked for Arnett Enterprises had something to lose if the truth were to get out, and having something to lose was the best incentive for keeping people quiet.

"Same to you, Lynn. Tell your grandfather I said hello," I said in passing with a small smile, making a beeline for the elevators.

Excited energy buzzed through my blood as I rode up

to the tenth floor, curious to know more about this woman. Considering that we didn't hire people without a familial connection to another executive here, it was baffling that a woman like that ended up in an administrative assistant position.

They were usually given cleaning jobs or working in the building's food court. I couldn't help but wonder what she might've known about the company, what she was exposed to, or whether or not she'd try to use whatever info she had in order to gain leverage in her current situation.

Just that quick, my excitement morphed into annoyance as I got off the elevator and stalked to Harold's office. He looked up at me with a raised brow when I entered without knocking.

"You know, on a normal day, this is usually around the time where the secretary comes in to suck my cock," he said, leaning back into his seat with a frown. "Unless you want an eyeful of shit you can't unsee, it's common courtesy to knock before you open closed doors."

I rolled my eyes and sat across from his desk. "We shared a dorm in college. There's nothing you can do that I haven't already seen. Now, the file; where is it?"

He handed me a folder with all of the information she'd submitted when she was hired. "What the hell has you in a mood that fast? I literally just got off the phone with you," Harold said.

I opened the file and scanned the contents. "On the way up here, I was trying to figure out how a woman that was an orphan ended up in the position she was in," I said idly, my eyes falling on her work badge with her picture on it.

"Through the program you set up a few years ago," Harold said with a dismissive wave of his hand. "Or have you already forgotten about that?"

Of course. A few years ago, I'd decided to help young adults aging out of the system by offering them a decent enough job to help them get on their feet. They were almost always assigned jobs that wouldn't require them to ever discover what went on behind the scenes. When one guy got a little too close to classified information and threaten to go to the news with what he'd found if I didn't give him more money, I'd killed both the program and him immediately. I shook my head.

"No. I just thought that I'd closed it and that we'd let go of anyone who was hired under the program."

"It's closed now, but somehow she slipped under the radar."

I read over her information.

Name: Lia McIntyre

Position: Administrative Assistant to Joyce Connor
Current Age: 26
Start date: 5-26-2018
Termination date: 1-21-2022
Termination reason: Embezzlement of company money valued at over $200,000.

"Yeah, long enough to embezzle money," I mumbled, looking back to her photo. She had dirty blonde hair that appeared to be a tad bit greasy, and a small smile on her lips that didn't reach her eyes. Nothing about her was memorable or stood out, and from this photo, she definitely wasn't the type of woman that would've been seen on my arm.

But there's nothing a makeover can't fix, I thought with a sigh, closing the folder and handing it back to Harold.

"What do you think?"

I shrugged. "She'll have to do for now. I'm sure she could use some cleaning up and refinement, but she'll work for now. She's better than the bullshit Jalen and Tommy have shown me lately."

Harold grinned. "Good. I'll keep you up-to-date so that you can prepare your team of people for her." Mischief twinkled in his eyes as he regarded me. "You know, finding a woman was the easy part. The hard part will be shaping her into your wife."

But it wouldn't be. I was no stranger to bending a woman to my will, either by false seduction or by force. And considering this bitch stole money from me, she'd have to pay me back in a good bit of blood before she and I were even.

"Like I said, she doesn't have many options. Either she submits and does what she's told or I'll make her life a living hell before I kill her."

Harold smirked and shook his head. "If only she knew that jail would've been her best option," he mused, which made me grin.

"She doesn't know that yet and by the time she does, it'll be too late." I looked at my watch. "Anyway, I have some paperwork to finish and phone calls to make so keep tabs on that for me," I said as I stood to my feet.

"Of course. You'll have to tell me how she settles in later on," he called after me.

I nodded to acknowledge I'd heard him as I made my way out of his office and strolled to mine. The corner office views were my favorite part of this building, smack dab in the middle of downtown with a beautiful city skyline view right from my desk. One wall was nothing but bookcases with a tinted glass covering over them, soft backlights casting a glow on the titles on display. The interior designer picked this bullshit desk that I personally thought was odd with its architectural-like build, but it still somehow fit into the space perfectly fine.

When I sat behind my desk, I pulled out my phone and called Maryse, one of the women who worked for me at home. There was so much shit that needed to be done for this woman and I knew she and the other women would be the perfect ones for this job.

"*Good afternoon, Mr. Arnett. What can I do for you?*" she said upon answering.

"I've finally found the woman I've been looking for, so she'll be arriving soon," I replied. "I need you and the girls to give her the works when she arrives. Spare no expense."

"*Of course, Mr. Arnett. If you're not here by the time we're done with her, do you have a preference on where she's put?*"

I ran my hand along the stubble growing on my jawline. "Lock her in the guest bedroom," I instructed. "And be sure to give her the manual I've created as well. I'll be sending you an email with an updated version of a few sections so that it's personalized for her specific situation. Please print them and put them in there as well."

When I'd first come up with the idea, I'd made this extensive binder filled with everything the woman in my possession would need to know. It was generic because I'd planned to take a random woman, but I wanted this woman to believe that this had always been personal. It would be a real eye-opener when she saw her name explicitly stated, solidifying how badly she truly fucked up.

"*Of course, Mr. Arnett.*"

"Also, call the doctor and have him give her a full check up. I need to ensure that everything is good in that regard since I don't have any medical records on her."

"*He's actually already here. One of the landscapers had a small accident and needed stitches,*" she said.

I nodded. "Good. Ask him to stay later and he'll be nicely compensated for his time," I ordered.

"*Will do, Mr. Arnett.*"

"Thank you, Maryse. I'll see you soon," I said and hung up.

I shook my mouse to bring my computer screen to life, opening my calendar to the yearly view. The sooner I could get this woman on board with things, the sooner I could work on creating an heir. My father built this company from the ground up while I created its underground empire myself. I wanted it to stay with the Arnett family instead of someone I didn't share blood with. I just needed one son to mold into the ruthless boss I was, one I knew would carry this empire forward long after I was gone.

Now that I had the woman, it was time to plan the wedding.

"Six months," I mumbled to myself, counting the months on the calendar. "A July wedding it is."

I marked the date on my calendar and turned back to my phone, finding Jerry Kingston's contact.

Me: July 16, 2022. Set the date. I'll be arranging a formal meeting with you soon to start the planning.

His response was nearly immediate.

J. Kingston: You've finally found the lucky woman! Looking forward to planning this wedding for you!

I smirked. Lucky would be the last thing this woman would call herself once she met me. I leaned back in my chair with a sigh, staring at the marked date on my computer's calendar.

Six months.

Both of our lives would change by the time this date rolled around. She had six months to become what I needed her to become, six months to fully accept the new life she would be thrust into. If she didn't, walking down the aisle would be the least of her worries.

Because you couldn't walk down the aisle if you were dead.

CHAPTER ONE
LIA

I*'ve really fucked up now.*

"Turn to your right, please," the female officer said, her voice flat and dry as she stood behind the camera. I swallowed the growing lump of anxiety sitting in my throat and followed her instructions, listening for the telltale click that would indicate my picture had been taken. I flinched slightly when an ear-pitching scream filled the space, a group of officers wheeling a restrained, screaming woman past the mugshot station, a spit bag secured over her head as she jerked against the straps that held her. This place was a nuthouse, a place I didn't belong in.

But I do. I'm not innocent.

I wasn't sure what the hell I thought would happen when I started embezzling money from my boss, but I had to have known it would've led me here. I thought it would've been harmless; I'd only skimmed a couple thousands here and there, sticking to low amounts so that I wouldn't raise any red flags. But then it became easy, especially when it went unnoticed for a complete year. I should've stopped while I was ahead, but I'd been so fucking stupid.

As the administrative assistant, I had access to the company's card to place business orders on their behalf for the main headquarters. At first, I'd been on the straight and narrow path, only fulfilling the orders and never looking at the card again. But when one of the executives asked me to check the payment date on an order placed and I'd actually logged into the account the card was linked to, my life changed forever.

I'd never seen so many fucking zeroes in my life. Growing up in foster care, I never had money of my own and went without a lot of things I desired throughout my life. I knew the owner of the company was a billionaire, but to see the actual number in an account that I had access to ignited an itch that I needed to scratch.

I wanted that kind of money.

It started off small, a couple hundred dollars every other month or so. Though I was scared shitless of getting caught, the thrill of doing something bad was addicting. They had so much fucking money, money I didn't think they would account for. I didn't see the harm in taking some here and there; the amounts were so small that I didn't think anyone would notice it or investigate too far into it. To my knowledge, the executives only checked the accounts if there was a problem with an order, and since that was a rare occurrence, I took that as the green light to continue.

But then I became greedy, stupid, and flashy. One thing I learned was that if I were going to steal money from my boss, it wasn't the best idea to come to work in designer clothes and bags when the salary they paid me didn't reflect that kind of lifestyle. Even though the executives weren't looking at the account, I damn sure didn't take their accountants into consideration.

Today started off as a normal morning at work. I'd clocked in, started on my tasks, and placed orders for one of the casinos they owned. There were no signs that anybody had been on to me, no signs that I'd reached the end of my embezzling gig. No warning bells went off when I was called into the COO's office after lunch. I didn't grow nervous when he introduced the accountant that also sat in his office, looking at me in what I now realized was disgust and contempt.

None of it clicked until Harold opened the binder on his desk and slid it across to me. Stacks of pages were filled with highlighted lines, all of them the transfers I'd made to my own personal account. There was nothing I could do to explain it away; the proof was in black and white in front of me.

No one spoke, and even when I tried to, Harold immediately shut me down and ordered me to continue flipping. Page after page. Transfer after transfer. The moment I realized the kind of situation I was in, fear and anxiety tightened my chest.

"Here's what's going to happen, Ms. McIntyre," Harold had said when I'd flipped to the last page. "You will be terminated immediately, and we expect you to return the..." he looked at his computer screen for a brief moment, "$674,982.59 you've stolen from the company."

"I...I don't have the money anymore," I'd timidly admitted.

Harold continued as if I hadn't said a single word. "The company will also be pressing charges against you for embezzlement. Law enforcement have already been called."

No sooner than he finished his sentence, two male officers appeared in the doorway, frowning at me.

And here I was, ashamed and humiliated as I went through processing for jail.

"Face forward, please," the female officer ordered again. I turned to face her, staring straight ahead as the camera clicked once more. None of my actions became real until I was in the back of a squad car, my freedom dissolving into nothing as they sped away from the Arnett Enterprises headquarters building. I had no idea what the maximum sentence was for this kind of thing, but I was sure the company would fight to imprison me for as long as possible.

"Follow me, please," the woman instructed.

I reluctantly followed her a few steps over to the fingerprinting station, wincing when she roughly gripped my wrist and took my fingerprints. My heart raced in my chest as my reality unfolded before me. Angry inmates banged on the shatter-proof glass of the holding pods, women shrieking demands and drunken nonsense. I'd never been in legal trouble a day in my life, and here I was on my way to prison for stealing over half a million dollars.

I knew how to go out with a bang, at least.

"Ma'am, you're hurting me," I said as she tightly squeezed my fingers as she pressed it on the ink pad.

"Maybe this pain will remind you not to steal from your employer, hmm?" she mused, continuing on with the process. I fought back tears as she finished with the rest of my fingers, relieved when she finally let go of me and handed me a wet wipe. "Let's go."

My anxiety mounted as she led me toward the holding pods. Catcalling and whistles sounded as we passed the men's pods, my heart rapidly pounding against my ribcage as the women's pod came into view. To my surprised, we walked past it, instead going to the intake area.

I frowned in slight confusion. "Am I able to try to bond out?" I'd asked. It was a stupid question, really. I literally had no money to do anything, and I had no family or real friends that I could call to get me out even if I had the money.

The female officer shook her head. "No. Because of the severity of your crime and potential flight risk, you're being held without bond." She gestured to the male officer that came to a stop next to her. "Officer O'Ryan will be handling you from this point forward."

She walked away before I could utter another word, leaving me with a man who had a look in his eyes that I'd seen plenty of times before in the different foster homes I'd ended up in. He had the eyes of a predator, one who could hurt people without remorse over and over again until they'd destroyed their victim's will to live.

"I need you to follow me to the changing station so that we can get you out of your clothes and into a prison uniform," he said.

Though his tone was professional, the look on his face was not. I was aware of the influence the Arnett empire had on Palmetto Beach, but I didn't realize the extent until

I was arrested. Out of all the inmates I'd seen since coming in here, they'd all been treated like a human being while the officers treated me as if I were the scum of the earth. From the way they roughly handled me, insulted me, and looked at me with disgust and contempt, you'd think I was arrested for a mass murder, not embezzling money from a fucking billionaire who didn't really need it.

I looked around, noticing there wasn't a female officer present. I'd watched plenty of crime shows and documentaries to know that this part was usually administered by a female officer since I was a woman. But the longer I stood there, the longer I realized things were a lot different here than they were on TV.

"I gave you an order, inmate," Officer O'Ryan stated through gritted teeth.

I shuffled from foot to foot. "I don't mean to cause trouble, but I'd feel more comfortable if—"

"We're not here for your comfort. Get the fuck in there and strip. Now," he growled. His hand moved to the butt of his gun, his piercing green eyes glaring at me as if silently daring me to disobey him again.

I suppressed the whimper threatening to escape and scurried into the changing room, growing nervous when he entered behind me and closed the door. The room was empty for the most part, but it made me extremely uneasy when I noticed the disconnected cameras in the upper corners of the room. I kept my back to him, my cheeks burning in shame as I slowly peeled my clothes off.

"Keep the bra and underwear," he stated when I moved to take them off. I bit my tongue from asking questions, as I thought inmates weren't allowed to come in with any garments of their own. I didn't move as the heels of his shoes clicked against the hard floor toward me. He kicked my pile of clothes to the side and walked around me. "Arms up."

I lifted my arms, blinking back tears as he roughly groped me for the sake of "frisking me." I forced myself to keep quiet when his hands roughly groped my pussy, his fingers rubbing and probing more than necessary. When I stepped back out of reflex, his hard eyes locked onto mine as he frowned.

"Don't you fucking move, slut," he growled between clenched teeth. He moved around to the back of me, firmly palming my ass and the back of my legs in a way that I was sure would be bruised by the morning. It made no sense why he was doing this in the first place; I didn't have anything but undergarments on. Once he finished, he moved closer to me until I could practically feel his erection poking my lower back. "You're so fucking lucky you don't belong to me. I'd rip you open like the whore you are."

"All ready to go, O'Ryan?" another voice suddenly

said from the doorway, flooding me with relief. The sooner I got to my own cell, the better I'd be. It was apparent that everyone in this precinct was either on Silas's payroll or just professional ass kissers, ones I needed to get away from if I wanted to make it to jail alive.

O'Ryan stepped back, the clicking of his heels retreating away from me. "Almost, Chief. She just has to get into uniform."

"Well, hurry up. Transport will be leaving in less than ten minutes."

A wad of clothing hit me in the back a moment later. "Get dressed, slut," O'Ryan ordered.

I wasted no time grabbing the uniform from the floor and pulling it on. If getting processed was this bad, I didn't even want to think about what awaited me in jail. A few tears slipped down my cheeks before I could stop them. I didn't deny that was guilty, but I still deserved to be treated like a human. Out of everything I'd experienced throughout my life, this was probably the worst day I'd ever had. I was about to be locked away and miserable for however long they deemed fit.

I had no family or friends to come visit me.

Nothing to look forward to.

And honestly? Not much will to live at this point.

O'Ryan stalked back over to me once I had the

uniform on and handed me a pair of flimsy rubber slides. "Put those on and give me your hands," he ordered.

I did as he said, wincing when he tightened a pair of handcuffs onto my wrists. He firmly grabbed my upper arm and led me out of the room. It was bizarre watching him smile and exchange greetings with other officers in a nice, inviting manner considering that he'd been a grade A asshole to me moments ago.

It was as if cops were a different breed. They were friendly with each other, but callous toward the people they had to process or transport. No one cared about our tears, our discomfort, or our problems. At the end of the day, we were just lowly criminals to them that didn't have a right to respect and human decency anymore.

The warm evening air washed over me the moment we stepped out of the precinct. A running bus sat a few feet away from the door, an older man standing outside of its open doors. O'Ryan gave me a shove in that direction, a silent command to move forward.

"We don't have all day, young lady," the older man said with sigh, his thick gray mustache hiding most of the frown on his lips.

I made my way over to him and went up the stairs on the bus, surprised to see it was empty. None of this shit felt right. From their treatment during my processing to now being the only one on this bus, my gut screamed that something was wrong.

"All good, Chief? Need me to ride with you?" O'Ryan asked outside the closing doors. I slid into a seat, moving over to the window to watch the chief and O'Ryan whisper amongst themselves before O'Ryan nodded and headed back to the building. My throat tightened with slight anxiety at what they could've possibly said to each other, but I forced myself to hold my composure.

The chief got onto the bus with a grunt, heading toward me. He didn't say a word as he secured my hand-cuffs to the chain in front of me before he settled himself into the driver's seat.

A tired sigh left me as we finally moved away from the building. I had no idea what journey was ahead of me as I prepared myself to face the music of my crime, but we were already on a bad foot after my time at the precinct.

The ride was a quiet one, which was well-needed after all the noise I was exposed to. The sun was setting, the sky a beautiful mix of oranges, blues, and pinks. I sadly looked out the window as we drove through town, watching as people left work, ate outside with their friends and family, or simply walked their dog along the sidewalk. It was so easy to take freedom for granted, which was delusional for me to do when I knew I was doing something illegal.

Regret pooled in my belly. All I'd wanted was a

different life, a better life than the one I'd lived. I'd had these grand hopes and dreams of working my way up the company and giving myself the life I deserved, but I'd completely fucked it up by making bad decisions. Even if I got out of prison after a couple of years, I could kiss working anywhere in Palmetto Beach goodbye. With the stronghold Arnett Enterprises had on the city, I'd be lucky if anyone would hire me to clean floors.

As the sun dipped lower in the sky, fatigue washed over me. We were surrounded by nothing but trees and a long stretch of road. I gazed at the sign ahead that read, *Palmetto County Prison, 2 miles.*

I'd better enjoy these last two miles of freedom, I thought to myself, fresh tears burning my eyes. But there was nothing to enjoy. I was chained to a seat and only surrounded by wilderness. I focused my attention on the sky, observing how the black ink of night inched its away across, swallowing the beautiful colors the sun left behind.

I couldn't help but wonder how different my life would've been if I'd had parents. I wondered if I would've had a loving life and eventually went on to college, working for the life I had instead of stealing to get it. I wondered if they'd be ashamed I was their kid if they'd known what I'd done.

I sighed inwardly. It wasn't like it mattered anymore.

They'd surrendered me days after I was born, robbing me of whatever life I possibly thought I could've had with them. Some days it made me angry that they didn't even have the common decency to come back for me or even try to find me years later. Instead, they subjected me to years of bouncing from home to home, abuse, and sexual assault from the people who were supposed to "care" for me.

It was no wonder I held a fucked up view of the world.

When the chief drove past the prison, I immediately went on guard. I sat up straight in my seat, looking at him and back to the prison building he was driving past. O'Ryan's threat echoed in my head, dread icing my veins as worst-case scenarios filled my head.

"Um, sir?" I started, but he didn't respond. I cleared my throat and tried again. "Sir, where are you taking me?"

"You'll see when we get there," he said.

There was nowhere to run, no way to escape. If this man decided to hurt me, I'd be left at his mercy with no way to defend myself. My brain conjured up all kinds of fuckery that only made my anxiety worse.

He could pull over and walk me into the dark forests surrounding us, putting a single bullet in my head and leaving me to rot. He could pull over and rape me before turning the bus around to take me to the prison. He could—

My thoughts halted when the bus slowed down, a

paved driveway coming into view up ahead. I looked on in both confusion and wonder as he turned down the driveway, a large house lit up in the distance. This damn sure didn't look like a prison or where I belonged.

My tongue burned to question where we were, but I didn't want to agitate him. My heart raced so fast that I grew lightheaded and nauseous. After stealing so much money, I'd expected to sit in a dirty cell with a bitch of a cellmate who was ready to make my life a living hell. There was no way this was where I would be serving out my sentence.

The chief didn't say a word as he parked the bus and killed the engine. A woman walked out of the house and stood in the driveway, waiting as the chief made his way off the bus. I leaned forward in my seat, watching them as the chief spoke and gestured toward the bus.

The woman only nodded, her eyes pointed in my direction as she listened to him. After a few moments, she passed him a thick, brown envelope and walked back into the house. The moment the chief pulled the wads of money out and began to count them, my stomach sank.

It all made sense.

He was never taking me to prison. Even though I wouldn't be in a traditional prison with other inmates and guards dictating my life, this house was probably going to be my prison. I'd been sold to someone, someone who probably had sinister plans for me that would've made prison a fucking cake walk.

"I'm going to die here," I whispered to myself, tears burning my eyes.

A tall, muscular man walked out of the house next, saying something to the chief. I idly shook my head as they both made their way back over to the bus, knowing if I didn't try to make a run for it, I'd never get another chance.

Think, Lia, think, I thought to myself. It didn't help that we were in the middle of fucking nowhere. Trees loomed in the distance everywhere I looked. Even if I ran, there weren't too many places I could go. I frantically looked around, noticing the keys were still in the ignition. As soon as the idea formed, it evaporated again. The keys wouldn't do much good while I was still cuffed, and the chief would probably be back behind the wheel by the time I had the chance to get close enough anyway.

Any opportunity to escape disappeared when the man and the chief stepped onto the bus. The chief unlocked the lock tethering me to the chain and pulled me out of my seat.

"Here you are," he said, thrusting me toward the waiting man. "Please give my thanks to Silas when he returns."

"Will do," the man said, his deep voice making the tiny

hairs on the back of my neck stand. A different kind of fear crashed into me at the sound of my boss's name. Prior to working for him, there'd been rumors around the city that he had a dark secret.

Some people said that he kidnapped girls and sold them, some said he was a secret mob boss, and some people even accused him of being a serial killer. I'd never seen him much while I worked because he was either holed up in his office or meetings or working outside the office. Anytime I did see him, he never said much or even looked my way. I knew he'd be angry that I stole from him, but not enough to pay for me to be brought to him and possibly killed.

Don't be dramatic. If he were going to have me killed, he wouldn't have gone through the trouble of having me arrested, I reminded myself, which brought me some comfort. If Mr. Arnett wanted me dead, I was sure he could've had someone break into my home and murder me or something else sinister. If this was his house, I couldn't begin to think of what he could possibly want me for, especially if he went through all the trouble of getting the police involved and putting me in the prison system.

I yelped when the man fisted my hair and damn near dragged me off the bus. Pain radiated over my scalp when I tripped, my hip hitting the top stair on the bus. He didn't slow his stride, simply pulling me down the remaining stairs until I fell into a heap on the smooth concrete.

"Fucking Christ!" I hissed. "I would've walked if you gave me a minute!"

"Another word out of you and you'll be punished," he snapped. "Get the fuck up."

I forced myself to my feet, wincing when he jerked my wrists to him and unlocked the cuffs. The bus rumbled back to life and the double doors closed, dread filling me as it backed out of the driveway. I didn't have much time to dwell on it before the man tugged me toward the house.

Aside from the lights spilling from the windows inside, everything else was coated in thick darkness. Even if I tried to run, I could hardly see anything beyond the yard. My shoulders sagged in defeat, hopelessness swelling in my chest as I followed him into the house.

Maybe if I do whatever they ask, they'll have mercy on me. He led me through the back door that opened into what looked like a mudroom of sorts. Four women dressed in identical maid dresses and aprons stood side by side in front of another door.

"We can take it from here, Donovan," the woman with red hair said, her voice even. The man let go of me without a word, walking around them to walk through the door behind them.

I swallowed hard as I regarded them. Their faces held

no emotion, which was both a relief and nerve wracking considering the situation. I nervously shuffled from foot to foot, suddenly feeling self conscious.

"You are now the property of Silas Arnett," the woman said after the long stretch of silence. My eyebrows nearly disappeared into my hairline.

"Property?" I squeaked.

"Mr. Arnett has instructed us to prepare you for his arrival." Her eyes traveled along my form, disapproval filling her eyes. "If you'll follow me, we can go ahead and get started. We have a lot of work ahead of us."

My feet grew heavy as I forced myself to move forward. *Property? What the fuck would that mean for me in the long run?* The real world would expect me to be in prison, not held hostage by my now ex-boss. Maybe the rumors about him were true; maybe he did have a dark side.

And at that moment, I wished for nothing else but to be locked behind bars, because my life as I knew it was over.

CHAPTER TWO
SILAS

I flicked a lighter, bringing the flame to life before extinguishing it. I tried busying myself with uploading photos of the women that would be up for the next auction, but I couldn't let go of the incompetence of the people who allowed the embezzlement fuckery to go on for as long as it did.

As my irritation grew, so did the number of times I struck up the flame in my lighter. Though I didn't smoke, the thought of the flame bringing pain to someone helped to ground me, allowing me to remain patient long enough to get the information I needed before throwing every responsible fuck off the rooftop as compensation for the inconvenience they'd caused me.

I fought the urge to grind my teeth as I attached a nameless woman's picture, filled in her bidding info, and submitted it. Most people would think that almost $700,000 was a drop in the bucket to a billionaire, but money was money. And if it was mine, I wanted every last red cent of it back.

Logically, I knew that wouldn't necessarily happen. I could easily make the money back, but it was the principle of the situation that pissed me off to no end. Even when I thought we were being careful in only hiring people I could trust, all it took was one bad apple to make the whole bunch rotten.

A light knock sounded on my door, cracking the silence that wrapped around me. "What?" I barked.

The door slowly opened before Amanda's timid head poked in. Her wide blue eyes looked at me with worry and nervousness.

"Um, you wanted to see me, boss?" she said, her voice holding an air of fear in it.

I swallowed down the irritation trying to bubble to the surface. In order to get the information I wanted, I needed to approach this conversation with a calm head. I didn't want her to tell me what she thought I wanted to hear; I needed to know what the fuck was going on within my company to where something like an embezzlement was able to go on for over a year.

"Come in, Amanda," I said with a sigh as I dragged a hand down my face, slipping my lighter into my pocket.

"Maxwell is here also," she noted.

I waved them both in and leaned back in my seat. *Good, I can kill two birds with one stone.* They both strolled across the room and sat in the two empty chairs across from my desk. I bounced my gaze between the two of them, a slight grin making permanent roots onto my lips.

Maxwell, my accountant, sat across from me with a smug expression on his lips, almost as if he thought he was called in here to be praised. I mentally scoffed. He had to be hitting a crackpipe if he thought I was proud of the fact that he'd waited until over half a million dollars of my money was gone before he busted the thieving bitch.

Instead, I focused on Amanda first, as I was more curious about her answers to my questions than I was about bloodying Maxwell's nose.

"I'm sure the both of you are aware that an employee was recently fired for embezzling money from the company," I started.

"Yes," they both said in unison.

I leaned forward and rested my elbows on my desk. "Amanda, you're in charge of the hiring and firing within the company. You work alongside the executives of this company when it comes to hiring for our many business locations." My fingers drummed on my desk as I held her nervous gaze. "When I ended the partnership we had with the city's foster program for aging-out kids, I asked you to let go any employee that entered employment with us through that program, correct?"

She swallowed hard before she nodded. "Yes, sir. But I swear I thought I did."

"If you had, the situation at hand wouldn't have happened, now would it?" I asked with a raised brow.

Her eyes watered as she wrung her hands together in her lap. "Mr. Arnett, I swear to you. I literally went through each file with a fine-toothed comb. All of the other applicants that came from the program had their foster home listed as a reference. Hers didn't have that."

I frowned. That didn't make any fucking sense. Considering the position she worked, she was at the bottom of the totem pole within the company. Those jobs were usually reserved for the people that came out of the program so that I could look like a good samaritan that cared about our new adults while also keeping them out of my fucking business so that it didn't cause problems later. To have a job within the company meant she'd come from the program, so it wouldn't make sense for her to have a reference that kept her here long after the others were fired.

"What do you mean it didn't have that? Every person that came into Arnett Enterprises through that program had their foster home listed as a reference. That's the only way they could've gotten hired."

"Then someone must've changed it because it wasn't there, sir. I swear it wasn't," she reiterated.

I tightened my jaw as I stared at her for a moment. After a few beats, I turned my attention to my computer, pulling up Lia's file and looking over it. I frowned when I noted the reference section on her most recent file, seeing that the name of the foster home she'd originally applied with had been replaced.

My blood boiled as I read Henry Catskill's name in black and white. I almost wanted to bring him back to life just to fucking kill him again. He'd worked for the company for years until we started bumping heads about how I ran my underground business.

First, it was him acting as if he had more authority than he did. Then, he used the women in the brothel like a fucking free-for-all, thinking he could do whatever he wanted simply because he was high ranking. But I didn't like anyone trying to ruin my business's reputation with the stupid shit they did, shit that nearly got us exposed.

And I didn't take too kindly to anyone fucking with my money.

The moment I realized what he was doing, I didn't even wait until he'd left the office to fire a bullet into his head. He was still sitting at his desk, surprised when I'd pulled my gun. There was no need for a conversation, no need to give him a chance to try to explain the bullshit he'd been doing for months. And now, it seemed as if he still managed to fuck shit up even beyond the grave.

Fucking bastard.

I closed my eyes and pinched the bridge of my nose. This wasn't on Amanda; I'd be a true asshole if I tried to pin this on her, especially when she was already having a rough time cleaning up the mess Henry left behind. I blew out a long breath to settle myself before I nodded.

"Thank you for making me aware of that, Amanda," I finally said. "In the meantime, I need you to activate a hiring freeze within the company. Nobody comes in until it's been clear that everyone who shouldn't be here are promptly let go."

Her shoulders sagged in visible relief as she eagerly nodded. "Yes, sir. I'll get on that immediately."

"And please double check any and all employee files that list Henry as a reference. Whether they came from the program or not, I want them all gone. I'm not chancing another incident to happen only to find out they're associated with him somehow."

"I'll do that."

I waved my hand dismissively. "You can go now," I said.

She wasted no time hopping to her feet and nearly teleporting out the door. I almost grinned as I watched her. It brought me both joy and amusement to see how nervous I made people. While Palmetto Beach saw the pristine, aspiring version of myself that I presented to them, everyone within Arnett Enterprises saw the real me. They knew what I was capable of and when people were called into my office, it usually ended tragically for them.

"Did you want a briefing on our findings, sir?" Maxwell asked, holding out a thick binder to me. "I've already presented this to Harold and—"

I held my hand to stop him, shaking my head. "I've already been briefed. I'm fully aware of what happened."

Maxwell looked at me as if he expected to be showered with praises, straightening his posture in his seat and holding eye contact with me. I scoffed as I stood to my feet, walking over to the large windows behind my desk.

Maxwell cleared his throat. "Uh, the team and I have—"

"How much was the pay raise and bonus I gave you last year when I made you head of the accounting department?" I mused, looking out at the pedestrians walking the streets of downtown. Even though I could see the cars and trucks moving along the street outside, I couldn't hear a thing in the office. It brought me peace to be able to see the ocean, even more so while being in a place that fucking stressed me out the most.

"You doubled my salary and gave me a half million dollar bonus," Maxwell answered.

I pulled my eyes from the distant ocean and turned around to face him, my hands in my pockets. "And why did I give you those things, Maxwell? To what?"

"To be on top of all things accounting."

I moved my hand in a circle impatiently. "For what? These short, choppy answers and pauses are pissing me off. If I wanted you to drag the answers out, I could've had this conversation over fucking email," I snapped.

The smug expression that once filled his face melted into hesitation and nervousness, his earlier confidence deflating. "You wanted there to be record of every penny coming and going, and wanted every purchase or money transfer verified."

I nodded and turned back to the window. "So, if that's what I paid you and your team to do—and paid quite handsomely at that—do tell; how does someone like a lowly fucking administrative assistant manage to steal almost $700,000 from me without a single one of you fucks realizing it until now?" I glanced at his reflection in the window, smirking when his eyes widened. I turned around to face him once more when he hadn't answered. "Well?"

He quickly opened the binder on his lap, and nervously flipped through pages as he stuttered through his explanation. "They, uh, some of the transactions were so small that they, um, flew under the radar when we—"

"I made clear instructions that all accounts within this company are monitored daily with a fine tooth comb. Every dollar was to be accounted for and logged. Am I right or am I right?"

Maxwell pushed his glasses up onto his nose. "Yes, sir."

"So, when I give instructions like that, there's no such thing as transactions 'flying under the radar' unless you're not doing your fucking job." I shook my head. "And this isn't even something that went on for a few months. She did this shit for two years. Two years and you've only now just caught it?"

"We were investigating—"

"And when did you think a good time to take action would be? When she stole a certain amount of money? When it was too big to continue ignoring?" He only stared at me, his skin growing pale the longer I talked. I stalked over to my desk, leaning down to pull up the minimized window on my computer before turning the screen to face him. "Or is it because you didn't want to bring attention to your own abuse of your company card?"

He looked at the screen with wide eyes, adjusting his glasses nervously. "I, uh, I—"

"I'm going to look into who gave you a card to begin with because what the fuck does an accountant need with a company card? In fact, give me the one you have." I watched as he fumbled with his pants pocket, pulling out his wallet and removing the card with shaky hands. I snatched it from him and dropped it on my desk. "But your personal bullshit isn't why we're here. I'm more worried about a woman you let fly under the radar when I'd paid you specifically to not let shit like this happen."

"Sir, we didn't want to jump the gun because it wasn't obvious that the bank account was personal—"

"Which was why you were supposed to look into that. Fine-tooth comb, remember?" He only swallowed hard at my words, his Adam's apple bobbing in his throat. I pressed my hands against my desk and leaned forward. "The question now is...how are we going to recover the money that you allowed her to steal?"

Maxwell adjusted his tie as he cleared his throat again, uselessly shuffling through the pages in the binder. "We could place an order with the courts to seize her bank accounts and—"

My laughter escaped before I could even stop it. This idiot had to be the dumbest motherfucker I'd ever come across in my life. It was obvious that woman didn't have a single dime of my money left for it to even be worth the court costs to get her account seized.

That was the difference between people who had money and those who grew up without it. They tended to buy shit they thought would make them look and feel rich instead of being strategic and finding ways to grow their money. She was one of the stupid ones who liked to have flashy designer shit to feel important. I could understand in a sense. When you'd spent your entire life in foster care because no one gave a fuck about you, it made sense to do whatever you could to feel like somebody important—even if it was on someone else's dime.

"Be fucking serious, Maxwell. I need real solutions, not bullshit your pea brain thinks it can skate by me," I said once I regained control of myself. His mouth opened and closed like a fish out of water, which only caused me to shake my head. "Great, so you have no kind of plan to recoup the money you, your department, and that thieving bitch cost me."

Maxwell shifted nervously in his seat. "Perhaps we could put the woman up for auction—"

"The woman is already handled so that's the least of my concern," I interrupted, rolling my eyes. "I still need to deal with the fact that you dropped the ball on this one, Maxwell. I didn't pay you all that money for you to just dick around and not do your job the way I told you to." I stroked my chin as I thought. "So, I brainstormed my own solutions."

"I'm all ears, sir. Whatever gets your money back the quickest has my support," he quickly said.

I grinned. "I'm glad you think that, Maxwell, because it's going to require your full support."

"Of course, sir. I want to do whatever I can to help make this right."

"Good." I paced the floor behind my desk. "Well, my first solution was to put Brenda in one of the brothels and have her make my money back," I mused, stroking my chin.

Maxwell's face blanched with shock. "Brenda? My wife Brenda?"

"Are you having an affair with someone else named Brenda?" I scoffed. "Who the fuck else would I be talking about?"

"Mr. Arnett, I'm begging you—"

"But then I realized that it would take too long for her to make my money back, as I can't make as much money on a woman who's pretty much washed up." I shrugged. "So, then I had a better idea."

"God, no! Please—"

"Shut the fuck up while I'm talking, Maxwell," I warned, pointing a finger at him. "So, then I thought, 'Maxwell has those lovely daughters.' Children aren't usually my targets, but there sure is a market for them. Men would pay millions to have a couple of hours with a pair of innocent little girls these days."

"Silas, I'm begging you humbly. Please don't include

my family in this. It's not their fault."

"You brought them into this by taking them to Disney World and other family-friendly fuckery on my dime, so why shouldn't they help you rectify this situation?" I asked, tilting my head to the side as I regarded him. After a few moments, I rolled my shoulders back. "You're very lucky I can tolerate your family, otherwise we wouldn't be discussing this. I would've simply done it and you would've had to deal with it or be executed."

I'd never seen relief flood a grown man's face as quickly as it did his. He pulled a handkerchief from his pocket and dabbed his glistening forehead before loosening his tie a little. "I'm forever grateful for the mercy you've displayed," he said, his voice trembling slightly.

"This is our first and last time having a conversation like this, Maxwell."

"I swear nothing like this will ever happen again," he promised.

I nodded, a slight grin on my lips. "Oh, I know it won't." *You have no fucking idea what I already have planned for you.* "Anyway, I need you to come to my house tonight. The judge is coming by to take Lia's guilty plea and I need you to give him your professional account of the situation so he can sentence her correctly."

He quickly nodded, probably glad the conversation

was no longer on him and his family. "Of course. Just let me know when I should be there."

"Eh, have your wife and kids come along and we'll have dinner. I assume I can trust someone who has broken bread at my table to ensure this fuckery can be put behind us."

He gave me a tight smile. "Of course, Mr. Arnett."

"Then I'll see you around 6:30." I waved my hand. "Now disappear before I'm tempted to change my mind."

He scurried out of my office like the mousy fuck he was, all but slamming the door shut after him. I sat back in my chair and pulled out my cell phone, finding Harold's contact.

Me: Fill Maxwell's position, please. It'll be vacant as of tonight.

I hit send and watched as his reply came in immediately.

Harold: Will do. Dinner?
Me: Dinner.

. . .

I grinned as I hit send and put my phone on the desk. That was what I loved most about Harold. He never asked questions and we were always on the same page. The only time I invited these fucks to do dinner was if I'd planned to kill them and scatter their dismembered bodies in the forest around one of my properties. Maxwell didn't know that. But soon he, his cunt of a wife, and his two bratty children would find that out soon enough.

I called Donovan, drumming my fingers against my desk as I waited for him to answer.

"*Ready for me to come get you?*" he asked when the call connected.

"Not quite." I spun around in my chair before looking to my computer screen. "Has the girl arrived?"

"*Yep. Chief just dropped her off. He asked me to send you his thanks for the compensation.*"

Having the PBPD chief in my back pocket had been the best investment I'd ever made in my underground business. To have so many important people heavily influenced by my checkbook, I could turn this whole city into a human trafficking ring right under everyone's noses and without much pushback.

It was amazing what being filthy fucking rich could buy you.

"That's good. She wasn't roughed up or anything, was she?"

"*Nah. The girls are with her now getting her ready for you.*"

"Good." I leaned back in my seat. "Speaking of prep, I've invited Maxwell and his family over for dinner."

"*Ah. Anything in particular you want on the menu?*" he asked.

Speaking in code was something that Donovan and I did fluently. When it came to inviting people for dinner, we had certain food dishes we used for certain situations.

"I'm thinking filet mignon for the adults and a ravioli for the kids," I mused, causing Donovan to chuckle. It'd been a long time since I'd brought out the "kill the parents, sell the children" menu items. I didn't usually involve kids in my plans, but what the fuck was I going to do with two mangy kids after I killed their parents?

"*You got it. How many kids?*"

"They have two daughters."

"*Cool. I'll get that sent in to the appropriate parties,*" he said.

"Thanks." I spun around in my chair again. "And the girl; what's her temperament?"

"*She seems more confused about what's going on and why she's at your place and not in prison.*"

"Any fighting or problems?"

"*Nah. I did have to drag her down the bus steps because the bitch wanted to act like she couldn't walk.*"

I chuckled and shook my head. "That's on her then. Anyway, I should be ready to leave in about forty-five minutes. I have a few more auction listings to make and then I'll be ready to head out. Please tell Maryse that I want everything done on that woman."

"*You know she'll yell at me if I, and I quote, 'tell her how to do her job.'*"

"Well, you tell her that I told you to tell her. If her job isn't done to my liking, I can add more items to the dinner menu," I said.

Donovan let out a low whistle. "*Aye, aye, sir,*" he teased.

I smirked. "I'll see you soon, asshole," I said and hung up.

I pulled up Lia's employee file and looked at her photo, studying the dead, uninterested expression on her face.

And I'll be seeing you soon, too, you thieving bitch.

CHAPTER THREE
LIA

For a brief moment, I almost forgot my fucked up situation as I took in my surroundings in awe. As the women quickly led me through the kitchen, I took in the black and dark gray room. The cabinets were black and the marble counters, marble floors, and state-of-the-art appliances were a dark gray. The clean, expensive space looked like something that came straight from my Pinterest board or a showroom floor. If it weren't for the chefs dressed in black preparing food, I would've thought this was some kind of model house and not one that someone actually lived in.

"Keep up, please," the ringleader of the women's group stated, snapping her fingers above her head without even looking back at me.

"Sorry," I mumbled, more so to myself as I quickened

my pace. She led me down a hallway, passing rooms so quickly that I didn't have time to register everything. I'd briefly saw a dining table in one room and a couch in another, but didn't note anything beyond that. Before I knew it, we stood in the middle of the brightest bathroom I'd ever been in.

White marble with light gray streaks covered every surface of the room—the walls, floors, even the shower wall. A deep white porcelain tub next to the large glass shower was already filled with steaming water. The women stood in a line side by side as they looked at me expectantly.

"Please removed your clothes and get in the bath," the leading woman said.

My gaze shifted from each of their faces, frowning when none of them moved. "Are...you guys going to step out in order for me to get undressed?"

"No."

"But I—"

"Ma'am, if you don't remove your clothes immediately, I will remove them for you," she said sternly.

I swallowed the knot in my throat and slowly removed the prison uniform, letting it pool at my feet. The other women moved around the bathroom, grabbing different bottles and brushes and putting them on the counter.

Once I was naked, I dipped my foot into the water and hissed as I jerked back.

"This is way too hot," I said, shaking my head.

"It's at the appropriate temperature needed for your exfoliating. Get in," the woman simply said.

I swallowed back my retort, knowing it wouldn't get me anywhere. I hissed in pain as I stepped into the hot bath, clenching my jaw so tight that I thought I'd break my teeth. It was an ongoing joke that women loved their bath water hotter than hell, but I definitely wasn't one of those women. It was as if I were bathing in acid, my skin burning as I submerged myself into the bath. As soon as the water hit the lips of my vagina, I jumped back up and shook my head.

"It's too—"

The woman moved quicker than lightening, firmly grasping my shoulders and pushing me down into the water. Water sloshed out of the tub as we struggled, another one of the women grabbing my legs and jerking them from underneath me. The hot water burned my skin and I screamed, hot water filling my mouth as my head went under. I resurfaced with a gasp, my nerve endings on fire.

The women walked back over to the door as if they hadn't just assaulted me. My heart raced quickly as I wiped my wet hair out of my face, glaring at the ringleader bitch.

"You'll soak for twenty minutes before we start our work. Do not leave the tub, and do not alter the temperature of the water. It'll only make your exfoliation painful."

Without another word, the four of them filed out of the bathroom, closing the door behind them. Heavy silence cloaked the room, almost to the point that I had to splash a little in the tub to keep my ears from hurting. I still couldn't understand why I was here. What the hell did this man have planned for me?

I forced myself to lay back in the tub in an effort to relax, but my mind ran a mile a minute. Just hours ago, I thought I'd be rotting away in a cell for years after I'd gotten arrested. Never in a million years did I think I'd be in the mansion of the man I'd stolen money from.

The optimistic part of me wanted to believe that he didn't bring me all the way here just to kill me. As expensive as this house probably was, I wouldn't want to ruin my expensive floors with blood if I were him.

He obviously has the money to replace anything he might ruin if he were to kill me, the pessimistic part of myself remind me.

Regret ebbed and flowed throughout my veins the longer I sat in the water. I knew I was fucked the moment I was called into the COO's office, but I had no idea the degree. There was no one who could help me out of this situation if this turned out to be something that was meant to harm me. The police seem to be working for this guy and if he had that much power, then I couldn't trust anyone in the city.

I sniffled as I shifted in the tub. While the water was still hot, my skin had finally adjusted to it. There were no bubbles in the water or soap nearby, so I had no idea what the fuck I was supposed to do other than sit here.

The women didn't give me long to dwell on it before they returned. No one said a word as one of them moved over to the tub and pulled the plug out to drain the water. She motioned with her hands for me to stand so I did, the cool air in the bathroom sending a shiver down my spine when it hit my wet skin.

They wasted no time getting to work. I always thought getting pampered like the women in the movies would be so relaxing and nice. I used to dream of going to a spa and having someone exfoliating my skin and treating me like a queen for a day.

This was the complete opposite of that.

It was as if they'd taken sandpaper to my skin, four pairs of hands scrubbing off what they claimed was dead skin. They'd scrubbed so hard and for so long that my entire body was red when they were finished. I was pretty sure I'd shed several tears during the process, but it didn't deter the women from the task at hand—nothing did.

I released a cleansing, shaky breath when they finally put the exfoliating mittens down. When one of them approached stirring a bowl of colorful wax, my stomach dropped. I couldn't even remember the last time I shaved, which only meant they were about to wax me bald.

"Can't we just take a moment to—fuck!" I hissed when she spread a glob of hot wax on my arm. I yanked away from her, fed up with this whole process. "Just wait a fucking minute!"

No sooner than the last syllable left my mouth, a sharp sting bloomed across my cheek. I held my face, looking at the ringleader with wide eyes. She only frowned at me, her face otherwise clear of emotion.

"Let's get one thing clear," she started, her voice eerily calm and even. "You are now the property of Silas Arnett. You will do what you're told and you'll be quiet. If you decide you don't want to do that, you will suffer the consequences. You don't want me to have to call Mr. Arnett; you're in enough trouble already as it is." She yanked my arm forward, allowing the previous woman to continue her task. "Now be still, shut up, and let us do what we've been assigned to do."

Silent tears rolled down my cheeks as I let them painfully rip hair from my body. To them, I wasn't even human anymore, only someone's property that another person could abuse. I definitely wasn't innocent, but I knew my crime wasn't severe enough to be subjected to this. If this was the shit I'd have to go through, I'd rather be sent back to prison. I'd rather take my chances with a prison system that at least had some kind of rules instead of a psycho billionaire and his equally psycho employees.

When I was fully exfoliated and waxed, my skin hurt so much that it was practically numb. Even as they rubbed lotion onto my body, it didn't provide any kind of relief from the trauma they'd caused. I just wanted to get out of this bathroom, wanted people to stop touching me, wanted people to just leave me the fuck alone. I wasn't even sure what this man wanted from me, but I already knew there was no way I was going to survive for long. I just couldn't.

A solid knock sounded on the door. Ringleader bitch broke off from the group and went over to the door, cracking it slightly. A male voice sounded on the other side as they spoke softly to each other, the woman nodding before closing the door again.

"Dinner is ready, and Mr. Arnett would like her to join him now," she said to the other women.

One of them handed me this plain white, thin nightgown and undergarments before they all filed out of the bathroom. I walked over to the mirror, taking in my red, angry skin. I ran my fingertips over it. Though it hurt like a bitch, my skin was baby smooth, smoother than I'd ever felt it in my whole life. I blew out a shaky breath and put on the bra and panties, surprised that it was a perfect fit. *Had he already planned this?*

My brain wanted to tell me that it was probably just a lucky guess or a coincidence; maybe the police from the precinct had told him my size when they confiscated my clothes. But I couldn't help but feel uneasy about this whole thing.

"Hurry up, please," a woman's voice said outside the door.

I rolled my eyes. I hadn't even been around these women long and I already hated them all, especially the leader of their little group. I stomped over to the door and ripped it open, glaring at the main woman. She looked back at me completely unfazed, simply turning on her heels and snapping her fingers as if I were some dog that was supposed to follow her on command.

Play it smart, Lia. Maybe you can appeal to your ex-boss and make the best of this situation if he's a reasonable man, I thought to myself as we made our way to the dining room.

Voices floated out into the hallway before we'd even approached, even a burst of genuine laughter. Nausea rolled in my belly. It took a really sick person to find some-thing to laugh about after they'd kidnapped someone and held them hostage. I was supposed to be the property of the state, not the property of my boss. When we entered the large dining room, I recognized my ex-boss, the stupid fucking accountant that ratted me out, and a man I'd never seen before. A woman and two little girls also sat at the table. From their plain, mousy appearance, I could only assume they came with the accountant.

My ex-boss gestured to an empty chair. "Sit," he simply said before continuing his conversation. I sat and put my hands in my lap, my stomach growling as I looked at the decadent steaks the adults had. I would've even taken the pasta the children were eating. But nothing happened for almost ten minutes, the men at the table continuing their conversation as if I weren't there.

I cleared my throat and shifted in my seat, sliding my gaze to the opening of the kitchen. *Maybe they don't know I'm in here yet,* I rationalized. One of the little girls looked at me, smacking on pasta as she stared at me. I looked around to avoid her gaze, not sure what to do with myself or what to focus on.

"That lady doesn't have food," she said, pointing at me. The other little girl looked at me before glancing at the empty spot on the table in front of me.

"Yeah, she doesn't have food," she chimed and looked to my ex-boss. "Is she going to get dinner, too?"

He didn't even bother looking at me, instead leveling a

hard gaze at the children. "Bad girls don't get to eat good food in this house," he simply said. He clapped his hands together, the sound so loud that I jumped. A chef entered the dining room with a thick plastic tray like the ones I'd seen when watching prison shows on Netflix. The entire room went silent as the chef put the tray in front of me, all eyes on me as I looked at the plain, dry bologna sandwich, luke warm corn, and an apple with multiple brown soft spots.

Angry tears burned my eyes as I only stared at the tray. Of course; why the hell did I expect anything differently when I was technically a prisoner? But to be given prison food while everyone ate a rich meal was dehumanizing and embarrassing.

"Ick," one of the girls said. I didn't even react when one of their forks appeared near my tray, poking at the dried out bologna that sat on top of a stiff piece of bread.

"Alana, that's rude. Worry about your own food, please," the woman next to them said.

"Sorry, Mommy," the girl mumbled before going back to smacking on pasta.

I kept my hands in my lap throughout dinner. I refused to touch anything on this tray. Every muscle in my body wanted to throw it in my ex boss's smug face, but there was only one of me and many of them. For now, I just had to play it cool and smart. I needed to learn my surroundings, learn the people around me, and figure out how to get the fuck out of here. I didn't care if running would land me in jail—where I should've been in the first place—but I knew that staying here wasn't in my best interest.

"That was a lovely dinner, Silas," the unfamiliar man sitting on the side of him said as he wiped his mouth. "It's always a pleasure when you invite me over."

"Of course, Judge. I appreciate you coming out here after hours to help me get this situation resolved once and for all." He wiped his mouth and put his napkin on the table. "Shall we go to the office and talk business?"

"Sure," the accountant said as he also put his napkin on the table. "We have to get the girls home soon anyway, so I'm ready whenever you are."

"Good. Let's go to my office then," Silas said and stood, the others following suit.

The accountant looked to the woman and children and held up his hand. "Honey, you and the girls can stay here—"

"Oh no, they're fine," Silas interrupted. "Besides, we need another witness to sign the documents anyhow."

The accountant appeared visibly uncomfortable as he forced a smile and nodded. "Very well then," he said.

Silas stalked over to me and tightly gripped my upper arm, yanking me out of my seat. I ground my teeth to keep from saying something. He held my arm so tight that it started to go numb under his grip. No matter how I tried to turn or reposition my arm to find relief, he only tightened his grasp, his own knuckles going white from the force. He pushed me into a chair when we got to his office before he moved over to his desk. I shook my arm out and glared at Silas's back, dropping my gaze to my lap when he sat down.

"I'll make this quick so that we're not here all night," he started as he slid his chair closer to his desk. "Judge Reilly, I'd like for you to go ahead and sentence this young lady so that we have the rest of the legalities out of the way. She's on record as being in prison right now, which I showed you earlier. So, now I only need a proper sentencing so that we can go ahead and bury this out of the spotlight."

The judge dabbed his forehead with a handkerchief as he nodded. "Of course. I just need the account of the crime since there are no lawyers here to brief me on charges."

Silas gestured toward the accountant. "Maxwell, please," he said.

My cheeks burned with shame and embarrassment as I listened to that accountant rattle off the details of my crime. The amounts, the dates, the frequencies. The air in the room shifted when the accountant listed the total amount I'd taken.

I hadn't even realized it'd been that much. I was only

taking what I'd needed in that moment, never thinking about how this would all add up and eventually get me caught. It was only supposed to be a few hundred here, a thousand or two there. But then I grew stupid and greedy, and started fucking up. *I'm such a fucking idiot.*

Once the accountant concluded his report, the judge took his glasses off and cleaned them with his tie. "Very well." He put his glasses back on and looked to Silas. "Do you have a sentence in mind that you'd prefer?"

My heart hammered in my chest, my freedom hanging in the balance. My freedom was already gone, obviously, but I didn't want to spend it in this expensive prison. I licked my dry lips, my fingers nervously fiddling with a loose string on the hem of my nightgown. The two girls giggled in the corner as their mother whispered to them, and I was almost jealous that they could be so fucking care-free in a moment like this. They were probably used to witnessing shit like this, as if kidnapping a woman from prison and bringing them to someone's home as property was normal.

"I trust that you'll make the best judgment," Silas responded.

The judge took the stack of papers Silas held out to him, multiple neon yellow strips displayed along the side of the stack. "How do you plea, young lady?" the judge asked without looking at me.

My mouth suddenly felt as if it were filled with cotton, my tongue stuck to the roof of my mouth. I cleared my throat. "Guilty," I murmured.

"I accept the defendant's guilty plea and will sentence her to nine years." He looked up at Silas. "Is that good for you?"

"That's plenty of time for what I need to do," he said, his words sending a chill down my spine. Suddenly, the uneasy feeling returned. What the fuck did he plan to do with me that would take him nine years?

"Very well." The judge signed the documents, flipping through it to sign all the papers with the neon tab on them before passing it to Maxwell. Maxwell did the same and passed it to his wife, who signed off as a witness. Once all the appropriate parties had signed, the judge stood and put the documents in a folder, slipping it in his briefcase. "I think that's everything. The woman has been sentenced and now your sale can be complete, Mr. Arnett."

"Thank you again, Judge. I've sent you that deposit to compensate for your time."

"You know the pleasure is all mine," he said as he headed for the door. "And thank you for dinner. One of these days, I'm going to steal your chef for a few days," he teased. Silas chuckled but it sounded unnatural and cold.

"We've talked about this, Judge," Silas said, pointing at him.

The man waved him off with a chuckle. "I know, I know," he said and opened the door to the office, jumping back when two large men stood in the doorway. "Jesus Christ, you two scared the daylights out of me."

"Let him through," Silas ordered with a wave of his hand. "He has to get those documents where they need to be."

The two men stepped aside and let the judge through before closing the space again, looking at all of us in the office. The accountant stood to his feet and cleared his throat.

"It's getting kinda late and the girls have school tomorrow," he said, looking over his shoulder at his wife and children as they headed for the door. "I'll see you tomorrow at work?"

The men at the door stepped aside once more, two more large men entering the office with briefcases. "Ah, Julius and Alexander. You're right on time," Silas said, holding out his hand.

Neither man said anything as they shook Silas's hand, glancing back at the girls. One of them glanced my way, the malicious look in his gaze raising goosebumps on my arms. He was bald, tall with a thick, muscular build. There was a scar across his eye, his eye socket filled with a milky colored prosthetic one.

"I assume the sale is ready to be completed, yes?" the

other man said. He looked the same as the other guy, except he had hair as well as both of his own eyeballs.

"It is. You have the money?"

"We wouldn't be here if we didn't, Arnett," the man growled.

"Mr. Arnett, I'm sorry for stealing from you," I started. Everything in my gut screamed that he was about to sell me to these two men, and they didn't seem like the friendly type. The way the bald one kept eying me made me sick to my stomach. "I know I fucked up, but—"

"Shut the fuck up. No one is talking to you right now," he said, his tone firm.

Any other words I wanted to say ran back down my throat to hide when he looked at me. The icy blue glare he gave me promised pain if I uttered another word, and after everything I'd already been through, I didn't want to press my luck.

"Can you please move?" the accountant said to the men standing in front of the doorway. "My business here is done, so—"

"Not quite, Maxwell," Silas said as he placed a money counting machine on his desk. "There was one more thing I'd wanted to talk to you about before you left."

Maxwell turned to look at him with a frown. "It can't wait until the morning? It's getting late, Mr. Arnett."

"If it could wait until morning, then I would've said it

could wait until morning." He opened the first briefcase presented to him and put it through the money machine, repeating the action until each stack was counted. No one said anything as he did the same thing with the second briefcase before he looked at the screen and nodded. "Looks like it's all here," he said.

"The paperwork?" the bald one said, his voice rough and raspy.

Silas slid papers over to them, papers that looked like the ones they'd just signed. *I'm really about to be sold into a human trafficking ring,* I thought, the realization sending a crushing wave of fear and helplessness through me.

"Now that I have my money, you can now grab your property from behind you and be on your way. Pleasure doing business with you," he said as he closed the briefcases.

I stared at them with wide eyes when they turned around, my heart beating so fast that I thought it would explode. But it wasn't until they walked past me and headed toward the accountant and his family that I'd realized what'd happened.

The girls screamed when each man grabbed one of the girls's arms and chaos ensued. Maxwell grabbed his daughters' free arms and tried to pull them against him. "What the hell do you think you're doing?" he shouted as his wife screamed.

"What I told you I was going to do when we were in my office this morning," Silas said coolly, sitting behind his desk.

"What the hell is going on, Maxwell?" his wife exclaimed. "They can't take my children!"

"They can and they are. As of twenty minutes ago, you signed away your parental rights to your children."

"We did no such thing!" Maxwell bellowed, spittle flying from his mouth.

"Did you really think I needed a witness signature from your wife of all people? Or even your account of what happened?" Silas asked, as if it was absurd for Maxwell to think otherwise. "I told you earlier that I needed to recoup the money you allowed this stupid bitch to steal from me. So, I put your daughters up for sale and these two gentlemen are now their new owners."

"And you have five seconds to let go of them before we have a major problem," the bald one sneered.

"You can't do this! They're just children!" Maxwell exclaimed, tears glossing his eyes.

Silas raised an eyebrow. "....and? Them being children doesn't negate the fact that you needed to get my money back. They've been sold and now my money has been replaced."

"You son of a bitch," Maxwell growled, storming toward Silas.

One of the men that stood in front of the door rushed behind him, hitting him in the back of the head with the butt of his gun. Everything seemed to move in slow motion from that moment, sounds blurring together. The girls sobbed as the two men ripped them away from their mother, throwing them across their shoulder as they kicked and screamed. The remaining guard at the door restrained the woman as she fought to go after her children, her screaming shattering my heart. The girls' screaming shattering my soul.

I'd caused this. I was the reason their family would be broken. I was the reason for their grief. I'd been selfish and thought a billionaire wouldn't quickly notice that I'd taken his money, never thinking that it would involve other people if I were to get caught.

Even as the girls' screaming floated down the hallway, Silas laughed—fucking *laughed* as their mother collapsed in grief on the floor. Her wailing filled every inch of the room, crawling into my ear and making permanent residence in my brain.

"I'm sure those bratty fucks weren't screaming when you were spending my money on family trips, huh, Maxwell?" Silas taunted as he stood and walked around his desk.

Maxwell brought himself up to his hands and knees, his head bowed. Before he could even utter a word, Silas kicked him in the head, the sickening crunch of nose cartilage bringing bile up my throat. I forced myself to swallow it down, as the last thing I needed was to bring attention to myself.

"The papers you signed as 'witnesses' were actually papers for you to relinquish your parental rights and approve an adoption to the pleasant men that just left," Silas explained, looking down at Maxwell. He kicked him again in the ribs as he continued to explain. "You fucked up and now you'll never see your children again. You see, those men are headed back to Canada. Your daughters will now be two more children in their orphanage, and they already have clients lined up to tear your little brats to bloody shreds."

"No!" his wife wailed from her place on the floor. "Please, we can pay you everything back—"

"Oh, we're well past that," Silas said with a dismissive wave of his hand. "Tie them up."

Tears blurred my vision as I sat frozen, watching as the two men wrestled with both the accountant and his wife, both of them screaming and begging for Silas to have mercy on them. He only looked at them with no kind of expression before turning his attention to me.

"See what you've caused?" he asked, taking a few steps closer. "I want you to think about what you've done and how you've fucked up. I want you to think about those two young girls being tortured, abused, raped, and eventually killed by perverts all because you fucked with the wrong person's money." He pointed at their mother. "I want you to think about their mother's broken heart because you got her children taken away after you thought it was smart to fuck with my money."

"Silas, please! We can work something out!" Maxwell called out when the guard pulled him to his feet after tying his hands together.

Silas shook his head. "We already did." He turned his gaze back to me, a small smirk on his lips. "There are things much worse than prison, and I intend on showing you just how worse it can get. I have you for nine years after all."

Tears rolled uncontrollably down my face as Silas grabbed my arm and roughly yanked me out of my seat. The two men dragged the accountant and his wife out of the office kicking and screaming.

"I didn't want anyone to get hurt," I wailed as we made our way through the kitchen. "No one was supposed to get hurt."

"Well, you're going to see what happens when you fuck with me or my money," he said, pulling me along.

Once we were back outside on the smooth, paved driveway, the guard pushed the accountant and his wife to the ground. Silas firmly grabbed my face and forced me to look at the scene before me. I watched in horror as the two men emptied a full magazine into the accountant and his wife, the gunfire sounding hollow in the darkness.

A ringing filled my ears as well as screaming, and it took me a minute to figure out that the screaming came from me. Never in a million years did I think my mistake would cost other people their lives, their freedom. Never in a million years did I think my boss would personally come after me with the sole intention of making my life a living hell. If he was capable of doing something like this, I couldn't begin to fathom what he had planned for me.

Dark red blood stained the driveway as it pooled beneath their lifeless bodies. I couldn't force myself to take a full breath, my body hyperventilating as Silas took me back into the house. It was then that I realized how fucked up my situation was, and how much danger I was in by being here.

He led me through the house, putting me in a large bedroom. He pointed at a thick binder on the bed before thrusting me further into the room.

"That's for you. Start reading and memorizing that shit. Pop quiz in the morning, and it's in your best interest that you pass it," he said. He stalked out of the room and closed the door behind him, locking it.

I looked at the cover of the binder, reading the plain letters that only said *Training Manual.* The longer I stared at it, the more angry I became. I picked the heavy binder up and threw it against the wall, not even caring when it chipped the dry wall.

I crumpled to the floor in tears after everything that'd happened today, after everything I'd witnessed. And as my hiccuping sobs threatened to strangle me, only one thought crossed my mind.

I was going to die here.

CHAPTER FOUR
SILAS

I paused in eating my breakfast when Maryse brought the pouting bitch into the dining room, unable to stop the smirk on my lips as I took in her appearance.

The last twenty-four hours had been rough on her, and it was evident in her bloodshot eyes, eye bags, and puffy face she had. She sat at the opposite end of the table, practically glaring at me as if that would do anything for her situation.

"Do you know your purpose here now?" I asked casually, cutting into the thick Brioche French toast on my plate. When she didn't immediately respond, I looked up at her and frowned. "Are you hard of hearing?"

The muscles in her jaws flexed for a fleeting moment

before she spoke. "Because you want to torture me for stealing money from you," she ground out.

I shook my head and released a light sigh. "Looks like someone didn't read the manual," I mused, putting the sweet, syrupy bread into my mouth.

I held her angry, tired gaze as I chewed. Considering that she didn't eat dinner last night, I was sure she was hungry. I clapped my hands to signal the chef to bring her breakfast, which was only two hard boiled eggs, a slice of toast, and oatmeal. She looked at the plate with a frown but didn't move to touch it, only going back to staring at me.

"I've also learned that you've damaged my wall in your room when you threw your tantrum last night," I continued. I grabbed my fresh squeezed orange juice and took a few swallows of it before placing it back on the table. "That'll be added to your punishment as well. I didn't bring you to my home for you to fuck it up."

"Then why bring me here at all?" she snapped. "I should be in jail, not held hostage by a psycho."

I ignored her comment and continued speaking, eating more of my breakfast. "Your purpose—which you would've seen had you read the manual like I told you to —is to become my wife and give me a male heir."

Her eyebrow raised as an incredulous look filled her face. "Is it crack you smoke? You're fucking insane. I stole money from you; you're acting like I killed someone you loved or something."

"My money is the only thing I love and you stole that. So yes, I'd say I'm reacting appropriately," I said with a shrug. "Either way, this isn't something that's up for debate or discussion. Become my wife or become a casualty. You've seen how easily I can make the latter happen."

"I'd rather die than subject myself to that," she muttered, folding her arms across her chest and looking away from me.

Laughter bubbled up in my throat until it spilled out of me, filling the dining room. "Oh, you delusional, thieving cunt," I said as I chuckled. "Do you think I'd really make your death so quick and easy to where you think you wouldn't have to suffer long?" I laughed some more as I shook my head, leaning back in my seat. "I spent a great deal of money to get you to be in that seat you're in right now instead of a jail cell. I have too much money already invested in you, and that's on top of the money you already stole. So if you eventually died by my hand, it would be due to your body being unable to withstand any other injury I could inflict upon it after I break you down to nothing."

Her eyes widened and she swallowed hard, her skin paling at my words. "What you're doing isn't legal," she said, her voice shaky.

I continued on as if she hasn't said anything. "Because you—Lia McIntyre—are supposed to be rotting away in jail right now, your name will be legally changed to Alyssa Mitchell."

"I'll never answer to that because that isn't my name."

I shrugged and took a forkful of scrambled eggs into my mouth. "Then you'll be punished until you do." I ate a little more of my breakfast, letting silence swell around us before I dropped the next bombshell on her. "You'll also be undergoing plastic surgery to look the way I want you to look. Since you'll be my property for the next nine years, you need to be someone I can stand looking at and right now..." I looked at the pathetic parts I could see of her from her seat at the table. "I'm not impressed."

"I'm not getting fucking surgery, you vain bastard," she snapped. "No doctor in this country would do surgery on someone without a consent form unless they want a lawsuit on their hands."

When I grinned and put my fork down, that previous fear she had moments ago returned. My hands tingled to choke the shit out of her and shut her up, but I had to play the long game. I didn't go through all this trouble to get her just to kill her in less than a week.

"Is that right?"

"It's common sense."

"Hmm, interesting." I stroked my chin. "You know,

was it common sense when the police decided not to take you to prison but instead brought you here? Or what about when the judge did your sentencing at my home office instead of in court on the official record? And let's not forget those two little girls that you caused to be sold off to recoup my money you stole. Nothing is common sense when you have the money to make a problem disappear. Everyone has a price."

"Well, I don't," she said defiantly.

"You've already been bought, so common sense would tell you that you do." I pushed my finished breakfast plate away from me. "Go wash the dishes."

She only continued sitting there, staring at me. If looks could kill, I would've been dead ten times over. Unfortunately for her, I had thick skin and wasn't a sensitive person. She could glare at me every day for the rest of her pathetic life for all I cared; there wasn't shit she could do about her situation. If she were smart, she would go with the flow and be on her best behavior. But it was already obvious that she wasn't smart.

Which would make it so much fucking fun to break her.

"Alyssa, wash the dishes," I stated again, my voice more firm. She looked around the room as if looking for another person before settling her gaze back on me. "You don't take directions very well. I told you to get up and wash the dishes. If I have to tell you one more time, we're going to take a trip to the mudroom for discipline."

She rolled her eyes before she pushed away from the table and stalked over to me. She snatched the plate from in front of me and marched into the kitchen. Even though I was fully dressed to head out for work, I slipped my shoes and suit jacket off. I unbuttoned my cuff links and rolled my sleeves up as far as I could past my elbows before I quietly stood from the table.

Her back was facing me when I entered the kitchen, inaudible grumbling coming from her mouth. My hands tingled the closer I moved to her, and I made sure to keep my steps light.

I roughly grabbed the back of her neck when I was close enough to her and forced her head into the hot, soapy dishwater the chef usually ran near the end of breakfast. She struggled against me, trying her hardest to pull her head out of the water but she was no match for my strength.

I closed my eyes and relished in the sounds of the sloshing water, her muffled screams, and her wet hands hitting against my hands and forearms. After a few moments, I ripped her head back. She gasped and sputtered, coughing as she forced herself to breathe.

"One thing I don't tolerate is backtalk, especially from a lowly bitch like yourself," I sneered before putting her back under. I held her down tight, pushing her down so far that I was sure her face touched the bottom of the sink. I pulled her out once again. "When I tell you to do something, you fucking do it and you do it immediately!"

"Wait," she gasped, but I didn't wait.

I thrust her back into the hot water, my homicidal urges begging to be released but I knew I couldn't kill her. Not yet anyway. When her movements grew jerky and weak, I pulled her from the water and let her go, watching as she fell onto her hands and knees. She coughed up water and gulped for breath before sobs wracked her body. Fisting her wet hair, I yanked her head back to force her to look at me.

"You better spend the day reading that fucking manual," I growled, my voice low and dark. "When I get back here, you better be able to answer any question I give you about the information in there. If I learn that you haven't done what I asked, I promise you your next punishment will leave you unable to sit for days. Do I make myself crystal fucking clear?"

"Y-y-yes," she stammered.

I let go of her with a slight shove and headed back to the dining room to grab my shoes and jacket. I needed to put space between us, otherwise I'd be tempted to torture her all day until she no longer had a pulse. As tempting as it was, I was in no mood to go through the tedious process of trying to find a wife again, especially when the previous attempts had gone to hell in a hand basket.

Once I was ready, I strolled through the kitchen and headed for the backdoor. She was still on the floor sniffling and sobbing like the pathetic bitch she was, which only irritated me further.

"You can't read the manual if you're on the floor being a crybaby bitch," I said.

Maryse appeared in the doorway between the dining room and the kitchen. "I'll make sure she reads it, sir," she promised.

"Good. I'll be back as soon as I can," I said and headed back out of the house.

———

When I arrived at the office, the entire building buzzed with news about Maxwell's death. Everyone murmured amongst each other, conjuring up conspiracies for why he and his wife were murdered.

"I heard it was a murder-suicide. You know that his wife was threatening to divorce him and take the kids," one person murmured as I walked past.

"I heard that he was also embezzling money with that girl and killed his family and himself before he got caught," another person speculated.

I almost wanted to chuckle at how absurd some of this shit was, but the fact that none of the conspiracies surrounded me was good news. Some employees from the accounting department stood in huddles, comforting each other. One of them looked up and flagged me down, their sad eyes meeting my gaze when they stopped in front of me. I couldn't remember this man's name if someone had a gun to my head and ordered me to tell them.

"Mr. Arnett, did you hear about Maxwell? It's terrible what happened to him and his wife," he said, folding his arms across his chest and shaking his head.

Of course I did. I was the one who ordered their execution. Instead of voicing my thoughts, I forced a frown on my lips and shook my head. "No, I haven't. What happened and why is everyone in a frenzy?"

The man looked around for a brief moment before leaning in closer. "He and his wife were murdered," he murmured, his voice low. I only looked at him with faux shock. "Rumor has it that he owed money to the mafia or something. He and his wife's bodies were found washed up on the shore near the bridge."

"Jesus Christ," I muttered. I had no fucking idea how normal people were supposed to react in situations like this. I didn't experience emotions like a normal person did. I didn't really know how to show empathy, compassion, or any of that shit. And I damn sure didn't know how to fake emotions I didn't feel. Even though I was winging an appropriate reaction to the news, the accountant seemed to accept it, which was good enough for me.

"Now that their bodies have been found, they're looking for their daughters," the man continued. "They're getting search and rescue teams to look for the girls in the event that they were also thrown over the bridge."

I shook my head and sighed. "I hope they find them safe," I said with a small shrug and turned to head for the elevator, a small smirk on my lips.

I'd always found it so amusing to be so unsuspecting when things like this happened. All I did was throw a few million to a few charities a year to be hailed as a saint. Even if someone did try to accuse me of something, no one would believe them. Silas Arnett a murderer? Oh no, not the philanthropist, business tycoon, and mentor! But people were fucking gullible, easy sheep that took little to no effort to lead to the slaughter house. They all just made it so damn easy.

Harold was standing in the hallway when I reached the floor that held our offices, grinning at me. I couldn't stop the smile that crossed my face because I knew he'd already heard the news. He silently followed me to my office and closed the door, taking a seat across from my desk as I sat in my chair.

"I'm assuming dinner was successful," he mused.

I grabbed the remote from my desk drawer and turned the TV onto the local news channel, where the reporter stood near the bridge.

"Very. I recouped my money from the sale of his daughters, and both he and his wife got their heads blown to bits." A delicious shiver shook my whole body as I remembered the massive holes in their faces after Donovan and Colt emptied their respective magazines into their victim. It was something about the gore of a kill that made me crave more. The high it gave me was something I was addicted to, something I craved more than sex. I regretted that I hadn't recorded the kill to watch it on repeat later.

We both stared at the TV, the reporter rattling on about the missing children. Video footage of boats and a dive team played on screen, the rolling headline displaying information about an Amber Alert for the missing girls.

"Are they still in the country?" Harold asked for a while.

"I don't know if they still are right this moment, but they won't be. The buyers are from Canada."

"Smart."

"*The police and community are frantically searching for the daughters of the deceased. Family members say that sisters JessLynn, eight years old, and Alana, six, have health issues that require daily medication. If you have any information on the whereabouts of these two girls, please contact the Palmetto County Police Department immediately. These two girls have now been reported missing and are assumed to be in grave danger following the brutal murder of their parents."*

"What did you do to Maxwell and Brenda?"

I shrugged, flipping through a couple of files on my desk. "They were both shot, something quick and easy. I just wanted to traumatize the girl to show her the kind of man she made the mistake of fucking with."

"I guess you showed her then," he said with a chuckle before he turned away from the TV and focused his gaze on me. "So, how's everything going with your soon-to-be wife anyway?" he asked, a playful grin hinting on his lips.

I frowned, a subtle throb starting at my temple at the thought of that bitch. "I haven't even had her for a full twenty-four hours and I already want to hang her from my helicopter," I muttered.

Harold barked a laugh. "She can't seriously be that bad, Si. It's more like you being impatience, not that something's wrong with the other person."

I shook my head. "She's mouthy, stubborn, and doesn't fucking listen. I nearly drowned her in the kitchen sink this morning when I got sick of her shit."

"Isn't it always more fun when they fight?" he asked,

tiling his head to the side. "Besides, you never liked women who were weak and submitted to you too easily."

"Yeah, as a partner. But I have no intentions of romance with this woman. There's no way in hell I could trust being with someone who's already stolen from me. She's just a resource right now and I'll use her until I have no use for her."

"Sounds like the best plan. And everything is squared away with her name and all that?"

I nodded. "I had the judge come over to get all the appropriate paperwork done, so he should be getting those filed."

"What happens next then?"

I ran a hand down my face. It was already exhausting to think about all the shit I needed to do to prepare her for our wedding in six months. I had to get her surgeries scheduled and done, meet with the wedding planners, call my lawyer to draft a pre-nup, train her, and make sure she was actually ready to walk down the aisle. The day I got married would be big news, so I absolutely refused to marry her before she was mentally ready to take on the role. Her mind was too independent right now, which still made her a liability. It only took talking to the wrong reporter who put out the wrong headline to send everything crashing down.

Harold continued looking at me expectantly, so I

shrugged. "There's so much shit that needs to be done that I don't even know where to even start. The main thing is working on her training. She needs to accept her life and the shit that will happen in it."

"Especially if she wants to survive long enough to walk down the aisle."

"Especially that," I agreed. "I need to schedule her surgeries and such, though. Those will need to be done ASAP. The last thing I need is for someone to recognize her and wonder why she's not in prison."

Harold chuckle and shook his head. "It's like you have your very own build-a-bitch," he teased.

"I mean, that's what she'll be essentially. She should be happy that she's getting a new body. Because she's definitely not doing shit for me right now with what she has now."

Her face was decent but her body didn't make me react in the slightest. Her breasts were barely a B cup and she lacked the curves I usually liked in the women I slept with. I had to make her fit the mold of the type of woman I liked in order to get away with this shit in the long run, so she'd get whatever surgery it took to reach that goal.

"Well, you'll have to keep me updated on how that works out. I'm very curious to know whether or not she makes it down the aisle."

At the rate she's going, that makes the two of us, I thought. "Only time will tell," I said instead.

He stood and stretched before taking a sip of the coffee he held. "Anyway, I just wanted to see how everything went with Maxwell since he's the talk of the office. You know what that means, right?"

I sighed inwardly. It was only a matter of time before the media swarmed the building, wanting to get a statement from me and others who worked here about how "tragic" Maxwell's death was. There was nothing I really wanted to say other than he fucked up and got what was coming to him. But I couldn't be the bad guy in public, which meant I needed to rehearse what I'd say when I ran into the media later while leaving the building.

"Yeah, unfortunately," I finally said. "I'll figure something out."

"I'll leave you to it then. You know where I am if you need me," Harold said, leaving with a wave and closing the door behind him.

I blew out a breath and turned my chair to face the floor-to-ceiling windows. The day was warm but gloomy, the sun hiding behind the thick clouds that threatened rain showers and thunderstorms. I watched the tiny figures moving along the street. Despite the death and missing children that were on everyone's lips right now, life still went on for everybody else. Maxwell and his family were just as insignificant to the rest of the world as they were to me and this company.

He played stupid games and it cost him and his family their lives. Wasn't much more to say about that.

I pushed the thought of him from my mind and dived into my work, allowing myself to get lost in a sea of video meetings with international suppliers and office meetings to talk about Maxwell's unfortunate death and what it would mean going forward.

But in the back of my mind, all I could think of was the little bitch that was still in my house and whether or not she'd been reading the manual like I told her to. If I were being honest, a part of me hoped she hadn't. There was nothing I wanted more than to go home and drag her to my mudroom to cause her pain.

But I didn't need a reason to hurt her. She was my property now, which gave me free reign to do whatever I saw fit.

"Mr. Arnett?" a voice called out.

I blinked and looked at the room full of faces staring at me as I stood at the front of the room. It was then that I realized I was standing there with a grin on my face, probably looking completely psychotic in that moment. I cleared my throat.

"What?"

"You were talking about the Jennings account and

then you just...spaced out," Jackson, the district manager of the hotels under Arnett Enterprises, said with a confused expression.

I pushed the thoughts of my new toy out of my mind so that I could focus on the task at hand, but I'd be lying if I said I wasn't eager to blow this place just to spend the afternoon making her scream.

And scream she would.

CHAPTER FIVE
LIA

I wasn't sure how long I'd stayed on the floor after he'd left the house.

My heart hammered in my chest as I fought to catch my breath, my lungs burning with each inhale. My brain was still trying to wrap itself around the fact that this psycho just tried to drown me in the kitchen sink just now. Everything happened so quickly that I couldn't react. One minute I was washing his plate and griping about him being a major dick, and then I was underwater the next.

I closed my eyes and ground my teeth. He'd completely caught me off guard and my brain froze, making it impossible to think logically enough to defend myself. I pulled myself off the floor, gripping the counter top tightly as I stood on shaky legs. A soapy knife taunted me in the empty side of the sink. Had I been thinking clearly, that should've been the first thing I grabbed instead of slapping at him. If I were going to be punished, it was only right for him to hurt, too.

So fucking stupid, I chastised myself, sniffling as I pushed my wet hair from my face. The bossy bitch from yesterday appeared in the kitchen doorway with a frown on her lips as she observed me.

"It's time to go to your room for the day," she said, her hands clasped in front of her.

"There's nothing to do in there." I shifted my weight from foot to foot. "Can I watch TV in the living room or—"

"Mr. Arnett wants you in your room only. Besides, you have plenty to keep you entertained, as you have your training manual to read."

I rolled my eyes. I was so sick of hearing about this stupid fucking manual. "I'm not his employee anymore," I countered, folding my arms across my chest in defiance.

"Of course you aren't. His employees have rights; as his property, you don't. If I have to repeat myself, I'll have one of the men forcibly escort you to your room."

An angry retort crawled to the tip of my tongue but I forced it back down my throat. This particular woman had already made it known that she'd hit me if I didn't listen to her, so I didn't want to press my luck. It was apparent that everyone in this house liked to abuse and threaten people, so the smartest thing for me to do was comply until I could figure out how to get out of this fucking nightmare.

I stepped into my room when she stopped outside the door of it, turning around to face her. "I didn't get a chance to eat breakfast," I said. A part of me hoped she would've brought me something that wasn't the disgusting prison-style bullshit Silas wanted to torture me with. But the woman only shrugged, her hand poised on the doorknob.

"Then maybe next time you'll remember to eat instead of provoking your owner."

"He's not my owner and I'm not a fucking prisoner in this house," I snapped back before I could stop myself. It was a stupid comeback really, because I *was* a prisoner in this house and as of yesterday, he *was* my owner.

The woman's eyes rolled up to the ceiling briefly before looking at me again. "Living in delusional denial doesn't make what I said any less true," she said and pointed to the binder that was still on the floor after I threw it last night. "Read the manual. I'm sure he'll quiz you on it just to be sure you did."

"Whatever," I muttered, sitting on the side of the bed. She stared at me before she closed the door, the light click of the lock seeming to echo around me.

I fell onto my back with a huff, gazing up at the ceiling.

He didn't fail in making this place feel like a fucking prison. If he were going to go through the trouble of making his home into a prison, he would've been better off leaving me where I was. It would've been less money and hassle that way anyway.

Being in this house would've been awesome if the situation were different. After spending my entire life in foster care, it was a dream to live in a house like this. I used to imagine my life would end up like Annie's, waiting for my own Daddy Warbucks to whisk me away to a lavish life filled with love and memories. But that day never came, no matter how many times I prayed, no matter how many times I was a "good girl," and no matter how hard I tried to think positive.

Instead, the closest I got to the billionaire family I wanted was my psycho ex-boss that was now obsessed with holding me captive and using me for whatever fuckery he conjured up in his head.

I finally pulled myself off the bed and looked over at the thick binder still on the floor. The simple text on the cover looked normal enough, but I knew the contents of it would do nothing but solidify how fucked up my situation was.

My mind rolled over potential options of how to acclimate to my current situation. I'd already seen what Psycho

Silas was capable of last night against other people, and he showed me earlier how easy it would be for him to kill me if he truly wanted to. On one hand, I could follow all of his rules and do what he wanted to be able to survive for the next nine years. On the other hand, there was no guarantee that he wouldn't torture me just for the hell of it. I *did* steal money from him after all. My best bet was to find a fucking way out of here before things escalated more than they already had.

There's literally no where for me to go, even if I did make it out of here, I reminded myself with a sigh. I was a prisoner of the state outside of this house—at least, that was what I should've been. Right now, I was a prisoner of Silas Arnett so he could fulfill this sick version of a family he wanted.

I was sure this man could have any woman he wanted. He was rich, handsome as hell, and seemed to be a great guy on the surface. But after seeing how evil and psychotic he was last night, I could very well understand why a deranged moron like him would be single.

The screaming of the accountant and his family filled my head as memories of last night filtered into my mind. I couldn't forget the tears and fear in the eyes of their daughters as those men ripped them away from their mother. My stomach flipped at the thought of what those men were possibly doing to them, memories of my own abuse trying to break out of the mental box I'd stuffed them in.

"May as well see what kind of fuckery is ahead of me," I muttered. I lugged the weighty binder over to the bed and opened it, rolling my eyes when I saw the first page.

For The Property of Silas Arnett

Welcome to my home. As my property, there are rules that must be followed and things that will change as you get settled in. Please be sure to read through this entire binder, as everything inside is of great importance to you. You will be quizzed on things within this binder at any moment, so be prepared. Your life could very well depend on how well you can follow directions and obey.

"This man is definitely on drugs. Probably coke since he's rich," I mumbled to myself, flipping to the next page.

Important Information To Know Immediately

Because you are supposed to be in prison, you will no longer be addressed as Lia McIntyre while you are

in my possession. Please take note of the following name and story you are to give people when you're given permission to speak.

"Permission to speak?" I scoffed and shook my head. This man had clearly lost his marbles.

New name: Alyssa Diana Mitchell
Purpose: To be my wife in public and to give me an heir. Male children only.

"You can't control biology, dickhead, but please go on about how I will only birth male children," I muttered, rolling my eyes.

The story of how we met: We met at a charity fundraiser event for the children's hospital wing almost a year prior. You were a volunteer helping the organizer and we hit it off. We kept our relationship a secret until we became engaged and now we're planning a wedding. Nothing more, nothing less.

. . .

I used to think that rich people had it all and had such cool lives considering they had money to do whatever they wanted. But this delusional fuck made me realize that rich people had nothing better to do with their time than to fuck with people and boss others around. I'd given him the benefit of the doubt to think he was doing coke if he thought this was reasonable for me to follow, but with him being as stupid as he was, maybe I gave him too much credit.

He was definitely on meth. Had to be.

I flipped to the next page to brace myself for the bull-shit list of rules.

<u>My rules</u>

1. We will not share the same bed.

2. You will not be entitled to or have access to a dime of my money. I will provide you with the basic things you need.

3. You can not leave the house unless I am with you.

4. You should not speak while in public unless I give you explicit permission.

5. You are to attend to my needs whenever and however I see fit.

6. Any disrespect or disobedience will be met with swift and brutal punishment.

7. You are permitted to stay in your bedroom unless there is a need for you to be outside of it.

8. You are to never address me by name, only Sir.

9. Do not speak to house staff unnecessarily. They are not here to be your friends.

10. Never reveal your true identity to anyone inside or outside of the house.

"Okay, that's enough of that fuckery," I said and closed the binder, pushing it away from me.

Who the fuck did he think he was? Permission to speak to people? Not using his name when talking to him? I scoffed and shook my head. "Fucking bastard."

I stood and moved over to the window, trying to open it but it was sealed shut. *Well, there goes any chance of escaping*, I thought bitterly to myself. The bedroom window faced the large backyard. Beautiful flowers and a large fountain sat in the middle of the healthy lawn, a sparkling pool not far from that. The beautiful backyard was probably just his version of "the yard" that I'd get to spend an hour in before being locked in my bedroom for the remaining twenty-three hours of the day.

"If only Danica could see me now," I murmured to myself.

She'd been my work friend for the last year, the both of us bonding over the bullshit our managers put us through on a daily basis at work. While we didn't see Silas often, we'd often joke about how we thought he'd be in bed or how lucky his rumored girlfriend at the time was.

But that was before I saw what he was capable of, before I realized how much of an asshole he truly was. He didn't have actual girlfriends because he preferred to keep his women hostage.

Maybe he had something to hide that he didn't want getting out in case the relationship went south.

I tapped a finger on my chin as I thought. There had to be a way out of this shit. Granted, it wasn't like I had much waiting for me outside of here. I was supposed to be in prison, for fuck's sake. But at least I had a chance of being treated like a fucking human in actual prison and not the property of a man hell bent on making my life miserable.

"It's not like prison is a cake walk either," I murmured with a sigh, turning to press my back against the window.

I looked around at the beautifully decorated room. This bedroom was probably bigger than the shitty studio apartment I lived in. Despite this room being my prison, it held a queen sized bed with sheets that had thread counts out of my price range. I'd slept like a baby last night despite the traumatic shit I'd witnessed. A bookshelf sat in a corner across the room with books and magazines I hadn't bothered looking at with a chaise lounge next to it. This room might've been a prison, but at least it was luxury.

"I just need to play my cards right," I whispered to myself as I paced the floor. There had to be someone within Silas' fucked up organization that knew all of this was wrong, someone who might could help me get out of town or even out of this state. I just needed to get far enough away to where I could possibly start over. I could get a new name, a new—

A solid knock on the door jolted me out of my thoughts, my heart racing once again. I only stared at the door but it didn't matter if I spoke or not. A lock clicked before it was pushed open, the woman from earlier walking in with a doctor of some sort. He almost looked like a plastic Ken doll, which made it a bit obvious that he was here for the plastic surgery bullshit Silas mentioned at breakfast this morning.

The woman said nothing to me, only gesturing toward me as she kept her attention on the doctor. "Here she is. Please let me know if you need anything else. Security is right outside the door if you have any trouble," she said.

"Thank you," he said with a nod, watching her as she excused herself before turning to me. The small smile on his lips seemed forced as he clasped his hands in front of him. "Hello, Alyssa. I'm Dr. Wynn. It's nice to meet you." When I didn't say anything, he cleared his throat and continued. "I'm sure Mr. Arnett has already spoken to you about this, but I'm here to do your surgery consultation. If you could remove everything from the waist up, we can get started."

"I'm not having surgery," I stated firmly, folding my arms across my chest.

I still thought Silas was out of his fucking mind to think he could alter my body just because he wanted to. Sure, I might be his property for the moment, but I wouldn't be forever. I still had human rights, rights protected by laws that he couldn't break no matter how much fucking money he had.

The doctor frowned slightly before pulling out his phone, scrolling through something before looking back to me. "Please don't make this harder than it needs to be, Alyssa. We're only doing a consultation today—"

"He can do whatever else he wants to me, but he's not surgically altering my face or body just because he has the money to. I don't consent to it."

Dr. Wynn shook his head and pulled out a silver vape. He took a deep puff from it before exhaling thin smoke, filling the room with a sickeningly sweet scent. "Do you know how many women would kill to be in your position right now?" he asked before putting the vape back into his mouth. "You're acting like an ungrateful bitch."

I scoffed. "Excuse me? You have no idea the shit I've seen in the twenty-four hours I've been here!" I snapped, my cheeks heating with anger.

"Alyssa—"

"Stop calling me that! That isn't my fucking name," I said, holding up a hand. "How dare you come in here and tell me I'm lucky because a psycho is trying to force me to have a surgery I don't even want."

"I know enough to know that your alternative is to die in prison. You're lucky Mr. Arnett even found you attractive enough to make such an arrangement." His burning gaze left a disgusting, imaginary film on my skin as it swept along my body. "And with my work, you'll be perfect."

"Well, I'm not having surgery. He wanted me so bad, so he can take me as I am."

He and I stood there in a silent stand-off as my refusal lingered in the air. After a few tense moments, he shrugged and grabbed his phone. I sat on the edge of the bed and watched him, already knowing he was calling Silas.

"Mr. Arnett, good morning," he said enthusiastically.

"I'm sorry to disturb you at work, but I'm running into a problem with your *fiancée*." I rolled my eyes at his use of fiancée. "Well, she's incredibly mouthy and refuses to allow me to do what you've sent me here to do." His brows furrowed as he lips flattened into a thin line as he listened to whatever Silas told him. "Uh huh, same thing I said. But you know how these disrespectful cunts can be."

I ground my teeth as the doctor laughed. Had we been outside of this house, a comment like that would've earned him a slap across the cheek. It absolutely blew my mind how crude and awful these men were, but then again, why was I surprised? Anyone in Silas's circle had to be as terrible as he was, otherwise they wouldn't be close enough to know the secret he was hiding in his house. Fucking bastard.

"Sure, one moment," the doctor said, pulling me out of my thoughts. I blinked at him when he held his phone out toward me. "Mr. Arnett would like to speak with you."

My heart hammered in my chest as I only looked at the phone. I already knew my refusal would give him a reason to do something to me when he got home, but I wasn't ready to hear his voice verbally lash out at me. When I didn't grab the phone, the doctor put it back to his ear.

"She won't take the phone," he said. After a few moments, he nodded and took the phone away from his ear, putting it on speaker. "She can hear you now, Mr. Arnett."

"*Thank you, Dr. Wynn,*" Silas's voice said from the phone. "*Alyssa, please be sure you're reading the manual. That's important for later.*"

I frowned, confused that he was talking about the manual instead of my refusal to have the surgery consultation. "I am reading it," I said cautiously.

"*Good. Dr. Wynn, I'll just reschedule this for another time. I'll call your office when things are ready.*"

Dr. Wynn's mouth opened and closed for a brief moment before he finally nodded, probably just as confused as I was. "O-okay then, Mr. Arnett. Just remember that my schedule can get pretty busy around this time of—"

"*I'll let you know when we're ready,*" Silas interrupted, his voice firm. "*You'll be compensated for your time. I appreciate you for making the trip.*"

"Of course, Mr. Arnett. I look forward to hearing from you," he said and then the line went dead. He stuffed his phone back into the pocket of his white lab coat before glaring at me. "Stupid bitch. You better not have screwed up my working relationship with him."

He roughly pushed me to the floor before he stomped over to the door and pounded his fist against it. It opened instantly and allowed him to storm out of the room, the woman outside the door looking at me with disdain before closing and locking the door again.

I slowly pulled myself off the floor and sat on the bed. Silas hadn't reacted the way I thought he would've after refusing to do something he'd set up for me. The naive part of me wanted to believe that he was simply respecting my wishes to not have my body altered, but I knew better. He was probably one of those "silent storm" type of men where they made you think everything was okay until they finally attacked you.

I glanced over at the manual next to me. The only thing he'd mentioned was that it was important to read the manual. I'd already gotten the gist of what it was that he wanted, so the rest seemed a bit redundant. But I reluctantly grabbed the manual and continued where I left off. Since he didn't threaten or scream at me after refusing the surgery consultation, the least I could do was read like he asked me to.

Majority of the pages were mock pictures of potential surgery looks, which slightly irritated me. How the hell did this man have time to have this thoroughly thought out when I hadn't even been here long? I hadn't even been in his house a full twenty-four hours and yet he had pictures of who I assumed to be me with various plastic surgery enhancements. *Maybe he knew I'd been stealing from him longer than I thought,* I mused as I flipped the page.

Plastic Surgery Recommendations

Though you are spending my money, I want to give you the option to choose how you'd like to look. The purpose of the surgery is to conceal your identity. You, thief, are supposed to be in prison. It would raise a few eyebrows to the public to see you by my side as my future wife instead of in prison where you belong. Surgery is not debatable, nor is it up for discussion. Feel free to fight against it if you'd like. You'll just leave me with no choice but to make the choices for you.

I scoffed as I stared at the page. All of this shit was wrong. I understood what he meant, but it didn't make any of this shit right. It only seemed as if he was trying to hide what he'd done, not protect me or keep me out of prison. Being in this house in general was a fucking prison. Being held captive by the man who had me arrested was a prison. Being forced to change my body to hide my true self in order to avoid actual prison *was* a prison.

Voices in the backyard peaked my curiosity, luring me

to the window. A woman in a sports bra and leggings stood in the back talking with a security guard and one of the women. She held two bright-colored mats in her arms as she smiled up at the security guard.

When their eyes moved toward my window, I quickly ducked down and crawled back over to the bed. I wasn't sure who the woman was or if she was here for me or not, but I wasn't a very athletic person. The last thing I wanted was to get all sweaty and sunburned for someone else's amusement.

When I got back on the bed, the manual was opened to the sheet that displayed my scheduled activities. My eyes quickly scanned it before looking at the round clock poised over the door. I frowned. The woman was definitely here for me.

Alyssa's Daily Schedule
7:00am - 7:45am—Wake up/morning routine
8:00am 8:40am—Breakfast
8:45am - 10:45am— Lockdown
11:00am - 11:20am— Prepare for workout
11:30am - 12:20pm—Workout with trainer
12:30pm - 1:15pm—Lunch
1:20pm - 6:00pm —Lockdown
6:00pm - 6:45pm—Dinner

7:00pm - 11:00pm—Owner's Open Hours
11:30pm—Light's out
*Schedule open to change as Silas Arnett sees fit;
schedule to be started immediately after capture.

"What the fuck are open hours?" I murmured to myself, just as my bedroom door opened. A different woman than the earlier bossy bitch walked in with an outfit in her hands. She placed it on the bed and gave me a small smile.

"Please get changed. Your yoga session will be starting soon," she said, her soft voice bringing me a hint of comfort.

"Um, can I ask a quick question?" I said when she turned to head back out of the room. She looked at me over her shoulder. "I'm sure you and the other woman will be the ones I'll see the most. I wanted to know if I was allowed to know your name."

Her lips pressed into a thin line before she nervously flicked her gaze to the hallway. "It's Aimee. Now please, get dressed. I don't want you to get in trouble."

She quickly skittered out of the room and cloaked me in silence once more. *I don't want you to get in trouble.* At least there was one person in this stupid prison house that had a sliver of compassion for someone.

Not wanting to cause her any issues, I quickly changed out of the gown and pulled on the sports bra and leggings. The instructor was outside talking with the security guard, twirling a lock of auburn hair around her finger as she smiled at him. I rolled my eyes. How people could find psychos attractive was beyond my comprehension.

"Are you ready, Alyssa?" Aimee asked, suddenly appearing in the open doorway. Out of the four women, she was the smallest. There wasn't anything too memorable about her. Her brown hair was thin and thrown back into a messy bun, a few tendrils cradling her face. Her skin was pale in an almost sickly way, her frame thin and hidden in the loose dress she wore. Her brown eyes were bright with hope, though, and a warmth that put me at ease with her.

"Yeah, I think so," I said, giving her a small smile. She gestured for me to follow her, standing off to the side as I stepped into the hallway.

The smell of roasted meat coming from the kitchen made my stomach growl, reminding me that I didn't have breakfast. I glanced at Aimee as we walked through the house and headed for the backyard, the smell growing stronger when we passed the kitchen. If I played my cards right, I could probably convince Aimee to give me something nice to eat other than the prison food Silas had given me lately.

The bright sun was blinding when I stepped outside. I shielded my eyes and continued toward the voices ahead. I wasn't quite looking forward to doing whatever this woman had planned, but I'd comply and do what I needed to do. I'd already pushed my luck with the surgery consult; I wasn't stupid enough to play Russian roulette with my life a second time.

The woman spun around toward me with a bright smile when the security guard walked a few feet away. "Good morning, Alyssa!" she beamed, clasping her hands together. "I'm happy to be working with you! Is this your first yoga class?"

I wrapped my arms around myself, shuffling my weight from foot to foot. "Yeah, I guess," I murmured.

The woman gave me a playful push. "Don't be shy, silly. We all have to start somewhere!" she exclaimed. "Well, I'm Taylor and I'll be your yoga instructor three days a week!"

I raised an eyebrow as I regarded her. "I only have to workout three days a week?" I repeated.

She shook her head, her auburn ponytail swishing at the back of her head. "You only have yoga three times a week. You have other instructors that'll do other things with you on the other days." She clapped her hands together and then gestured to the lavender mat next to me. "Let's go ahead and get started."

She took me through various poses I had no clue my body could move into. She moved so effortlessly from pose to pose while I struggled embarrassingly. She at least gave me words of encouragement that prevented me from dying of embarrassment. The women in the house watched me from the kitchen window and the security guard watched us a few feet away, though I was sure he was mostly looking at the instructor's ass more than he was paying attention to me.

The sun beat down on my skin and sweat dripped down the middle of my back. I used to think yoga was just good for stretching and not much of a workout, but my muscles burned and felt like jelly by the time it was over.

"Alright, we're going to close our session out by doing a little meditating to prepare us for the rest of our day with a relaxed mind," she said with an even breath. I put my hands on my knees and nodded, trying to catch my breath. Taylor lowered herself to a sitting position on the ground before looking up at me, shielding her eyes from the sun. "Go on, sit."

I plopped down on my mat without a shred of grace, relieved to finally be off my legs. I copied her crossed leg position and placed my hands in my lap, closing my eyes.

"Right now, I want you to imagine something relaxing and allow yourself to imagine how calm it makes you feel. You can imagine being at the beach, curled up in front of

A WIFE FOR SILAS

the fireplace with your favorite book, or anything that makes you happy and at ease."

I swallowed the growing lump in my throat as tears burned the back of my eyelids. The only thing I could imagine was how great my freedom had been. I'd hated the life I lived because I was nowhere close to being where I wanted to be in life. I was stuck in a dead end job, wasn't making much money, didn't have a ton of friends or any family. Now that I was in captivity, I'd do anything to have that life back. I'd do anything to have my shitty apartment back, my shitty job back. I just wanted the relaxation of freedom, something I'd lost the minute I stepped foot on this property.

If only I could go back and tell the past version of myself not to be tempted to touch that money. If only I knew the can of worms I would open by financially fucking over my boss. If only I'd stopped before I got ahead of myself and returned the small amounts I'd taken while I still could.

But what ifs didn't matter anymore. I'd done it and now I was paying the consequences of my fucked up choices. One of my old foster moms once told me that I could make whatever decision I wanted, but I couldn't control the consequences I got from them. She always told me that when I'd done something she deemed to be bad. The last time she'd said it was right before she dropped

117

me back off at the foster home after accusing me of seducing her husband—after she caught him raping me.

"Now bring yourself back to the present, bringing with you the calm and peace you filled yourself with as you rested in your happy place," Taylor's soothing voice said, bringing me out of my darkness. I quickly wiped away a stray tear that managed to fall and opened my eyes just in time to see Taylor exhale slowly and smile. She opened her eyes and looked over to me. "Great job on your first day! Even though it was your first time, I think you did great."

"Thanks," I mumbled, dropping my gaze to the mat.

"Let's go," a gruff voice growled before a rough hand tightly gripped my forearm.

"Jesus, you don't have to be so rough, you asshole," I snapped. No matter what kind of reprieve I got whenever I was around someone who wasn't in the house at all times, the assholes within the house quickly reminded me that I wasn't here to have fun or enjoy myself. I was here as a prisoner only, and was treated as such.

"It was nice meeting you, Alyssa!" Taylor called out behind me, but the security guard quickly whisked me away before I could even respond.

He didn't stop until we reached the dining room. He let me go with a slight shove and pointed to a chair. "Sit. Your lunch will be brought to you."

Since Silas wasn't here, I said a silent prayer that I

could eat something decent for once. I looked around to see if Aimee was around, but I'd only seen the other three women. After a few minutes, the chef came into the dining room with another prison tray and plopped it in front of me.

I grimaced at the mush that was supposed to be some kind of pasta dish, a stale chunk of bread, fruit cocktail that seemed to be more juice syrup than fruit, and a limp salad with lettuce that was browning a bit at the corners.

I slumped in my chair, my stomach growling and swirling with nausea at the same time as I just sat there staring at the tray. If Silas kept feeding me shit he knew I wouldn't eat, then maybe I wouldn't even have to worry about marrying him or any other bullshit he had planned for me. I'd either starve to death or kill myself eventually.

And the latter sounded like a good fucking idea to me.

CHAPTER SIX
SILAS

My mind conjured up the many ways I could hurt Alyssa when I got home.

She was already on thin fucking ice when I learned she hadn't read the manual and chipped a wall in her bedroom during her tantrum. The incident in the kitchen was only a taste of what could happen to her, one I thought would startle her enough to force her to be on her best fucking behavior while I was at work today.

That was on me for thinking she had common sense.

My home appeared in the distance, my irritation growing as we turned onto the long, smooth driveway. I used to think I wanted a woman that was a little stubborn to give me something to do from time to time when she disobeyed, but this bitch was already pushing my buttons to the point that it pissed me off more than excited me.

Feisty women were always fun until they were fucking annoying.

I looked down at my watch to see that it was 6:20pm, which meant she was probably in the dining room having dinner. Donovan looked at me in the rearview mirror with a raised brow.

"Something wrong?" he asked.

"Why would something be wrong?"

"I mean we've been sitting here for about two minutes now and you haven't moved," he said with a small shrug. I glanced out the window and realized we were parked, the car's engine no longer running. I'd been so caught up in my thoughts that I hadn't even realized the scenery stopped moving outside.

"Just trying to prepare myself to deal with this infuriating woman before I actually go in the house," I finally said when Donovan's gaze never left me in the mirror.

"You know you can always get rid of her," he reminded me, but I rolled my eyes.

"That would be stupid at this point. There's too much money invested into her now," I growled.

He raised his hands as if to surrender. "It was just a suggestion, man. It seems like she's stressing you out more than anything else."

I shook my head. "She hasn't been around long enough to stress me out. More like annoying the fuck out of me." I looked toward the house. "Well, sitting out here isn't going to make her disappear, so I may as well go inside. I need to decide on her punishment anyway."

Donovan got out and opened my door, closing it behind me when I stepped out. I rolled my shoulders, trying to release the tension that'd settled there. Maryse looked up at me when I entered the kitchen.

"Could you come with me to my office, please?" I asked her as I passed. She put down the knife in her hand and wiped her hands on a towel before following me to my office. She stood on the other side of my desk with her hands clasped, waiting for me to speak.

"So? How was she today?" I asked her as I sat behind my desk.

"I'm sure you know she refused to cooperate with the surgeon during her consultation this morning," she started.

I nodded as I rubbed my temples, a small headache brewing. "Yeah, he called me," I said with a sigh. "I'll get that rescheduled because it needs to happen soon. There's an event coming up that she'll need to be present for in a couple of months and I need her completely healed from whatever she has to get done." I focused my gaze on her. "What else?"

"She refuses to eat anything given to her. I'm not sure about breakfast since I wasn't with her then, but she refused to eat lunch and dinner. At this point, I don't think she's eaten since she's been here."

I ground my teeth. She was probably holding out in hopes that I'd give her the food she'd seen me eating, but she'd be in for a rude awakening. She could starve herself until she was skin and bones for all I cared. She was in prison after all. Had she been in a real prison, she wouldn't have a choice about what she ate. Regardless of the luxury that surrounded her, she was here to serve out a prison sentence and would be treated as such.

"I'm not surprised," I finally said.

"There were also a few instances were she was disrespectful and rude. She mentioned numerous times throughout the day that she hated everyone in this house and that she was going to either run away or kill herself." Maryse frowned. "Should we put her on suicide watch or something? You never know what someone in her predicament will do."

"No," I said, shaking my head. "I'll deal with her. Besides, her running away if the last thing I'm worried about. There's literally nowhere for her to go."

"But the suicide?"

"She's helpless, not stupid," I said, but even I wasn't too sure. A woman with common sense would simply do whatever she had to in order to stay out of trouble. This woman was practically fucking begging for it, almost as if she were a glutton for pain.

"Okay then," Maryse said with a small shrug. "I sent the security feed from her room to show you when she was throwing her tantrum earlier in case you wanted to see it."

"I'll take a look at it, thanks." I slumped down in my chair and loosened my tie. "I need you to tell Donovan to take Alyssa to the mudroom at eight. Her instructions are simply to prepare herself."

"Will do," Maryse said with a nod before turning and heading to the door.

"And Maryse," I called out. She paused and looked at me over her shoulder. "Tell him not to tell her what that means. Had she been going through the manual like she was supposed to, she'd know what to do. He's to only give her that instruction and lock her in until I get there."

"Yes, sir," Maryse said and headed out of the room, leaving me in silence.

I closed my eyes and tried to settle myself. There was so much shit I needed to do to both get this woman ready to present her to the world as well as planning to walk down the aisle. The dynamic of a relationship wasn't something I could easily grasp, even when I was younger. Making money was always easy because there were multiple ways it could be done. But emotions and being in relationships wasn't something I spent time on.

Most women I interacted with would say that I was cold, empty, and lost, and they were probably right. I'd never been in love, lust, or anything else distracting. A woman may have caught my interest every now and then, but once I fucked her, she was no different than any other bimbo walking down the street.

Now I had to convince the world that this woman was the one I loved enough to marry, to have children with, to be seen in public with. I wasn't good at pretending, but if she could do what she needed to do, it would make everything else easier for me. But first, I had to break her in order to mold her into what I needed her to be.

With a quick glance at the clock, I saw that I had about an hour or so to kill before I dealt with her. I flipped through my contact book on my desk and called the surgeon, drumming my fingers on my desktop as I waited for him to answer.

"*Mr. Arnett, good evening!*" Dr. Wynn exclaimed, his boisterous voice causing me to cringe slightly. The headache bloomed in the front of my head as I pinched the bridge of my nose and exhaled deeply.

"Dr. Wynn, good evening. First, I want to apologize again on my fiancée's behalf. I know how valuable your time is, so I hate that it was wasted this morning."

"You owe me no apologies, Mr. Arnett. I know how moody women can be about certain things," he said with a chuckle. I rolled my eyes.

Sometimes, it was slightly annoying how easily other people bent to my will just to maintain a working relationship with me. Some of the strongest, well-respected men always cowered before me like a pussy. It made it so hard to respect men who were more of a bitch than women were.

"Well, I'm calling to get her appointment rescheduled," I said as I rubbed my forehead. "Is it possible for you to come in the evening instead of the morning? I want to be able to be present to make sure this gets done."

"I usually don't make evening house calls, though."

"That's fine. I can see if I can find someone else to—"

"On second thought, I could make some arrangements," he quickly interjected. I scoffed inwardly. *Of course you would, you pathetic fuck.*

"Are you sure?"

"I'm sure I can move some things around. When would you like to plan it?"

"In three days," I said. "After the punishment she's getting tonight, I'm sure she's gonna need a few days to recover."

"Try not to strike her face too often," he warned. *"Facial*

swelling can make it hard to give her an accurate consultation."

"I'm not touching her face, so that won't be a concern," I said.

"Okay, then. What time?"

"Around eight is good. I should be home and settled by then."

Dr. Wynn let out a low whistle before he sighed. *"Okay then."*

I frowned. "If it's too much of an inconvenience, I can truly find another surgeon, Ronald."

"No, no. There's no problem, Silas," he quickly said.

"Then stop with the exaggerated bullshit every time I say something," I ground out. My patience was already thin; the last thing I wanted to deal with was a mother-fucker who wanted to act as if my business was an inconvenience to them.

"My apologies," Dr. Wynn said and cleared his throat. "I *have you down for a home visit in three days at 8 p.m."*

"Good. I'll see you then," I said and hung up before he said another word.

A solid knock sounded before the door opened, Donovan stepping into my office.

"You okay in here?" he asked.

I nodded as I shrugged out of my suit jacket. "Yeah, I'm good," I said. "Did Maryse tell you what I asked of you?"

"Taking the girl to the mudroom soon? Yeah, she did. I wanted to ask you if you needed me to restrain her or anything or just take her in there and lock the door?"

"Just take her in there and lock her in. She can't prepare herself if she's restrained." I shrugged. "My gut tells me she hasn't read that part of the manual so she won't even know what that means."

"What do you plan to do?"

I smirked at him and shook my head. "That's between me and my prisoner, Donny," I said, earning myself a wicked grin.

"I'll be able to tell from the way she screams," he said and chuckled.

"Oh yeah, while I'm thinking about it," I snapped my fingers. "You were outside when she was doing yoga, right?"

He nodded. "Yeah, why?"

"She didn't do anything stupid, did she?"

"No, she was fine. It looked like she was crying when they were meditating or some shit, but other than that, she was fine." He tsked and shook his head. "That yoga instructor was something else, though."

I frowned. "What about the yoga instructor?"

"That's between me and the yoga instructor's pussy," he said with a smirk. I stared at him for a long moment before I burst into a hearty laugh.

"Why the fuck am I surprised?" I said with a chuckle when I finally got myself together.

"You should try fucking a yoga instructor. Their flexibility can make sex interesting," he said with a grin.

I shook my head. "I'm good. I'm sure Alyssa will be flexible soon enough."

"Anyway, I'm about to make my rounds on the property before I have to get Alyssa to the mudroom. If you need me before then, just shoot me a message."

"Will do, thanks," I said and turned to my computer.

Silence cloaked my office once more when he closed the door behind him. I spent the next half hour reading and replying to emails, my headache growing the longer I sat there looking at my computer. I pulled the top drawer of my desk open and grabbed a bottle of pain reliever, popping two in my mouth and forcing them down my throat before focusing on my computer screen again.

A slow grin spread across my lips when I saw an email from one of the men that'd been here the night before to buy one of Maxwell's daughters.

Silas,

. . .

Thank you again for such a seamless purchase. They were exactly what my boss was looking for. He sends his thanks, as you've just given him two top money makers for the next few years.

-Julius

I typed a quick response and promptly deleted the email. It always made me happy when customers were happy with the money they spent. I didn't usually sell children, but Maxwell and the money he'd lost me caused me to make a small exception.

At a few minutes past eight, I finally shut my computer down for the evening and stood to my feet. Tension slowly melted from my muscles when I rolled my shoulders, my mind shifting from work mode to punishment mode. If she thought her small punishment this morning was bad, she had no idea what I had in store for her.

The girls all smiled and spoke to me as I passed. I nodded to acknowledge them, unfastening my cuff links and rolling my shirt up to my elbows. When I reached the mudroom, Alyssa looked exactly as I expected her to—lost and fucking stupid.

I looked at her and frowned. "Were you not given instructions when you were put in here?" I asked.

She gave me a one-shouldered shrug. "He only told me

to prepare myself but didn't tell me what the hell I was supposed to be preparing for. I figured you'd have more instructions when you came back in that would make more sense."

"Interesting." Her eyes followed me as I circled around her. "So, I assume you haven't had a chance to go through the rest of the manual like I told you to, right?"

She shuffled from foot to foot, biting the inside of her cheek as her eyes nervously looked around the room. "I mean, I didn't have a chance to read all of it, but I did read some of it."

"Well, one would think you'd wait to be a disobedient asshole until you knew how things worked around here. But I'm coming to learn that some people aren't very bright," I said with a light sigh. She frowned at me but she didn't respond. I waved my hand around the room. "This is the mudroom. Anytime you're in here, you're here for punishment."

"But I—"

"Shut the fuck up," I snapped, pointing at her. "Don't speak when I'm fucking talking. Understand?" She only stared at me, blinking. "Are you fucking deaf? I asked you a question."

"Yes," she ground out.

"As I said, anytime you're in this room, you're here for a punishment. Had you read that part of the manual, you'd know what to do when someone tells you to prepare yourself when you're brought here."

"Okay, fine. I didn't read that part yet." She folded her arms across her chest and frowned. "Why don't you tell me what it means so that I know for future reference then?"

I only shook my head. "That's for you to find out when you do what you're supposed to do. All I'm going to say is that not preparing yourself will make this punishment very painful for you."

Her skin paled as her mouth opened and closed a few times. "Okay, so I had a bad day," she rushed out, taking steps back as I stepped forward. "I mean, can you blame me in my situation? I'm being held hostage in a—"

"Remove your clothes, please," I said, my voice calm and even. She gaped at me for a few moments, still moving backwards even though I'd stopped moving.

"I promise I won't be anymore trouble. I just...I—"

"Remove your clothes, please," I repeated, folding my arms across my chest.

The longer she stood there staring at me, the more my patience dissolved. My fingertips tingled at the thought of choking her out, but I wanted her conscious for every ounce of pain I planned to bestow upon her.

"Please," she begged. "I'll do anything. I'll—"

"Then remove your clothes," I stated. "If I have to

repeat myself again, I will soak this fucking room in your blood. Clothes. Off. Now."

Her eyes widened as her breath hitched. I raised a brow and cocked my head to the side when she didn't move immediately. After a few moments of hesitation, she finally pulled her t-shirt off with shaky hands and let it fall to the floor. I ground my teeth as she took a million years to unsnap her bra and pull it off, covering her chest with her hands.

My frown deepened as annoyance heated my skin. "Everything," I said firmly.

The muscle in her jaw tightened as she slowly moved her hands to the waistband of her leggings, pulling everything down and stepped out of them. I noted the faint scars that covered her thighs, and zeroed in on the freshly healing ones curling downward to her inner thighs.

Her cheeks reddened as she kept her eyes trained on the floor, her arms draped across her chest. If those fresh scars were from self harm, I could already assume the lack of satisfaction this punishment would cause me.

"Bend over the table in front of you," I ordered, gesturing to the table. She only looked over at it briefly before looking back to me, unmoving. I pinched the bridge of my nose, my headache rearing its ugly head as I grew more annoyed. "I really hate repeating myself, Alyssa."

"That isn't my name," she stated plainly.

I clenched my jaw as I stared at her. Most people possessed a survival instinct to keep them alive if they were in dangerous situations. This infuriating woman didn't even know what I'd planned to do to her and yet, she still decided to fight me at every turn. A smart woman would've simply complied in hopes of lesser punishment.

This bitch seemed to like the hard and painful route.

When she refused to move, I blew out an annoyed breath and stalked over to her. She flinched when I roughly gripped the back of her neck and yanked her over to the table, forcing her head onto the wooden tabletop. I let go of her neck long enough to yank her wrist to secure it with the leather strap attached to the table, doing the same for the other. Once she was restrained, I took a step back and observed her.

Her back and the backs of her legs were covered in faint scars, some bigger than the others. A part of me was curious about her past and what she'd gone through to have earned these. If her mouth and behavior was any indication, it was probably something she deserved.

I moved forward, tracing a scar on her upper left asscheek with a single finger before sliding it down her warm skin. She tensed when I parted the lips of her pussy and I grinned. She was nowhere near prepared to take me the way she would've needed to be, which would make her screams deliciously satisfying.

"Take this as a lesson to read the manual," I said as I unbuckled my belt, the sound hollow in the mudroom. "If you would've reached that part—which you would have had you started last night when you were first told—this next part wouldn't hurt as much as it's going to."

A scoff came from her. "What you're about to do is no different than what's already been done to me," she stated. Though her words were firm, her voice was thick with tears.

I shrugged. "We'll see about that," I said.

I walked over to back corner of the room and grabbed a condom and the bottle of lube from the shelf before going back over to the table. Her sniffles filled the swelling silence as I prepared myself for the first half of her punishment. Excitement buzzed through my blood as I pulled out my cock, stroking it in my hand as I looked down at her. There was something addicting about breaking my victim for the first time. She wasn't the first woman I'd destroyed, but she was the first one that was an unwilling participant.

The ones before her were ones who'd begged me to have my way with them, completely oblivious to what I was capable of doing to them. But this time, this woman had no say. Once I was finished, I wouldn't have to remind her of any NDA she'd signed prior to our activities and I wouldn't have to pay her any hush money to keep her from trying to blackmail me later.

I'd simply just drag her back to her room until I was ready to break her again.

"What is it with you men who think raping a woman will make them bend to your will?" she said as I rolled on a condom on. I didn't bother responding, putting a little lube onto my hand and stroking my condom-covered cock. "Does it make you feel powerful to know that you've traumatized someone?"

"You'll be thoroughly traumatized if you don't shut the fuck up," I growled. I moved to stand behind her, fisting her hair into my hand. She whimpered when I yanked her up. "All you have to do is do what I tell you and this will be the easiest prison sentence you'll ever serve. But you prefer to do things the hard way."

"Forcing me to be your wife and surrogate isn't what I signed up for," she snapped back, her voice tight.

"You should've thought about that before you stole over half a million dollars from me," I retorted, slamming her head back against the table. She whimpered and squirmed in my grasp. She muttered more shit under her breath, but I didn't bother listening, instead positioning myself behind her. Her shaky breaths filled the hollow space around us and echoed in the corners of my mind as I lined the head of my swollen cock against her tight, unready entrance. "Let this be a lesson for you to obey."

A sharp gasp flew from her mouth when I forced myself inside of her. I groaned, her walls collapsing against my intrusion before immediately tightening around me. She jerked against her wrist restraints, satisfaction licking up my spine as I slowly pulled back and thrust back into her.

"Not so mouthy now, huh?" I ground out as I fisted her hair and pounded into her.

"Fuck. You." Anger and tears laced her voice, heating my blood with ecstasy.

She was so fucking tight and warm, but the only thing my mind could focus on was the silence that surrounded me after a while. Aside from what she'd spoken, she hadn't screamed, sobbed, or did...anything.

I ground my teeth as I picked up my pace, squeezing the back of her neck as I pounded into her. There was no way this wasn't hurting her. Her blood lubricated my cock with each rough thrust I put into her, but it didn't conjure up the sounds I needed to get off. Not a peep, a squeak, a whimper, nothing. It drove me up the fucking wall.

The only indication of her pain was the scratches her nails left behind on the wood and the coppery scent of her blood mingling into the air, but that wasn't enough for me. I needed her tears, her agony, her screams. I reached around her and found her clit, pinching her tight bundle of nerves tight between my fingers until she cried out.

I closed my eyes, relishing in the sound as I repeated my actions. She jerked against me, trying to dislodge my fingers from her clit as I squeezed, pulled, and twisted it in ways I knew would be painful. The fine hairs on my arms stood on end as her screams and pleas spurred me on, my cock throbbing as pleasure ebbed and flowed through my veins.

"That's the sweet sound I wanna hear," I moaned. The more she fought, the tighter her pussy gripped my cock. "Keep screaming, darling. Show me how much this hurts."

"Please stop doing that!" she begged, her tears clogging her throat.

"Fuck me, remember?" I reminded her, my voice tight. My fingertips dug into her fair skin as I pounded into her, pinching and twisting away on her clit as that familiar tingling oozed throughout my body. "Your screaming and this tight little pussy you have is gonna make me come so hard."

"I've learned my lesson!"

"You haven't, but you will." I pulled out of her and released her clit, smirking when her body went limp with relief. No sooner than her body sagged against the table, she tensed up once more when I angled the head of my cock against her asshole.

"No, no, no—"

Her sentence was cut off with a blood curdling scream when I forced myself into her ass. A satisfied smile settled on my lips as I soaked up the sounds she'd previously denied me of.

"Had I known you could get your voice that high, I would've started here first," I mused, firmly slapping her ass. "I'm gonna enjoy destroying your holes every time you fucking disobey me."

"I'm sorry!" she cried, but her apology fell on deaf ears. I held her hips in a tight grip, pounding away to the rhythm of her screams. Her muscles violently protested against me in an effort to push me out, the challenge almost akin to riding a bucking bronco. I followed her every move—not that she could move much. It was the most erotic tango I'd ever danced in. A step to the left, a wiggle to the right, a jerk forward, only for me to impale her with my thick cock once more.

She was a fighter, I'd give her that. Fighters were always so much more fun. They also made me come the hardest.

Once the tingling overwhelmed me, I thrust into her a few more times and came with a groan, filling the condom as I trembled from the aftershock of it.

"Fuck, that was good," I panted, planting my hands on either side of her body on the table. She shook beneath me, soft, hiccuping sobs emanating from her as she laid there. I slowly pulled out, my cock threatening to thicken again when she flinched. "When you look at your bloody holes in the mirror, maybe you'll think twice before you fuck with me, hmm?"

She didn't respond, only continuing to sob and tremble as I rolled the condom off and tied it. I frowned at the bit of blood staining the bottom of dress shirt, mentally cursing myself for not removing it beforehand. She didn't lift her head as I fixed my pants and she didn't say a word as I moved over to the coat rack near the shelves, plucking a thin leather belt from it.

"Now on to part two of your punishment," I said with a light sigh.

"Part two?!" she squeaked.

"What, do you think the shit you did today was only worth getting raped?" I asked with a chuckle. "That's a delusional thought to have, don't you think?"

"I can't take any—"

"You'll receive lashes until you either pass out or until I get tired," I interrupted her, moving to stand behind her again. "Luckily for you, your perfect asshole sucked me dry. Maybe you'll get lucky and it won't be as bad."

"Wait—"

But I didn't wait. The thin leather whistled through the air as I brought it down on her left ass cheek, marveling in the deep shade of pink it left behind. Her scream was a backdrop to the wonder that filled my mind as I struck her, watching the different patches of skin light up like Christmas lights synchronized to her beautiful caroling of screams. The agonizing music made me feel like I was conducting an orchestra of pain, of horror, of terror.

The low grunts, the sharp shrieks, the strained whimpering all swelled into a thunderous cacophony of torture that filled me with renewed energy and peace. Sweat slicked my brow as fatigue slowly settled. Her screams weren't as loud as they were, as she was barely standing on her feet. Had she not still been cuffed to the table, she would've been a useless, bloody heap at my feet. I dropped my arm, panting as I examined my work.

There wasn't an inch of space along the backside of her body that wasn't an angry red hue or covered in welts. Blood beaded along a good bit of the raised welts, a sharp cry coming from her when I ran my finger along it to smear the blood on her skin.

"If you need to learn this lesson again, the mudroom is always open for you," I said as I undid the leather straps bounding her. She fell to the floor and screamed when she fell onto her ass, immediately rolling over onto her stomach. "Get up."

"I can't," she sobbed,

I blew out an annoyed breath and grabbed her arm. "Fine. Then I'll fucking drag you."

She screamed all throughout the house, Donovan smirking at me as I passed and the women averting their eyes. I tossed her bedroom door open when we reached it and pulled her inside, leaving her on the floor at the foot of the bed.

"It's lights out at 11:30." I strolled back over to her door, my hand poised on the doorknob. "Get yourself cleaned up and read the fucking manual. I'm not going to ask you to do so again."

She only replied by sobbing. I frowned at her, the pathetic state of her irritating the shit out of me. I slammed her door closed and locked it before stalking to my own bedroom.

I wasted no time peeling out of my clothes and stepping into a hot shower. My muscles relaxed as the scalding water beat down on me. Every stress and negative emotion swirled down the drain with the dirt and grime of the day.

As I lathered my body with soap, my mind replayed the sounds of her screams, a smile sliding into place as my cock thickened once more. I reminisced about the beautiful shade of red her skin turned as I struck her with the belt.

My cock throbbed in my palm as I stroked it at the

memory of her blood beading to the surface, the same blood I had to wash off of me. Just thinking of her fighting me, her pussy and ass squeezing me, her skin breaking for me, sent a hard shiver throughout my body that curled my spine forward as I came hard once more.

"Fuck," I moaned, jerking the last of my release out of my cock and watching it swirl down the drain.

I stood there for a couple of minutes with my eyes closed, allowing the water to cascade over my head. I took deep breaths to ground myself, taking the steam in and releasing cool air in a slow, steady stream. Tonight was just the beginning for her, a taste of what was to come in between her duties. Sure, she was here to serve a purpose, but she was also here to serve time for her crime against me.

I reached forward and pressed the touch screen in front of me to lower the water's temperature, grinning to myself as I continued to shower.

I couldn't fucking wait for her to see the punishment I had planned for her tomorrow.

CHAPTER SEVEN
LIA

I looked at myself in the mirror of my small bathroom. Music thumped upstairs as my parents continued their Halloween party, sending me and their biological daughter to bed at ten. I turned from side to side as I admired my Marilyn Monroe costume.

Halloween was my favorite holiday because it allowed me to be anything I wanted to be. I didn't have to be Plain Jane Lia for a little while. Tonight, I was America's sex icon, a blonde bombshell with more confidence than I contained on a normal basis.

All night, my foster parents' friends would ask me to recreate Marilyn's iconic scene of her standing over the windy subway grating. I felt desirable, wanted. That was more than I could say after feeling invisible my whole life.

"*I'm Marilyn Monroe, America's sex icon and bombshell,*" I said before puckering my ruby painted lips in the mirror.

"*Yes, you are,*" a gruff voice said from the doorway.

I jumped back, my heart racing in my chest as I looked at my foster father. He looked at me with heavily lidded eyes, probably drunk out of his mind as a cigarette hung from his mouth. He leaned against the doorframe and took a puff from his cigarette, blowing the smoke my way.

"*D-Daddy, I was just getting ready for bed,*" I stammered.

"*Were you, now?*" He flicked the rest of his unsmoked cigarette into the toilet before putting his hands in his pockets.

He'd dressed up as the phantom of the opera, something my foster mother complained about since he'd always chosen that costume. His mask was on top of his head instead of on his face, his tie now loosened.

"*Yes,*" I quickly said, my heart beating so fast I thought I'd pass out. "*I was just about to wipe the makeup off and get changed for bed.*"

He shook his head. "*Leave it on for a little bit longer.*" He took a step closer into the bathroom, his large stature swallowing up most of the space in the small bathroom. "*You know, I used to have a huge crush on Marilyn Monroe when I was a teenager.*"

A chill slid down my spine as I swallowed the ball of anxiety growing in my throat. I was trapped between him and the shower door, his body blocking the door. I forced a small grin on my lips and nodded.

"She was my idol," I said, noticing how shaky my voice was.

His wolfish eyes ogled my breasts as his tongue flicked out to wet his lips. "Your idol, huh?" He stroked his chin. "I assume you know a lot about her?"

I shuffled my weight from foot to foot nervously. "Um, not a lot," I admitted. "I just thought she was really pretty and she was popular in pop culture."

"Hmm." He took another step forward. "I thought she was really pretty, too," he started. "In fact, I had this big cut out of her wearing the same dress you're wearing from that iconic scene."

"Oh," I said, not knowing what else to say.

"I used to look at that cut out every night before I went to sleep," he continued. "It was always so comforting to look at while I jerked my cock to it."

"I-I think I should probably get ready for bed," I said. I had to find a way out of this bathroom. The way he'd looked at me made me feel gross, reminding me of how the guardian at the group home would look at us whenever he was around.

I thought I would've been safe once I left the group home, but my foster family wasn't much better. Up until this point, their abuse had been subtle with hurtful words and yelling here and there. But my current predicament felt gross, dangerous, and I needed to find a way out of it quick.

To my surprise, he stepped off to the side and gestured outside of the bathroom. "You're right. It's getting late," he said. I hesitated for a few moments before I scurried past him, only for him to grab me by the arm. "Aren't you forgetting something?"

I tried to get myself to swallow but it was as if I couldn't get my throat to work. He held his cheek toward me and tapped it, glancing at me expectantly. I pressed a quick, soft kiss on his damp skin and gave him a small smile.

"Goodnight, Daddy," I murmured. When he let me go, I all but ran to my bedroom and slammed the door, leaning against it as my heart pounded against my rib cage. I listened for a while, not hearing anything else in the basement before I let out a sigh of relief. I kicked off my shoes and pulled off the blonde wig, tossing it onto my dresser before moving over to the small mirror on my wall.

I stared at my reflection with a frown. Even though I hadn't taken off my makeup, I still looked so plain without the wig. I picked it up and put it back on, going back to posing in the mirror. I sighed after a few moments.

"I wish I were as pretty as Marilyn," I whispered to myself. I squished my breasts together, which wasn't much, to see if my sex appeal would grow. I was nowhere near as developed as Marilyn *was, but a girl could dream. "Everybody would want me, even the president." I untied the knot at the base of my neck and allowed the top half of the dress to fall, exposing my small breasts. "What was that, Mr. President? You want me to sing to you?"*

"Yes, why don't you sing to me?"

I spun around to see my foster father standing in my room. My arms quickly flew up to cover my chest as I stared at him with wide eyes.

"I-I was going to bed, Daddy—"

"Why don't you sing for me, Marilyn?" The crooked grin on his lips was malicious and hungry, chilling me with fear. "In fact, you were so keen on showing everybody your undies at the party tonight. Why don't you show Daddy, hmm?"

"I-I was just doing what she did in the movie," I squeaked, taking a few steps back.

He fully stepped into my room and closed the door, clicking the flimsy lock into place. "Since you know her movies so well, maybe we can do a little role playing."

"Daddy, please," I said as he stalked toward me. Everything happened in a hazy blur when he crossed the room and grabbed me by the throat. I whimpered when he roughly turned me away from him and bent me over my bed, his hand roughly pulling at my panties. "Daddy no!"

"Shut the fuck up," he growled in my ear. "I don't want to hurt you." I shivered as he ran the tip of his nose along my skin,

inhaling my scent. "Out of all the kids we've fostered, you're my favorite. I don't want to hurt you."

"Daddy, please," I begged in a whisper.

"Shhh." He clamped a hand over my mouth with one hand as his other moved between my legs, quickly rubbing my clit. After a few moments, the head of his cock pressed against my entrance. "Daddy wants to show you how much he loves his favorite girl."

I awoke with a gasp on the marble floor of my bedroom, pain firing on all cylinders. My skin was slick with cold sweat, my heart racing as haunting memories disintegrated into nothing as I became aware of my surroundings. I whimpered when I moved my legs, remembering everything that'd happened to me hours ago. Being raped wasn't new to me; my foster father and others had taken plenty from me in my lifetime. All I could think about was my foster father's words to me while Silas assaulted me, which rendered me quiet.

"You're so perfect for Daddy, princess."

"I always love fucking tight, young pussies, especially when you fight me."

"Shh, shh, shh. Daddy is only giving you what I know you want."

"When you want to dress up like big girl Marilyn Monroe, you'll get fucked like she did, too."

It was as if I were transported back to that bedroom in the basement, back to that pain, that torture, that humiliation and shame. It was as if I were in foster care all over again now that I was in the possession of a sadistic egomaniac set on making my life as miserable as he could.

All the skin on the backside of my body burned, as if I'd been scrubbed with acid and left to dry in the sun. The room was dark other than the moonlight filtering in from the window. I lifted my head, clenching my teeth when the simple movement sent a fresh wave of pain over me.

My bladder screamed at me to empty it, prompting me to prepare myself to get off the floor. Pulling myself to my hands and knees was rough, tears rolling down my cheeks by the time I finally stood to my feet. As I slowly shuffled to the bathroom, every step I took sent pain ricocheting all over. I hadn't felt pain this bad in a couple of years, but it wasn't the worst I'd felt. I shielded my eyes against the bright light of the bathroom when I flipped it on. It was then that I hated the fact that the bathroom was so white.

I couldn't bring myself to look at my reflection as I passed the mirror, crossing the bathroom to sit on the toilet. I planted my hand on the wall next to the toilet as I slowly sat, fresh tears cresting my eyes as more pain lit up. I practically had to hover over the toilet seat, unable to fully sit down without pain. I bit down hard on my lip when a scream threatened to slip out once I let go of my bladder. The intense burning between my legs told me everything I needed to know about the damage Silas left behind.

"Such a fucking bastard," I whispered to myself as a single tear rolled down my cheeks. I had no idea how this man expected me to be a good wife to him if this was what he'd do to me when he didn't get his way. How did he expect me to fall in love with a monster like him? Why would he even want a wife who feared and hated him? Nothing he did made much sense and yet, everything I needed to know was "in the manual."

I had to get the fuck out of here by any means necessary.

I ground my teeth as I forced myself to stand once more, flushing the toilet before moving over to the large tub. I ran a cool bath, hoping it would soothe my burning skin. It was always my routine whenever my foster father did something to me. At least if I was cold, I'd be too numb to focus on the pain.

It took a long while to get comfortable enough in the tub to be able to relax. There no epsom salt or anything to put in the bath to help the welts I had, but it was soothing enough. My teeth chattered after soaking for five minutes, silent tears rolling down my cheeks. I looked around the pristine bathroom.

What a beautiful prison I'm in, I thought to myself, my eyes growing heavy once more. *Such a beautiful prison...*

"What the fuck are you doing?!" my foster mother screamed when she burst into my room.

I sobbed as my foster father jumped away from me, his cock tinted red with my blood. Someone was finally here to stop the nightmare that'd been my life almost every night for the last four months. Every night my foster father came into the basement, raped me, and came all over me before leaving me in heap of tears, filth, and shame. But instead of my foster mother rushing to my aid, she only screamed at me and my foster father.

"Joyce, I—"

"No, don't you say a single word you sick bastard!" she snapped, her voice thick with tears. "I'm going to stay with my parents for the night. Please feel free to continue fucking a minor!"

She slammed the door shut behind her, leaving me alone with a monster. My sniffles were the only thing that filled the room but I didn't dare move. Since we'd been caught, I thought he'd just fix his pants, tell me not to speak of this again, and then leave me alone. My tears started once again when I felt the dip of his weight on my bed. I whimpered when he pushed back into my sore pussy, squirming against him as if that would help me get away.

"She doesn't understand, Princess," he moaned in my ear, thrusting into me. "She doesn't know how good your perfect pussy feels on my cock. She doesn't understand how good you make Daddy feel. She doesn't understand our love."

Except she had understood his sick obsession with me. The next day when I'd come home from school, she was sitting at the kitchen table smoking a cigarette, her eyes pink and puffy. She looked at me with disdain, her face disappearing briefly behind a cloud of smoke.

"You know, I try to do the right thing and be a good person by taking in children who don't have family," she started, a single tear rolling down her cheek as she tapped her ashes in the ashtray. "I should've known you were trouble when we first saw you. You prancing around in your short skirts and shorts and crop tops, advertising the whore that you are. You didn't want a family to love you; you wanted to seduce my husband and ruin my family." She took another pull from her cigarette and exhaled with a shaky breath. "Was that your end game, slut? To destroy my family?"

"I didn't want him to do that," I retorted, tears rolling down my cheeks.

"But I didn't see you trying to get him off of you either!" she screamed. "You laid there because you liked having his cock inside of you. Your tears didn't fool me."

"Your husband has a problem!" I screamed. "There's nothing normal about your husband raping a sixteen-year-old girl whether you think I liked it or not!"

She was on her feet in an instant, slapping me across the cheek. "You watch your mouth, you little bitch!" she snapped. She straightened her posture and ran her hands along the front of her shirt. "Go to the basement and get into position against the pool table for your discipline."

"I didn't do anything wrong!" I cried, holding my cheek.

"Get in the basement now!"

She'd always held an air of resentment and jealousy toward me ever since I'd come here. She'd always favored her biological daughter more than me, always excluding me from the things the two of them would do together. When we got to the basement and I bent over and put my hands on the green felt of pool table top, she flipped my uniform skirt up and pulled my panties down to the middle of my thighs.

There was no warning before she struck me with the paddle. I bit my lip to keep from screaming as she delivered blow after blow, her rage and hurt evident in the pain she put upon me. After the twentieth strike, my legs threatened to buckle from the pain. She simply forced my chest onto the pool table and continued, striking me until she was exhausted.

"You're no longer welcome in my house," she finally said

when she caught her breath. "I'll be talking to Raymond when he gets home and you're going back to the group home." She stalked toward the stairs, pausing to glare at me. "Now you'll be reminded of how you've ruined my family when you feel the pain from your lashing when he fucks you tonight."

And true to her word, they left me on the doorstep of the group home at two in the morning after my foster dad fucked me for the last time, with nothing but the school uniform I had on.

"Ma'am?" a soft voice said, gently shaking my shoulder. I jumped, the pain immediately grounding me and shaking the rest of the sleepy fog from my head. I looked around with wild, wide eyes before Aimee came into focus. Water sloshed out of the tub as I moved, the cold water raising goosebumps on my skin.

"W-what?" I finally asked.

Aimee looked at me with concerned eyes. "It looks like you've been in the tub for a long time. I wanted to make sure you were okay and see if you needed help getting out."

I expelled a slow breath and closed my eyes. "I'm sorry. I-I didn't realize I fell asleep," I murmured.

"It's okay. Let's get you out of this freezing water and into something warm," she said, giving me a soft smile.

I was relieved to have her help. After being in the cold water for so long, everything actually hurt more than it had before. Along with my skin, my bones and joints were achy and stiff, making each movement more painful than the last. Aimee was gentle in the way she helped me out of the tub and dried me with a soft towel. She led me to my bedroom, where the comforter was already pulled back on my bed as if preparing me to get into it.

"What time is it?" I asked when I noticed the sun and chirping birds outside.

"It's 7:15, ma'am."

I frowned when she helped me into bed. "Shouldn't I be at breakfast? I don't want to get in trouble."

"Mr. Arnett asked that you spend the day in your room, so your meals will be brought to you," she said. "Would you like some salve on your welts? It will help them feel a little better."

I shrugged. "Sure, that's fine," I said. I rolled over onto my stomach, my eyes on the door as I listened to her open a jar. I hissed as she smeared cool ointment over every welt. Even though the ointment itself was cool, it stung the broken skin she spread it across.

I knew they were all over the back of me, but it was almost as if she'd slathered every inch of skin on the backside of my body by the time she was done. I clenched my jaw as a stinging sensation buzzed along the surface of my skin, my fist clenching the comforter in my hand.

"It'll burn for a little bit, but it'll help you heal better with minimum scaring. You have a good bit of bruising, so I can get a heating pad if you need one."

I released a humorless chuckle. "I don't think you have a heating pad big enough to cover the areas he's bruised."

"I can get you a heating blanket instead if that'll help."

"That'll work better," I said.

She quickly made her way out of my room and left me in silence once more. I sighed and closed my eyes, silently praying for the pain to melt away. When I'd aged out of foster care, I'd vowed to myself that I was going to live a good life. I was determine to not end up a statistic like most of the other orphans I'd grown up with.

There were girls I used to see every day in the group home who were now either hooked on drugs, prostituting, or both. Some of the guys I grew up with were hooked on drugs or in and out of prison, sometimes both. I thought I was going to be different from them, wanting to make a life for myself to put my painful past behind me.

But all I managed to do was fuck it up and put myself in another hell for the next nine years.

Getting the job at the Arnett Enterprises Headquarters was a dream come true as a high school graduate. It was terrifying graduating from high school and then having nowhere to go afterwards because you'd aged out of the system and had no family.

Getting a job in general had been rough. I didn't have a permanent address, moving from shelter to shelter for a little while, and I didn't have a phone. I got lucky and got into the transitioning program the city had that helped new adults like me find our footing in society once we were on their own, and I managed to snag a job in a place that was hard to get into.

Now I wished I'd never met Silas or stepped foot in his bullshit establishment.

His abuse did nothing but trigger memories I tried to leave in my past. Every time I thought I was okay and could breathe again, something always happened to bring those forbidden memories to the surface. Raymond was nowhere near me, but the thought of him made me nauseous. I could still smell his cheap cologne if I thought too hard about him. My skin crawled at the thought of his slick, sweaty skin slapping against my ass as he violated me. Disgust held me in a chokehold as memories of the only time he'd managed to make me come crossed my mind, and the urge to kill myself bloomed bright and loud.

"Okay, here we go," Aimee said when she re-entered the room. I blew out a relieved breath as the memories subsided and tried to give her what I hoped was an appreciative smile. She walked in with a heating blanket and a tray of breakfast, putting them both on the bed next to me. Surprisingly, the breakfast tray had pancakes, eggs, and a sausage patty. The pancakes were obviously the frozen kind, but it was a lot better than the bullshit Silas had them give me yesterday.

"Thank you. I really do appreciate it," I said as I slowly rose myself up onto my elbows. I sighed softly. "It's comforting to have someone be nice to me in this house."

Aimee was quiet for a moment before she reached over and patted my hand. "I know things seem hard right now. I won't tell you how to feel, but I will say that as long as you do what you're supposed to, Mr. Arnett can be a good guy."

I scoffed and shook my head. "I know you don't mean any harm, Aimee, but that's the last thing I want to hear after what he did to me last night. It's also easy for you to say that when you're not his prisoner due to stealing money from him." I doused the budding flames of annoyance flickering to life within me. "Silas didn't bring me here to be nice to me when I should be in prison. He brought me here to punish me."

Aimee's cheeks turned a light shade of pink as she dropped her gaze to the comforter. "I'm sorry. I didn't mean to upset you. I just wanted to help."

"It's okay," I murmured, poking at the luke warm pancakes. I couldn't blame her for the negative feelings I had about Silas. She had a completely different experience with him than I did, so I couldn't hold that against her. Out of the four women in the house tasked to help me, Aimee was the only one who was kind and helpful to me. I mean, she was the only person who'd told me their name so that she wasn't a nameless face responsible for me during the day.

She cleared her throat and smoothed her hands along her dark dress pants. "Anyway, Mr. Arnett wants you in your room for the day. One of us will retrieve you at eight for your open hours with him."

Just as I was about to ask her what open hours were, I lightly bit my tongue to stop myself from bringing the question to life. I already knew it was probably something in the manual; everything seemed to be in this fucking manual.

"Okay, thanks," I said. She nodded as she plugged the heating blanket in and draped it over my body.

"I'll be back to check on you from time to time. Please let us know if you need anything," she said with a slight bow and left me alone once more. I shoveled food into my mouth with a sigh. Relief slowly seeped into my bones as the heat from the blanket soothed my sore skin and bruises. It definitely didn't take the pain away, but it was comforting to have something that eased it a little.

I spent the day sleeping and flipping through the

manual. Even while I read the ridiculous bullshit Silas put into this manual, my mind kept jumping back to my conversation with Aimee. There wasn't a guarantee that Silas would treat me better if I followed his rules, but it was in my best interest to be on my best behavior just in case.

A part of me wondered if he saw something in me that made him want to make me his wife. We had little to no interaction in his office, so I never imagined I'd be on his radar. Here I was in his home to be trained to be his wife when he could've chosen anyone else, particularly someone who hadn't stolen money from him.

Flipping the page, I paused when I read the definitions of what some of these things meant.

<u>Things To Know</u>

1. Open Hours With Owner: Activities during this time can vary depending on Silas's choice. If you have behaved during the day and Silas is in a good mood, this could lead to rewards for you. Rewards are up to Silas's discretion. In the event that you've had a bad day as reported by the staff of the house, open hours will be when you'll receive your punishment. Activities are ultimately up to Silas regardless of behavior,

but it's always wise to carry yourself appropriately to be safe.

2. In the event that you're taken to the mudroom with the instructions to prepare yourself, you should prepare yourself for anything kind of punishment. There are numbing creams, vibrators, and lubricants on the shelf to prepare your body for a number of physical assaults. While Silas is a brutal man, he is also fair. He gives you 10-15 minutes from entering the mudroom to prepare before he joins you to conduct your punishment. Plan accordingly and expect the worst.

I scoffed and shook my head. "That would've been helpful to know yesterday," I muttered to myself. One thing that I found odd despite having a shit ton of rules and tedious fuckery I had to know and abide by was that Silas gave me choices in big decisions. In the manual, he'd said I'd get to choose what I wanted done for my surgery. After the stunt I pulled yesterday with the surgeon, I wasn't too sure if that option was still on the table. But excitement fluttered to life in my gut when I saw I'd be able to plan the wedding with wedding planners myself.

When he'd told me I was to marry him and bear a son for him, I thought he'd handle all the details and the only thing I'd have to do was show up. But the wedding section of the manual was blank aside from the section introduction that he'd typed up.

Arnett Wedding Details

You and I will be married in six months. This is the section where you'll put your wedding wants and desires. You'll be planning the wedding however you'd like with the help of the best wedding planners money can buy.

As the fiancée of a billionaire, the wedding needs to reflect as such. There is no spending budget for this wedding, so you're free to have whatever you want. Now that I own you, the least I can do is be a good future husband and give you a dream wedding. By the time you walk down the aisle—granted that you make it down the aisle, that is—you'll have deserved the best wedding money can buy.

I was too hopeful about the prospect of having my dream wedding to be annoyed by his veiled threat. Every woman at one point daydreamed about what their dream wedding would look like. Being in a situation like this was the last thing that would've been a part of my dream wedding, but all I could do was make the best of it.

"I just have to survive long enough to make it down the aisle," I whispered to myself as I read the last line again. Dread settled in my stomach the longer I stared at the page. Marrying him was one thing, but how the hell would I be able to fall for someone who could hurt me the way he had? I couldn't wrap my mind around someone like him loving someone like me, which made this arrangement even more weird.

Closing the manual, I flopped onto my back, hissing when the pain reminded me why I was lying on my stomach in the first place. I used to dream that I'd find someone to give me all the love I missed out on growing up. I'd imagined having a loving husband who showed me there were good men in the world and having children that would never know what it felt like to be abandoned and alone.

I had a chance of having something like that with Silas if I could find a way to get through to him. There had to be some kind of humanity underneath all the psychotic tendencies he possessed. I just had to figure out how to reach him without him destroying myself in the process.

———

Just like clockwork, a different woman came to my room at eight. I blew out a shaky breath and winced as I forced myself to sit up, already knowing why she was here.

It was open hours for Silas to do whatever he wanted with me. A part of me dreaded tonight's activities. I was far too sore to have him fuck me and I hadn't done anything that warranted a punishment. I'd actually hoped he wouldn't bother with me since he'd kept me in my room all day anyway, but I was quickly learning that I wouldn't always get what I wanted.

"Mr. Arnett would like you to meet him in his office. Please put this on," the woman said, placing a neatly folded outfit on the foot of the bed.

"Can I ask your name, please?" I asked.

She frowned at me before threading her fingers together, clasping her hands in front of her. "My name isn't important, ma'am. Please get dressed quickly."

"If you're responsible for taking care of me through the day, it is important for me to know your name," I said, returning her frown. "If there was an emergency, I wouldn't know who to alert to help me. I don't think Silas would be very happy to know his investment could've been saved but wasn't because she didn't know who to call for help." I ended my statement with a shrug before clenching my jaw to prepare myself for the fresh pain that moving would cause. Sure, I was probably being dramatic in what I'd said, but I wasn't exaggerating.

The woman sighed deeply after a few moments. "Valorie," she finally answered. "The one who came in earlier this morning was Aimee. Our boss—the woman with the red hair—is Maryse and she's Silas's eyes and ears. Lastly, there's Kora, but she won't be super involved in your care."

"Thank you. It's nice to know who everyone else," I murmured. I slowly pulled on the silk pajama set. My heart beat a little faster at what Silas had in store for me tonight. I'd done everything he'd asked of me today and didn't cause anyone any issues. While I wasn't expecting any pleasure or rewards, I didn't think I was out of the woods for earning a punishment either.

"Ready?" the woman asked me once I was dressed.

I released a shaky breath and nodded. "As ready as I can be," I responded. She opened the bedroom door and gestured for me to leave the room. Anxiety tightened my chest as I followed her. *Just survive for now,* I reminded myself, chanting the phrase over and over in my head. With a man like Silas, survival wasn't promised or guaranteed.

I needed to hang on long enough to either turn this situation around or find my way out of here. My life depended on it.

CHAPTER EIGHT
SILAS

I clenched my teeth the second my father's name popped up on my phone screen.

I already knew why he was calling. After he'd retired five years ago and left me and Harold in charge, he'd spent the first two years micromanaging shit because he was worried I'd "run his legacy into the ground." It was only a matter of time before the company tripled its income, which finally allowed him to respect me enough to not snoop around or doubt me.

He didn't know the changes I'd made to the company that brought that extra income. Besides, what he didn't know wouldn't hurt anyway.

With Maxwell and his wife's murder being all over the news, I knew it was only a matter of time before he called.

I simply watched the phone ring a few more times before I sighed and picked it up before it went to voicemail.

"Good evening, Dad," I said, hoping my displeasure wasn't evident in my tone. If it was, my father didn't mention it.

"Hello, son. How are you this evening?"

I leaned back in my seat and loosened my tie. "As well as I can be considering everything going on. How are you and Mom?"

"Great, great. We just returned from Greece last night. Lovely place." He cleared his throat. "But imagine my surprise when I turned on the evening news to see that the head of our accounting department and his wife are dead and the children are missing?"

I closed my eyes, pinching the bridge of my nose as I prepared myself for this conversation. "Yeah, it's been hard for the employees. Reporters have been swarming outside the company."

"Why would they swarm the company?"

I shrugged and dived into the response I'd rehearsed. "Just trying to see if anyone knows something or knows where their children are," I started. "He was pretty angry when we let him go, so—"

"Wait, let him go? For what?"

"Because he wasn't doing his job, obviously," I said, rolling my eyes. "Along with him using the company card to pay for his family vacations, him not doing his job cost the company almost seven hundred thousand dollars. One of the administrative assistants had been embezzling money for almost two years unnoticed, which should've been caught by him had he been doing his job."

"Jesus Christ," my father muttered. "Well, good call then. I hope the little bitch is in prison."

My office door opened and Alyssa walked in, standing near the door when Valorie closed it behind her. She looked as if she were in pain still, shifting from foot to foot uncomfortably.

I waved her over. "I talked with the judge and convinced him to give her the maximum when she pleaded guilty. It's only nine years, but it's better than nothing."

"I suppose."

As my father continued blabbing on about his displeasure about the state of the news and the office, I frowned at Alyssa, who still stood near the door. I took my phone from my ear and hit the mute button, looking to her.

"Get over here," I stated, my voice firm. She slowly shuffled across the room, fear and hesitation dancing in her eyes. *Good.* She stopped in front of my desk, nibbling on the inside of her cheek as she watched me. I pushed back from my desk and turned my chair, undoing my belt.

"Silas, are you even listening?" my father fussed.

I unmuted my phone as I rolled my eyes. "Of course I'm listening, Dad."

"So what do you plan to do to recoup the lost money then?"

"Harold and I have been talking about it." I pulled my cock out and motioned for Alyssa to come to me. When she walked around my desk and saw her task, she looked at me with wide eyes. I raised an eyebrow at her before pointing to the spot on the floor at my feet. "He and I are supposed to have a meeting with the board in the morning about it amongst other things."

Irritation flickered within me as I watched her get on her knees painstakingly slow. I could only imagine the pain she was still in after last night. Maryse had reported she'd spent majority of the day sleeping and reading the manual, which was the main reason I wasn't pushing her down to her knees to get her there faster.

I guess she'd learned her lesson after all. It was interesting to see how pain motivated people to do what they needed to in order to avoid feeling it.

She took my cock into her timid hands, slowly stroking me in her warm palms. I relaxed a little into my seat, my father's voice becoming less annoying as my cock thickened in her grasp.

"Are you going to tell me now or later about what you plan to talk about at this meeting?" he said.

I ground my teeth. There was no way in hell I could tell him we planned to move the auction up that we'd planned for the girls we were replacing. He had no fucking idea about the criminal empire I'd built behind his precious company. Harold and I used to joke about it in college, thinking it would've been hard to set something like that up. But we quickly learned that there were more dirty people in high positions here in Palmetto Beach, and once we forged those relationships, we were fucking invincible.

"For fuck's sake, Dad," I ground out. "We're going to bounce ideas on how to recoup the money we lost."

"You can lose the attitude, Silas," he stated, his voice firm. "As the founding member of—"

"Yeah, a founding member that no longer has a part of the company anymore," I reminded him with a frown. "Once you sold your shares to me and fully retired, Arnett Enterprises was no longer a concern of yours. What I plan to talk about with the board members isn't your business."

"It still reflects on me, Silas!" he snapped, his voice raising a bit louder. "We still share the same last name. Everyone knows I founded that company. I no longer have a stake in the company, but that doesn't stop the phone calls from others asking me what's going on with the company for it to be in the news."

I glanced at Alyssa and snapped my fingers to get her

attention. She looked up at me with sad eyes, watching as I pointed to my mouth and then my cock. Confusion colored her features as she only continued looking at me.

"I understand, Dad. Give me one second; my house-keeper is trying to tell me something." I muted the phone and looked down at her. "Why are you using your hands? I can give myself a handjob. Use your mouth."

"Did I do something wrong?" she asked, her voice small. "I-I behaved today and—"

"Does it look like we're in the mudroom?" I asked with a raised brow. "You're serving a prison sentence; being here isn't a fucking vacation. I can have you do whatever I want you to during my open hours, and right now I want my cock sucked. So, get to it."

She looked at my hard cock for a moment, her mouth shut tight. A mixture of different emotions flickered across her face before defeat and shame colored her irises. I fought the urge to smirk. If she felt shame and embarrassment now, she had no idea what was in store for her soon.

I closed my eyes and rested my head on the headrest when she put me into her mouth, unsure hands stroking my cock as she sucked. I unmuted the phone and put it back to my ear. "I'm back with you, Dad," I said.

"Good. Is Maryse still working for you?" he asked, his voice more calm than before.

"Of course she is. If it weren't for her, I'd forget to eat

most days," I said with a light chuckle, swallowing down the groan that threatened to leave my mouth when I hit the back of Alyssa's throat.

"Good, good." He sighed. "Look, I know you'll handle this situation appropriately. Just get this media storm under control. We don't need bad publicity."

"I know. I have something for that to switch the narrative," I said. I watched Alyssa take more of my cock into her mouth, finally getting into a rhythm. "I got engaged."

"Engaged?!" My father's boisterous laugh filled the line, loud enough to hide the moan that slipped from between my lips. "My boy! You know, your mother and I was losing hope about you settling down and giving us grandchildren," he said with a light chuckle. "Mary Anne, get in here! Our son's getting married!"

I smirked at his excitement. I'd always found it interesting how my father always saw the best in me despite all the bad I'd shown him and my mother while they raised me. While my mother was always on edge and apprehensive when it came to me, my father was always excited when things seemed good on the surface.

I already knew my mom would be suspicious about me being engaged. I'd never been in a committed relationship, simply fucking women and sending them on their way. Many therapists and psychiatrists they'd sent me to throughout my childhood and teen years liked to throw around the word "sociopath" when talking about me, and maybe they were right. At least, that was what my mom believed. She loved me from a distance because I "scared the hell out of her," and that was absolutely fine with me.

Besides, they had no idea what I was truly capable of these days.

"Dad, it's not a huge deal," I said, threading my fingers through Alyssa's hair as her head bobbed in my lap.

He scoffed. "Are you kidding me? This is the best thing I've heard in a while! So? When do we get to meet the lucky lady?!"

"Soon. Things have been super busy lately, but it'll be soon."

"Mary Ann, get in here! Silas is engaged!"

"It's fine, Dad. I can tell her when I bring Alyssa to meet you both."

"Alyssa! Wow!" he exclaimed. "Mary Ann, his fiancée's name is Alyssa!"

I chuckled, a moan cutting it short. "Dad, I hate to cut this call short, but Alyssa's calling on the other line. I'll let you know when we're able to meet with you."

"Oh no, son, you go right ahead! Please tell your lovely fiancée that we can't wait to meet her!"

"Yeah, will do. Talk soon," I said and quickly hung up before he could say anything else. I looked down at Alyssa and licked my lips. "I think I finally found something you're amazing at." She only looked up at me with wet eyes, continuing her task. "If you do a good enough job, I may reward you during tomorrow's office hours."

A whimper left her mouth and she quickened her action, pleasure flooding me as I gripped her hair tight in my fist. I groaned, the muscles in my legs twitching as she deep throated my cock. Her hands skillfully pumped my cock as her eager tongue quickly brought me close to the edge.

"Oh fuck," I groaned, moving her head quicker by her hair. "That's a good girl; just like that." She responded in a purr that vibrated across the head of my cock. I grinned. "Well, look at that. I think my prisoner has a praise kink."

"Mhm," she said around my cock.

A solid knock sounded, causing Alyssa to jump. I almost growled in annoyance when her mouth disappeared from my cock.

"What?" I snapped before looking back to Alyssa. "Get back here and finish."

"But—"

"Now," I stated firmly. Maryse opened my office door and gestured to someone in the hallway.

"Your guests are here for your meeting," she simply said, closing the door once Charlie and Leland stepped into my office.

Leeland looked at me and smirked. He, Charlie, and

Harold were my closest friends since college. We'd shared everything back then—a suite dorm room on campus, secrets, girls, everything. It wasn't the first time they'd caught me with my dick out and a girl on her knees, so I wasn't in a rush to try to cover myself. Instead, I frowned at Alyssa, who hadn't done what I'd told her.

"Are you deaf?" I snapped, growing impatient. "Finish your fucking job."

She nervously looked over at Charlie and Leeland before looking back to me. "Even with them watching?" she asked.

"If you're worried about them watching, I can send you back to your room until I'm done with this meeting and we can pick back up in the mudroom."

"No, no, no, no, no," she quickly said, shaking her head.

"Then get the fuck over here and finish," I said, my voice rough.

Charlie cackled and shook his head. "You dirty dog. I see you haven't changed."

I grinned at him. "Did you really expect me to?"

"Of course not," Leeland said as he and Charlie moved over to sit in front of my desk. "But if you need a minute, we can wait."

I waved him off. "I want to get this over with," I said

and hissed, frowning at Alyssa. "Less teeth unless you want me to remove them."

"How you're able to convince a woman to fuck you with that mouth of yours is still a mystery," Charlie teased.

"I'm a charming bastard, what can I say?" I chuckled with a shrug. "Plus, being a billionaire certainly doesn't hurt."

"Being a millionaire doesn't hurt either," Leeland added. "Anyway, have you thought about what you plan to do to recoup the money you lost that can be put on the books?"

I stroked my chin, closing my eyes for a brief moment when I hit the back of Alyssa's throat again. My entire body tingled as she sucked and stroked my cock and it took every ounce of willpower to keep my composure in front of my friends and business partners.

Once I'd collected myself, I cleared my throat. "We're going to move that auction up at the Baldwin Casino," I started. "And then on the surface, run a promotion to get more people in the casino."

Our Baldwin Casino was our most successful business. Lots of locals and tourists spent a lot of time there since it was right on the beach and the gambling, food, and alcohol was endless. Even though I'd already made the money back by selling Maxwell's daughters, I still needed something on the books to recoup the loss, even more so now that the embezzlement situation was bound to hit the news soon.

"I'm not sure if we can move it up sooner," Leeland said, shaking his head. "We're gonna need to properly promote an event that will bring people in droves in order for us to be able to make that kind of money in a single night."

I frowned. "Lee, we make a couple million a night at that place. Why the fuck would it matter?"

"Because we need to make double that for it to cover up the money we'd filter in through the auction." Leeland tapped his temple. "Think, Silas. Maybe you should pause in getting your dick sucked because you're not making much sense right now with your logic."

I ground my teeth and stared at him for a long moment. "Step out into the hall for a moment," I said through gritted teeth.

Both men men stood and left the room, leaving me with a Alyssa. I released a long sigh and closed my eyes, placing both of my hands of her head.

"Go ahead and finish me off," I said, my voice low.

She hummed a response and quickly went to work, sucking and stroking me in a way that made my toes curl in my shoes. My breath quickened as I forced her mouth further down my cock, fucking her throat.

"That's it. Look at you swallowing my cock like a good girl."

"Mmm," she hummed, looking up at me with wet eyes. My entire body tingled as I forced myself to stand in front of her. Surprisingly, she didn't lose her stride. I quickly pumped into her mouth, feeling her gagging on my girth that sent a chill throughout my body.

"Oh fuck, I'm almost there," I moaned. I fisted her hair in my hands so tight that I wouldn't be surprised if I pulled out clumps of it.

She whimpered and tried to keep up with my assault on her mouth. When her throat relaxed and the head of my cock stroked the soft tissue of it, a shudder ripped through my body as I shot ropes and ropes of cum down her throat with a strained moan. She attempted to pull away from me to try to spit but I kept her still. She tried prying my hands out of her hair, whimpering around my cock.

"Do you know how many women would kill to have my cum in their mouth?" I asked, my voice low. "How many women would kill to have my cum in their pussies? Their asses? And here you are being an ungrateful bitch when you have a billion dollars in your mouth." I pulled out of her mouth and quickly clamped my hand over it. "Swallow. Now."

But she only looked at me with tears in her eyes, her

mouth still held in that stupid position that people usually did when they were holding something in their mouth that they needed to spit. I clenched my jaw and exhaled deeply. Now wasn't the time to yell or berate her when there were guests here. The only person who knew Alyssa's true identity and purpose was Harold.

Everyone knew an assistant had embezzled money, but most people didn't even know who the assistants were unless they were their personal assistant or if they were fucking them. Alyssa hadn't been on anyone's radar; she hadn't even been on mine. The guys probably thought she was a random woman I'd brought home to suck me off, which was probably for the best.

The fewer people I had in my personal affairs, the better.

I shook my head. "That's a shame. I thought you were my good girl," I said with a light sigh before letting go of her. "I guess you aren't after all."

She quickly nodded and grabbed my hands, swallowing with a slight cringe that she tried to hide. "I am," she finally said, her voice soft.

"If you want to truly be a good girl, I should only have to tell you things once. Understand?"

"Yes, sir."

"Good." I stuffed my softening cock back into my

pants and fixed them before going over to the door to let Charlie and Leeland back in.

"Ready to focus now?" Charlie asked as he walked past me.

I scoffed and closed the door when Leeland walked in. "I was focused before."

"Hardly, but whatever." Charlie flopped back down in his chair with a sigh. "As I was saying before, we need to do a commercial for the event at the casino. The auction is gonna make a shit ton more than what you're trying to recoup, and we need a way to wash that money. If we have a large promotion on food and drinks, and even lower the price of the table games a bit to encourage people to play more games, it'll be easier to clean the dirty money because the whole city will know about the event. But we need to be smart about this shit, though. We don't need the IRS digging too deep."

"Second what he said," Leeland said, nodding.

I sighed deeply. "When you put it like that, I guess it makes more sense." Alyssa sniffled next to me, which reminded me to start the next part of her punishment. I looked to Charlie and Leeland. "You guys up for a handjob?"

"I'm flattered, Silas, but you know I'm married," Leeland said with a chuckle.

"Not from me, dickhead." I nodded toward Alyssa. "From her."

Her head snapped over to me as her eyes widened. "What?"

"Well, in that case, hell yes. It'll help me last longer when I fuck my wife tonight," Leeland said.

Charlie shook his head. "Nah. I'm already in the doghouse with Sarah and I'm sure she'd take a UV light to my dick to see if she can detect fingerprints or saliva of another woman at this point."

I chuckled. Hearing Leeland and Charlie's horror stories about marriage made me glad I didn't have that kind of burden. Even though I would be married soon, it wasn't a marriage built off of love like theirs were supposed to be.

It was only an arrangement to get the things I wanted before I disposed of her. I didn't fall in love; I wasn't sure if it was because I wasn't capable or because I found love to be a weak emotion, but I knew it didn't have a place in my life. I'd never be obsessed over a woman because I was in love; I was only obsessed with my money and my property —which was exactly what Alyssa was.

My gaze fell back to her, who'd paled and looked as if she were about to shit herself at any moment. It was comical, really. If she and I were to marry in six months, she needed to get with the program fast so we could get everything done in time. The mudroom was the first step, but I needed to show her I could punish her on a whim if I felt like it. I could imagine she was so confused considering that she'd behaved, but she'd behaved simply because she didn't have a choice.

One couldn't really disobey or talk back if their pain kept them asleep.

"You heard him. Go jerk him off," I said, nodding toward Leeland. "And if I have to tell you more than once, I can go ahead and wrap this meeting up and we can go to the mudroom."

She swallowed hard before she forced herself on shaky legs and slowly moved over to Leeland. He wasted no time pulling his cock out of his slacks, looking at Alyssa with hungry eyes. She glanced over at me nervously before looking at Leeland's cock. After a few moments of hesitation, she finally reached out and took his cock into her hands, slowly pumping it.

I turned my attention back to Charlie. "So, who can we hire on short notice to plan this commercial then? Either way, the auction is in a week or so. I'm not sure how much interest we can drum up for this event."

"I don't know if a week is enough notice for the public," Leeland piped up before frowning at Alyssa. "Can you be any more unenthusiastic, slut?"

Alyssa paled when she met my glaring gaze, quickly

putting more effort into what she was doing as tears glossed her eyes. "We can't move the auction because it's already been moved twice in order to accommodate the big spenders. We're going to have to think of something else." I stroked my chin as I thought. "Maybe hire entertainment for the night. Or make a men's night with the promise of cheaper game tables, discounted food and booze, and dancers."

Charlie snapped his fingers and pointed at me. "Now there's a fucking idea," he said. "Men would go broke just to get into the door."

"We can—shit—we can send out flyers and make sure businesses heavily populated with men get the memo. Fuck, that feels nice," Leeland said with a sigh.

I rolled my eyes. "You don't say another word until you're finished over there," I said. "But I do agree. We can send flyers to gyms, shooting ranges, country clubs, and of course the surrounding businesses that aren't run by uptight dickwads."

"We can do that. It'll be cheaper anyway," Charlie said.

"Oh, for fuck's sake, just get the fuck off me," Leeland snapped, pushing Alyssa away.

I looked to the both of them, a frown pulling my lips down. "What's the problem?"

Alyssa sniffled but didn't respond. Leeland scoffed. "How the fuck does she except me to stay hard when she's fucking crying? I don't want to see that shit when I'm trying to get off."

"Hold on a second," I said and picked up my phone from my desk. I shot Maryse a quick text before putting my phone down. In less than two minutes, Maryse entered my office and handed me a folded pillowcase before excusing herself. I stood and walked around my desk as I unfolded the pillowcase, putting it over Alyssa's head. "That should help you not see it. I can't guarantee it'll keep her quiet, but you at least don't have to look at her."

A sob spilled from her mouth as her shoulders shook, which did nothing but piss me off. I gripped the back of her neck tight and bent down until I was close to where I assumed her ear was in the pillowcase.

"If you keep crying, I'm going to give you a reason to. Either you jerk him off or he can take you to the mudroom and fuck you," I growled. "And considering what I did to you last night, I'm sure you won't be able to handle that."

Even though her sobbing ceased, she still hiccuped and trembled in my grasp. I let her go with a little shove and continued my meeting, ignoring her random hiccups and sniffling as she continued having her meltdown under the pillowcase on her head.

"Silas, I hate to interrupt, but I don't want to ruin my pants," Leeland panted. "Think I could use her mouth?"

"No!" Alyssa said quickly.

I shrugged. "Knock yourself out," I said.

Leeland snatched the pillowcase off of Alyssa's head and fisted her hair in his hand, roughly bringing her mouth to his cock. "Open up, you bitch," he growled.

"He better not have to ask you twice, Alyssa," I warned. Another sob shook her body as she sat there and shook her head.

"I can't do this. I can't," she wailed.

"If I have to get up, you won't be able to do much of anything for a couple of days," I said, growing impatient. "Do what he tells you."

"I'll take the punishment. I'm not doing it," she said, scooting away from Leeland.

He let out a frustrated huff and shook his head. "Fuck it. I'm not going to fight with a bitch when I have one at home who'll do it willingly."

I continued staring at Alyssa, the muscle in my jaw ticking the longer I looked at her. "Let's pick this up tomorrow. It's getting late," I finally said.

"Fine with me," Charlie said, jumping to his feet. They both walked over to me and shook my hand, Leeland glaring down at Alyssa when he passed her. When they left the office, I leaned back in my seat and smirked at her.

"Well, well, well," I started. "I guess someone read the manual after all."

She didn't say anything, only staring at me with wet

eyes and a frown on her slightly swollen lips. There was a section in the manual that gave her an idea of potential punishments she could face. A rule I'd put in the manual was that in the event that I loaned her to one of my friends or business partners, she was only limited to hand jobs. The only person that could violate any of her three holes was me—unless she revealed her true identity to someone. She didn't know that little stipulation, though.

"Am I going to be punished every day?" she asked with a small voice, sniffling.

"Most likely," I said with a shrug. "Like I told you before, you're here to serve your sentence. I'll do whatever I want to do to you during my office hours. Maybe it'll be pain, or maybe it'll be something nice for you. Everyday will just be a delicious surprise, won't it?"

"Please," she whimpered. "Can we, I don't know, start over or something? I'll do whatever it is that you need me to do. I'll be whatever you need me to be. I'll—"

"You'll do all of that regardless." I stood up and walked over to stand in front of her sitting form on the floor. "In six months, you'll be going down the aisle. It's up to your own actions that'll determine if you're walking down the aisle to marry me or if pallbearers will be carrying your casket down it."

Goosebumps raised on my covered arms as I watched that orgasmic look of helplessness and defeat color her features. There was nothing that turned me on more than breaking someone's will and spirit. I wasn't sure if she thought she would just experience a couple of bad days because of her disrespect, but she had so much to learn about me. Despite what I'd done to her so far, she hadn't even met the true monster that I could be.

"Get up," I ordered, snapping my fingers. "I'm done with you for the night. You'll be resuming your regular schedule tomorrow, so you may want to turn in early tonight."

I stalked over to the office door and pulled it open. Maryse paused in her dusting when I stuck my head out into the hallway.

"Are you ready to send her to her room for the night, sir?" she asked.

I nodded, stepping off to the side and putting my hands in my pockets. I watched in silence as Maryse came into the room and gathered Alyssa off the floor, guiding her to the door. Alyssa looked at me with a gaze filled with misplaced betrayal, suppressed anger, and defeat before she walked past me.

"Oh, and Maryse?" I called out as stepped out into the hall. She paused and looked over her shoulder.

"Yes, sir?"

"Run her a bath to soak in. She's to restart her schedule tomorrow regardless of her pain level."

Something that sounded like scoff came from Alyssa, but I didn't dwell on it. Maryse nodded.

"Of course, Mr. Arnett," she said and ushered Alyssa away.

I ran my hands through my hair and gripped it tight. Pain blossomed along my scalp, grounding me and calming me. As the days went on, this idea was turning out to be more problems than it was worth. But I was too deep into it to turn back now. I'd paid for her to get out of prison, went through the trouble of getting her name legally changed, and greased too many pockets to turn back now.

"One thing at a time, Silas," I mumbled to myself as I headed to my bedroom. "One thing at a time."

I was still on track with everything and it was only the third day. I still had plenty of time to mold her into what I needed her to be. She just needed the right guiding hand and time to adjust to the new life I was creating for her.

And for her sake, hopefully the work would be worth it for the both of us.

CHAPTER NINE
LIA

"*It's a sad day for the single ladies of Palmetto Beach. Billionaire bachelor Silas Arnett is now engaged to be married.*"

I rolled my eyes as I continued walking on the treadmill in Silas's home gym, fighting the urge to wince with each step. After the soak Maryse had made last night, the pain wasn't as bad as it was yesterday, but my body was still pretty sore.

It was ridiculous that this engagement was breaking news. Any other woman could have him if I could find a way out of this hellhole. I listened to the women news anchors continue to gush about the man ruining my life.

"*For the longest time, he was dubbed The Ice King because every woman that'd been seen with him said he was incapable of love. It's surprising to see that he's due to be married when he hadn't been seen with a woman for the last few years,"* one woman said.

"Perhaps the secret to a lasting relationship is to keep things private," the other news anchor added. *"Whatever the case, Silas Arnett is officially off the market to one lucky woman. The single women of Palmetto Beach will mourn the loss, but we here at Palmetto 27 News wish him and his fiancée all the best. I bet that wedding will be one to remember."*

Had I been at my apartment watching this, I would've been a little excited. It was always exciting to learn about other people's lives, especially the ones you didn't have easy access to. It was like those who were obsessed with pop culture and the lives of celebrities, thinking they lived much more interesting lives than they actually did.

It was so easy to think rich people lived drastically different lives as if money solved every problem they could have. Money could be a blessing and a curse. In my case, it'd been a curse. Not only did I fuck up my own life trying to live a life I hadn't earned, but now my captor used his money to further my suffering.

The camera view switched to Silas standing outside of the Arnett Enterprises headquarters, surrounded by reporters.

"We're helping the police any way we can and we hope his

sweet girls are found safe and sound," he said. "We here at Arnett Enterprises are working with the family to help cover the funerals for Maxwell and his lovely wife Brenda. Maxwell wasn't just the head of accounting for our company; he was also a dear friend. It's a tragedy that someone would destroy a family this way. Everyone here at the headquarters are grieving the loss."

I scoffed. "As if you aren't the one who did it," I muttered under my breath. It was infuriating seeing him lying through his teeth so easily and faking sadness and concern over a situation he caused. The man was a certified psychopath regardless of what anyone said about him. "Nice guy" my ass.

"We've also supplied the reward money for the search of their two daughters, whom are still missing," he continued. "They deserve to be with their remaining family after losing both of their parents. Their family is worried sick about them, so it's important that we bring them home quickly and most of all, safe."

I scoffed. "Should've thought about all of that before you sold them off and killed their parents," I mumbled under my breath.

"What was that?" Maryse said from the corner of the room.

I rolled my eyes and turned my gaze away from the

television. "Nothing," I said, my voice flat. I had to watch what I said and did, as Maryse, the resident snitch, would give Silas reports on me every evening. Anything she said would determine what would happen during open hours with him. Even though I didn't look back to the television, the sounds still filtered over to me.

"*How are you and your employees remaining in good spirits after losing an employee in such a brutal fashion?*" a reporter asked.

"*We're trying to remain positive and grateful for the life we still have,*" he said and I cringed. "*I'm recently engaged, so I'm looking forward to marrying my beautiful fiancée in six months. I used to think love wasn't for me but this tragedy just reminded me that I made the right decision in wanting to settle down, as tomorrow isn't promised. So I'm grateful to have many days of loving her and creating a family of my own to enjoy.*"

Seeing how easily he could pretend to be something he wasn't was scary to watch. On the outside, he didn't look like the man who'd essentially kidnapped me from prison. He didn't look like the monster who'd raped and beat me in the mudroom. He didn't look like any of the things he'd shown me he could be. If people knew the danger they were in anytime they were in his proximity, they'd run for the hills and never look back. But most of them were blinded by his handsome looks, his money and status, and his fake charm. I used to be one of them whenever I saw him in passing at the office.

Crazy how someone's perception of another could change after a single night with them—especially when you witnessed them order the murder of two people and then sell their children to people who would violate those girls well into adulthood.

I cleared my throat when my own past tried to rise to the surface. "Maryse?" I called out. "Could I ask something?"

"You should be focusing on your workout," she said, her voice flat and uninterested in continuing with me. "In fact, I'm sure you can walk a little faster than that. Had you not been injured, you'd actually be running today."

I ground my teeth to keep from lashing out. She was such a bitch for no reason. "I just wanted to ask a question about the people around me." I debated on the next part, wondering how it would affect me if it were to backfire. "In the manual, he did tell me that you guys weren't here to be my friends, which is fine. But he didn't say I wasn't allowed to ask anyone questions."

She was silent for a long moment before I heard her slam the book she held shut. "What is it?"

I increased my speed a little on the treadmill, the

quicker speed activating more soreness along the back of my thighs. "How long have you worked for Silas?" I asked first.

She didn't immediately respond but finally sighed before she did. "I've worked with him since he was a teenager," she admitted.

I frowned and looked back at her. "Seriously?!" I asked in genuine shock. When she nodded, I shook my head and turned back to face forward. "That's insane. Whatever you use to look as young as you do, I need to know your secrets. I literally thought we were close in age. You look amazing." I glanced over at the mirror nearby to watch her reflection. A small smirk settled on her lips before she opened her book again.

"The best remedy to staying young is minding your business," she said matter-of-factly.

"Or you're some kind of supernatural being who feeds off the blood of her victims," I said with a shrug. "That's more badass anyway if you ask me."

"Hmph," she said in response.

"So if you've been working with him that long, then you've seen the kind of women he's dated then," I said.

"I would assume so, yes."

I bit my bottom lip as I thought out my next question. "So, thinking back to all the women he dated, do you think he has a type of woman he's attracted to? Like, as far as what they looked like?"

When Aimee came to get me for breakfast, she'd informed me that the surgeon was coming later tonight and asked me to be on my best behavior so that I wasn't punished during open hours. I'd never really had much desire to have plastic surgery simply because I was scared of being put under general anesthesia. Silas hadn't really given me any kind of references to what he wanted for surgery, only giving me examples of what kinds of things I could have done. Since he was the one that wanted to change my body, I thought he would've given me things to choose from that he wanted, but he hadn't. My gut told me if he were more physically attracted to me, maybe he would be a little nicer. I wasn't holding my breath for him to fall in love with me, but him being nicer would be a nice compromise to having this surgery.

"I can't say I've noticed anything like that," Maryse finally said, deflating my balloon. "Mr. Arnett has dated many women in his time. Every woman he has entangled with served a specific purpose for that point in time."

"Has he ever even had a long-term relationship with anyone?" I asked with a slight frown.

"Mr. Arnett doesn't date. He simply uses a woman for whatever he needs them for, pays them, and sends them on their way." She closed her book again in her reflection. "You will be the longest woman he's kept for a purpose."

I cringed inwardly at the honor that tried to bloom in my chest. The only reason I'd be the longest woman he would keep was because I was here to serve a long-term purpose. Once I was used up and he no longer had use for me, he would probably throw me out on my ass or worse —kill me. It definitely wasn't an honor to know that I'd be the longest person a psychopath kept in his possession.

"I see," I finally said around the knot in the throat. I cleared my throat a few times to even out my voice before I spoke again. "I guess I was trying to get an idea of what to tell the surgeon when he comes tonight. I just...want to look any way that would please Silas, but I'm not sure what he wants."

"Then that sounds like a conversation you should have with Mr. Arnett when the time comes."

"Will he be here when the surgeon comes?" I asked with a raised brow. "And if he isn't, is there a way you can call him or something to ask?" I swallowed hard. "I just don't want to choose the wrong thing and make him angry."

Maryse rolled her eyes. "The plastic surgery is simply to disguise your identity. It's not something that Silas is doing to become physically attracted to you. You could choose to turn yourself into the Hunchback of Notre Dame if you wanted. As long as you don't look like your current self, I'm sure he'll be pleased." She waved her hand toward the treadmill. "Please focus on the rest of your workout. Your time is winding down."

I ground my teeth and turned my attention to the floor-to-ceiling windows in front of me. The sparkling blue pool and lush green lawn out back looked so inviting. The multi-colored flowers near the bench further back made me wish I could sit outside and soak up some sun rather than staying in my cold room.

I thought back to my old life and everything I'd taken for granted. I used to think living in a studio apartment with leaking pipes, questionable mold spots, noisy neighbors, and weird smells was the worst situation I could be in. It was dramatic thinking, especially considering the kind of life I came from, but I used to think it was miserable living. That was what happened when you spent the majority of your life living in fantasy and delusions, thinking that life would've magically changed the moment I aged out of foster care. All that happened was that I left one hell and jumped into another one completely alone with no idea what to do next.

I worked a dead-end job surrounded by rich, out-of-touch assholes who had everything but still weren't happy. I thought if I had more money, life would be different. If I had a better place to live, I wouldn't have been so unhappy. It was so hard to not want more when you opened Instagram or Tiktok and saw influencers live these glamorous lives online. Wanting a similar life to them was the main thing that influenced me to sneak a few dollars here, a couple hundred dollars there.

But growing up as an orphan did me no favors. When you spent your entire life wishing for things, once you got a taste of it, it became addicting. Instead of doing something productive with the money that would've made me more money so that I wouldn't have to keep stealing from the company, I spent it on shit I didn't really need.

Designer shoes replaced my two pairs of shoes I'd left the group home with. Take out from the best restaurants in town replaced the microwaveable ramen cups I used to eat for breakfast, lunch, and dinner, granted that I even had enough of them to have three meals a day. I replaced my furniture I'd snagged from thrift stores with opulent furniture I would've never been able to afford on my own salary.

But even when I filled my shitty apartment with beautiful things, it didn't change how I felt. I was still stuck in the shitty apartment because I had no idea how to prove where I was getting the money to afford a nicer place. That alone should've stopped me but it didn't. I continued with my materialistic bullshit and was caught. Now I was stuck with a psychopath, walking on a treadmill and wishing I had the shitty life I'd tried so hard to get away from.

I'd thought the grass on the other side was so much more greener. But the moment I hopped over the fence, I quickly learned that there was nothing but cracked, dry earth, the grass simply an illusion and metaphor for suffering and death.

I looked out at the pool, lost in thought. Many times throughout my life, I wondered about my parents. I wondered what they looked like, if they had other children, and why they didn't want me. I wondered what made a mother give her child away to strangers. I wondered why she didn't at least try with me.

What was so bad in her life that made her subject me to the life she put upon me? People loved to harp about life being so precious, that every life deserved to be born. But what was the point of being born when you were abused by different people simply because your parents didn't want you? Being born didn't do unwanted children any favors. All it did was set us up for pain, abuse, neglect, and trauma that most of us never healed from.

I'd spent my whole life feeling as if I weren't enough. I mean, my own parents didn't think I was worthy enough to try to be parents to me, simply surrendering me days after I was born. My constant feelings of wanting to be wanted and loved opened the door for people to abuse and manipulate me with false affection and love bombing. It opened the door for me to fall for people who hurt me because my fucked up brain tried to rationalize their abuse as a different form of love, no matter how wrong it was.

No matter how much it hurt.

I should've been used to men like Silas; men like him were all I knew. They were always attracted to women who were easy to break, easy to hurt, easy to lure back in. The only reason I'd gotten out of my last abusive relationship almost a year ago was simply because he got bored of me. When he got upset that I wouldn't steal more money for him and his drug habit, he tried to threaten to leave me if I didn't. Anytime I didn't obey him, I'd come home from work to a meeting with his fist or his cock, ready to tear into me.

Even when I told him I thought it was a matter of time before I was caught with the amounts I was taking, he didn't care. He continued draining me while he was cheating on me. Once he'd convinced his shiny new victim to take him in, his visits were less and less frequent until he disappeared altogether, sending me a text telling me to lose his number because he was done with me. I was still stunned that I was devastated and depressed over that son of a bitch leaving. After that breakup, I'd lost hope in finding a decent guy. Besides, maybe I was delusional to think I deserved something different and healthy.

Being with Silas did nothing but solidify that thought.

At first, I thought I'd be able to reach some part of him that had compassion for others, but the longer I was around him only made it more obvious that there was no changing a man like that. I had no idea why I was so obsessed with trying to fix broken men, thinking that love, affection, and kindness would make psychos less...psycho.

Trying to reach a softer side of Silas would probably destroy me in the process. There was no need to aid him in my destruction; he seemed to already have that covered if the last few days were any indication. All I could do was hope that he'd loosen the reins on me once I proved to him that I was trustworthy. If I could talk to people outside of this house, there could be a way to get far away from this place, preferably somewhere he didn't have influence.

"Please power down the treadmill. Your workout session is over," Maryse said as she stood from her seat.

I blinked to bring myself back to my fucked up reality, pressing the appropriate buttons to lower my speed until the treadmill stopped. I stepped off with shaky legs and followed Maryse to the dining room, sitting at the table.

Lunch was the same disgusting thing it'd been for the past couple of days—a dry sandwich, an orange, a scoop of canned vegetables, and a bottled water. After choking down only half of it, I looked up at Valorie, who'd switched off with Maryse to watch me over lunch.

"I'm not feeling really good. I'm starting to feel sick," I lied.

I'd much rather starve than eat the poison they called food. I had no idea what I had to do to convince Silas to let me eat regular food, but I knew I'd be punished if I kept refusing food. If he was this ornery over money he'd gotten back when he sold the little girls, I didn't want to imagine what he'd do if he thought I was wasting money by wasting food.

It's no different than what I would've gotten had they left me in prison, I bitterly thought to myself once I was alone in my room. It was so easy to forget that this was another form of punishment as a part of my prison sentence when I observed the opulence around me. In regular prison, you knew you were in prison every day you woke up. But every morning I woke up in my soft queen bed alone, my own en-suite bathroom I didn't have to share, personal trainers, and a billionaire fiancé who doubled as a psycho, it was easy for a split second to think I was living in a fairy-tale—at least, until Silas snatched me out of my delusions and put me back into the fucked up reality he'd created for me here.

When Valorie clicked the lock in place, I sighed and walked to the bookshelf. It was filled with wedding magazines, a blank journal with a pen attached to it with a ribbon, and a few mystery books, which wasn't what I usually went for whenever I decided to read. I plucked a few magazines and the journal from the shelf and carried them over to the bed, flipping through them.

As I flipped through the pages and looked over the different dress designs and venue ideas, a part of me couldn't help but feel excited. It was almost like a dream —although a fucked up one—but a dream nonetheless. How many women could say they were marrying a billionaire, regardless of the reason? How many women could say they were planning a budgetless wedding that would allow them to create the wedding of their dreams?

Knowing I didn't have a budget for this made me feel like I was living someone else's life. Never in a million years did I think I'd end up with someone with so much money that they had endless spending budgets for something like a wedding, especially a wedding for a person they weren't even close to being in love with.

It's not like I chose this bastard for myself, I reminded myself, which quickly brought me out of the delusional cloud of excitement I was on. I was only here because of circumstances. Had I not stolen his money, I would've remained an unknown name and face around the office, completely off his radar.

I would've still been hating my mediocre life, wishing

my abusive ex would come back, and wishing death on my neighbors every time I heard them having sex through our thin walls. I couldn't imagine a man like Silas being capable of something like love after my conversation with Maryse, which made this upcoming wedding just another part of his agenda for me.

Sadness tingled throughout my body, which was confusing. I knew it wasn't healthy to love a man that could hurt me the way Silas seemed set on doing, but it was what I was used to. Toxic love seemed to be my vice, and everything in me wanted to be what he needed.

Maybe he just needed someone to accept all the bad parts of him to make him vulnerable enough to show his good parts. Maybe he saw something in me that made him want to marry me despite my crime. He could've left me in prison if he didn't think I was the right fit. There was also nothing stopping him from sending me back to prison if he was tired of me. It wouldn't hurt to ask him.

I sighed as the thought fizzled out. He'd made his intentions clear since our first conversation. It was stated in the manual; I was only here to serve a purpose. In public, I was his wife and the mother of his future heir. Otherwise, I was a prisoner confined to this bedroom. It shouldn't have made me sad; after everything I'd gone through in life, I deserved someone better than Silas. I deserved someone who didn't get off on hurting me, someone who saw me as their equal. I wanted someone who would actually love me the way I'd craved all my life.

I closed the magazine and stretched out across the bed and grabbed the journal instead, unraveling the pen from the ribbon it was attached to. I opened it to the first blank page before clicking the pen. There were so many things I wanted to get off my chest but I wasn't even sure where to start. So many traumatic things had happened in the last few days. From the treatment I'd received when I was processed in the prison, seeing two little girls be sold to child traffickers, witnessing their parents' murder, and having my captor rape and beat me all in a span of 72 hours.

It was like something straight out of a movie or a fucked up book. If I were someone different who came across this journal after I'd written all that'd happened to me in it, I'd think it was either exaggerated or a fiction book in the making of some sort.

Crazy how something so extreme was my actual life right now.

"No need to write about shit that's already happened," I mumbled to myself.

Silas had already traumatized me enough in ways I wouldn't easily forget; there was no need to write about it to further traumatize myself later. I closed the journal and pushed myself off the bed to take a quick shower. I peeled my clothes off and left them in a trail as I made my way to the glass shower. It took me a good while to figure out the digital pad that controlled the water and the temperature, as I'd only used the tub before now.

Once I finally got everything working the way I wanted, I let the cool wash soak my hair. Goosebumps rose along my skin as I stood there. The rainfall shower was soothing against my skin despite the usual soreness. It was soft and comforting, almost as if each drop of water knew of my pain and wanted to bring me comfort with each one that splashed against my skin.

The temperature quickly warmed up until there was a perfect amount of heat and steam in the shower. I lathered my body, inspecting my body for pain and soreness with each area I touched.

The water hitting the backside of my body didn't make me jump out of my skin the way the bath had the night Silas violated me. Even then I carefully cleaned between my legs, the pain I expected to be there wasn't as bold as it was before.

Whatever Maryse put in my bath soak last night definitely helped with a lot of the pain I had, which was both a blessing and a curse. It was great because I hated being in pain, but it only opened the door for Silas to prepare me for more pain.

As I washed my hair, my scalp was sore in certain places. I'd immediately thought back to last night. Last night's punishment was probably about humiliating and degrading me, which was fine considering what he could've done instead. But I'd be lying if I said I didn't think it was sexy to know how much pleasure I brought him.

Having him call me a good girl made something tingle inside of me. No one had ever called me that except my disgusting foster father, but even then, it made me feel as if I were making them happy. For that moment, I felt wanted, as if I were doing such a good job at whatever they made me do that they'd want to keep me around. That moment with Silas was the only time he'd talked to me in a soft yet deep voice.

His moans made my clit throb. Had I not been hurting down there last night, I was sure I would've touched myself at the sound of his vocal ecstasy. Even thinking about it now made me want to touch myself, but the thought of sexual satisfaction only made me wonder if that were his plans for me tonight.

So much for not being in pain, I thought with a sigh and returned back to rinsing the shampoo from my hair. Noise and voices coming from my bedroom made me pause, putting me on edge. I knew after lunch, I was on lockdown for the evening. Since I'd been here, Silas hadn't come home from work early and someone being in my room right now wasn't on the schedule.

No one had said anything about any doctors coming to visit other than the surgeon coming later tonight. The thought of Silas coming here to punish me for talking to Maryse the snitch was enough to freak me out and cause me to end my shower earlier than I wanted to.

I snatched a fluffy towel from the towel rack and tightly wrapped it around me. Being wet and freshly out of the shower would've been a huge disadvantage for me if it were Silas in my room right now. My heart pounded against my rib case as I stood in the middle of the bathroom, water dripping from my soaked hair and wet skin. After a few moments of hesitation, I grabbed another towel and worked to get my hair and skin as dry as possible. Sounds of metal clicking together further raised my anxiety, and if my heart rate went any higher, I was bound to pass out.

An unfamiliar man in a white coat stood in my bedroom near the door, looking down at his watch. A portable exam table was also in my room, which explained the metal noises I'd heard earlier. He wasn't the same doctor as the surgeon who was here the other day, so I wasn't sure if Silas had sent another plastic surgeon to get the job done or if this doctor was here for something else entirely. He only looked at me, as if he expected me to know what to do or why he was here.

I clutched the corner of my towel in my hand as I shifted nervously from foot to foot. "Um...are you here for my surgery consultation?" I asked nervously.

He shook his head. "No. I'm Dr. Horton, Silas's personal doctor. I'm here to get a little blood and to check your vaginal health," he said and gestured to the table. "Please remove the towel and get on this table, please. I will cover you with a sheet."

Not wanting a repeat of what'd happened the last time I refused to cooperate with a doctor, I dropped my towel and did as he asked. Modesty seemed to go out the window here, so I couldn't even feel shame or embarrassment. Besides, a few moments of embarrassment now was a lot better than a few hours of pain and torture later.

Once he had me prepped on the table, he pulled out a speculum from his bag. "Are you on birth control?" he asked, positioning himself between my legs.

I watched him as he squirted a little jelly on his hand from a small packet and rubbed it on the speculum. I squirmed and winced as he worked the speculum inside of me and then spread it to open me. I blew out a tense breath before answering him. "Um, yes. An IUD."

"Good." He plucked a Q-tip from his bag and swabbed the inside of me. "Any history of STDs or STIs?"

"No."

"Any history of pregnancies?"

"No."

He paused and looked up at me. "Ever?"

I swallowed hard and shook my head. "Never."

"Hmm." He moved his attention back to his task. "Prior to being with Mr. Arnett, were you sexually active?"

I shrugged. "Not for the last eight months or so."

He was quiet while he worked between my legs, finally pulling the speculum out. He moved from his spot at the foot of the table and came to stand next to me. "You can sit up now. I just have to draw a few tubes of blood, and I'll be on my way."

I sat up and held the sheet over my chest. "May I ask why all of this is being done?" I asked. "I thought Silas didn't want to try for a baby until after we were married, which isn't for another few months."

It didn't make sense for him to check all of this right now. He'd already chosen me to be his wife; I would've thought this would've been something he chose to do before deciding to force me into his plan.

"This isn't about having children right now," the doctor said, his tone flat. "Mr. Arnett wanted to be able to have unprotected sex with you and wants confirmation that you're clean."

I fought the urge to scoff, unable to help feeling

offended. He was being responsible with his sexual health, which I couldn't blame him for. But I couldn't help but think that he thought I was dirty simply because of my background.

Sure, most people who grew up in the foster care system turned to drugs or prostitution if they were exposed to extreme trauma growing up. But some of us beat those odds. Some of us tried to make better lives for ourselves despite what we'd been through. How would I know if he were clean? As the biggest manwhore in the city, I'd bet money that he'd probably contracted a few things or two with the way he went through women.

"I see," I ground out instead, keeping my sharp words dancing on the tip on my tongue.

He was going through all of this just to be able to fuck me however he wanted without protection, probably wanting to feel the pain he inflicted upon me without the barrier of a condom. A knot lodged itself in my throat. Did he want to have sex with me during his open hours tonight?

It would've made more sense for him to have had this done when I first arrived here, even before he first raped me. The fact that he was having this done now only furthered my fears about tonight's open hours.

He'd told me that anything can happen during open hours, even him giving me pleasure, but I was starting to think that everything was only about him and what he wanted.

And what he wanted most was to hurt me.

Dr. Horton quickly filled a few lab tubes before removing the tiny needle and placing a bandaid over the needle site. He didn't say much else as he gathered the rest of his things. I slid off the table when he motioned for me to move, watching him as he folded the table.

He knocked on the door and it opened, revealing one of the security men. The guy's gaze was hard when it washed over me briefly. He walked over and grabbed the table before exiting the room. Dr. Horton gave me a nod before he also disappeared, leaving me alone again.

It was only then that I realized I was still naked when the security guy saw me. I rushed to my large walk-in closet and found a pair a leggings and a loose t-shirt, pulling them on after I'd slipped into a matching bra and panty set.

I looked up at the clock, noting that I had four hours until dinner and five hours to mentally prepare myself for whatever fuckery open hours had in store for me to tonight. I climbed back onto the bed and grabbed the journal, opening it again. My hand started writing before I could even stop myself.

. . .

Day 3 in Hell

I now belong to a psychopath. As long as I'm confined to this house, I will never have a true chance at getting away from him. It seems the only means of escape is through death—whether that be him or me. For now, I have to play my cards right. Everyone has a weakness, and I'm smarter than they probably think I am.

I just have to be patience. Before this is arrangement is over, Silas will get what he deserves.

I'll make sure of that, even if it kills me.

Signed,

a desperate prisoner

CHAPTER TEN
SILAS

Ever since the announcement this morning, my phone had been ringing off the hook. Every publication in Palmetto Beach wanted the exclusive rights of an interview and pictures with my new, anonymous fiancée. No matter what news channel I turned to, most of them were harping on this engagement and having full segment think pieces about what they thought she looked like or what made her different from any other woman I'd been seen with.

The buzz was nice; it at least took a lot of the focus off of Maxwell and his wife's death and the disappearance of his daughters. It gave my employees something else to focus on, everyone congratulating me and excited about the prospect of me finally settling down.

They were so fucking naïve that it hurt sometimes.

I'd never been more relieved in my life to be home. I didn't want to hear another ringing phone for the rest of the night, making sure my phone was on *Do Not Disturb* the moment I stepped foot inside my house. I was in dire need of a stress release after the day I'd had. Even though the switched focus was well needed, it only reminded me of all the shit I needed to do.

The reporters wouldn't get off my back until this "mystery woman" was revealed, which meant I needed to get the ball rolling on this surgery for Alyssa. I shot a quick text to the surgeon to remind him that he'd better be here at eight and not a minute later before trekking to my office for my evening debrief from Maryse.

She appeared at my side with a look on her face that made me curious. A part of me hoped that meant Maryse had a bad report. I wanted nothing more than to make Lia bleed tonight, but I knew that wasn't the best thing right now when I needed to prepare her for surgery. The more I broke her body, the longer I'd have to push out her surgery. Between my father and these fucking reporters, I needed to leave her alone long enough to get this surgery done so I could finally show her to my world—to her new world.

"So how was it today?" I asked as I sat behind my desk.

"Drink?" she asked instead, moving over to the small

bar in the corner of the office. I eyed her carefully, a slight frown settling on my lips.

"I guess," I said. She busied herself making a whiskey neat before bringing it over to me. I took a sip and watched her from over the rim of the glass, waiting for her to speak. When she only sat across from me and stared at me, I put the glass down and tightened my jaw. "Are you going to answer me today or tomorrow? I don't have all night, Maryse."

"As far as behavior, she was fine," she started. "She did everything that was asked of her and didn't cause any trouble for any of us today."

"So if she was 'fine' today, what the fuck is up with this weird ass vibe coming from you?" I asked, my voice growing tight.

Maryse tucked a lock of auburn hair behind her ear. "Sir, if I may speak freely...I don't trust this woman being here." She steepled her fingers in her lap as she dropped her gaze. "I personally don't think you've fully thought this plan out in wanting to keep a woman you've essentially kidnapped from prison."

I rolled my eyes and pressed my fingers against my temples as I narrowed my gaze at her. "If I paid you to think, Maryse, you would be in a position to think," I stated firmly. "It doesn't matter what you or anyone else in this house thinks about Alyssa being here or whether or not you trust her. She's here for a specific purpose; nothing more, nothing less."

"But it's dangerous," she continued with a frown, holding my gaze this time. "You've worked so hard to build what you have right now, something you could lose because of this woman. Out of all the women you could choose, you chose someone who's supposed to be in prison right now." She sighed softly. "What if this plastic surgery isn't enough to conceal her identity?"

I ground my teeth and closed my eyes for a moment. Had Maryse been one of the other women that worked for me, I would've reached across my desk and choked her by now. But because she'd worked with me for so long, I'd grown accustomed to her lecturing and other bullshit.

It was just a matter of retaining some kind of self control in the heat of the moment. I'd always looked to her as a second mom, as she was my nanny when I was younger. I knew she only wanted the best for me, but sometimes she pissed me off with her flimsy concerns that I'd already handled.

"It'll be enough for what I need to do," I finally said when I'd gotten a grip on my annoyance. She looked at me for a long moment before she spoke again.

"You don't have every employee at the prison in your back pocket, honey," she said, her use of endearment making my eye twitch.

It always annoyed the shit out of me when she or my mother called me pet names. They only used it when they were trying to get me to be reasonable by their standards, which usually meant doing things their way. There was a reason why I always kept Maryse out of the specifics of certain things, mostly because I didn't want to deal with bullshit like this current conversation about my dealings. "It's only a matter of time before someone either doesn't know any better or a new guy realizes an inmate is missing for everything to crumble to the ground."

"For fuck's sake," I mumbled. "This is why it's important for you to mind the business that pays you, Maryse," I stated, unable to mask the irritation in my voice. "Do you really think I didn't handle all of that prior to that bitch being brought here?" A humorless chuckle left my lips. "You must think I'm a fucking idiot incapable of coming up with fool-proof plans, huh?"

"Not at all, sir," she quickly said, shaking her head. A waterfall of fire shook around her shoulders at the action before she narrowed her eyes at me again. "I'm just worried, is all."

I frowned. "It's not your business to worry about." I leaned back in my chair. "Besides, Lia the inmate isn't 'missing.'"

Maryse blinked a few times, confusion etching itself into her soft features. "What do you mean she's not missing? Was she not processed and put into the prison system?"

"Alyssa is here and Lia is still in prison," I said, a smirk sliding across my lips as Maryse continued to look at me, confused. "Do you not think I'd anticipated that already, Maryse? All of the shit you're 'concerned' about are things that have already been thought out and handled."

"I don't understand."

"When I made the decision to have Lia brought to me, I knew I couldn't just leave her spot empty. It would raise too many questions." I drummed my fingers along the top of my desk in silence, adding to the suspense before I continued. "Another woman is currently in her place. It was a hell of deal for this woman, too. She was going away for twenty-five years to life for murdering a taxi driver while she was high out of her mind. In exchange for her becoming Lia, I arranged for her sentence to be swapped from her current one to Lia's nine years instead. She also gets money monthly for commissary or whatever she wants to spend it on, special privileges that'll be carried out by the guards on my payroll, better living conditions, and protection." I shrugged. "You can't beat a deal like that."

"Oh." Maryse shifted in her seat before she shook her head. "I still don't think it's a good idea. You're gambling a lot on a person you don't know."

"She's the least of my concern," I said, waving her off. "If she knows what's good for her, she'll get with the program quickly."

"You shouldn't underestimate someone who is desperate and without hope," she said as she stood to her feet. "Those kind of people have nothing to lose and will do whatever's necessary to take you down with them."

"You give her too much credit," I said with another shrug. "As I said, mind that business that pays you, Maryse." I looked down at my wrist to see that it was nearly six. "In fact, it looks like it's time for you to escort your business to the dining room for dinner."

The muscle in her jaw ticked as if she was forcing herself not to say anything else, only giving me a tight nod before she hurried out of the office. I stared at the closed door for a moment. I wasn't sure what prompted Maryse to talk about not trusting Alyssa, but I'd be sure to keep an eye on her in the meantime. Maryse usually went with the flow with whatever fuckery I was up to, but this was the first time in a long time that she'd questioned me about anything.

Maybe it was only because of the method in which I'd gotten Alyssa, but it wouldn't have been any different than me snatching someone off the street. Alyssa still met the criteria I'd required for a woman in my possession in the first place. There would be no one looking for her, she was young enough to have children, she was easy enough to grab, and with a little work, she'd easily slip into my elite circle as if she'd always belonged there. I brushed the thoughts off as I stood and headed for the dining room myself. Maryse would just have to get over herself. But if she continued questioning me the way she'd just done, Alyssa would be the least of her worries.

The chef placed a plate of perfectly cook garlic and parmesan-crusted salmon with a side of creamy lemon pasta in front of me, the smell alone making my stomach growl. "Thank you, Angelo," I said with a nod.

He only nodded in response before disappearing back into the kitchen. A few beats later, my fiancée finally arrived in the dining room, sitting in the seat at the opposite end of the table as she had for the past few meals. She was wearing a t-shirt and what looked like tights or some shit, which made me grind my teeth. It was so fucking unattractive when a woman dressed down outside of working out.

I pulled my eyes from her attire and focused on my dinner instead, making a mental note to talk to her about it later. I was surprised the women let her come to dinner like that, especially since they knew I hated for her to wear that aside from her working out. It almost seemed as if they were trying to sabotage her in an effort to get her out of the house sooner.

"Good evening, sir," Alyssa said, her soft voice breaking the overall silence. I only glanced at her before taking a forkful of the flaky salmon in my mouth. The look of that fucking t-shirt at my dining table pissed me off once again.

"Never wear that outside of your workout block," I stated. She glanced down at her clothes before looking back to me.

"Sorry. I didn't know you wanted me to wear something else," she said softly. "I figured you didn't want me wearing pajamas to dinner again."

I rolled my eyes. "You have a whole fucking closet of clothes. Do you think I want you wearing pajamas or workout clothes when you're in my presence?" I scoffed. "If I wanted you to look like shit, I would've filled your closet with prison uniforms instead of the designer shit that's in there. I mean, that's what you wanted, right? That's what you were spending stolen money on, right?"

Her cheeks turned a medium shade of pink as she dropped her gaze to the table top. "I'm sorry. It won't happen again," she murmured.

"I know it won't."

Angelo came back out with a regular plate, placing it in front of Alyssa. She looked up at him in surprise before looking back to me. "I..thank you," she stammered.

I took another forkful of salmon. I'd had Angelo

prepare rigatoni pasta with Beyond Meat sausage and baby kale, switching her to a plant-based diet. Luckily for her, I just wanted to get off tonight, which didn't really require me to hurt her. But I knew I'd have to prep her myself, which I wasn't looking forward to.

The usual women I spent the night with were either plant-based or completely vegan. If I fucked a woman who ate meat, I typically didn't put my mouth anywhere near their pussy. Women who ate meat usually tasted like fucking battery acid to me, and if I was stuck with this woman for the long haul, she'd have to change the way she ate if she wanted me to give her the pleasure I knew she wanted.

"You're now on a plant-based diet," I said casually, still eating my salmon.

She was quiet for a moment. "What does that mean exactly?"

I paused mid-chew and looked up, frowning. "...are you dense? It means exactly what I just said."

"So, is that like a vegan or something?"

I rolled my eyes. "Veganism goes beyond food, airhead. To be vegan, you don't eat meat nor use products that either come from an animal or tested on animals. Plant-based is just related to food. You won't be consuming animal products anymore."

She looked down at herself. "Is this for diet purposes or something? I didn't think I gained any weight."

"No. It's simply because I want you eating a plant-based diet," I said and continued eating. She stared at me as if waiting for me to continue, finally sighing and eating her food when I didn't say anything else. I watched her poke at the sausage in her dish before stabbing it with her fork, bringing it to her nose for a slight sniff. She took the tiniest bite out of it before she made a face. I rolled my eyes. "You'll eat that entire dish before you leave this table. I don't think you want to risk what'll happen if you don't."

Her face paled a bit before she looked back at her plate, reluctantly sighing and taking a some into her mouth. We ate in comfortable silence for a while, and for a moment, things felt...normal. I assumed this was what people in a relationship usually did at dinner time, having small talk and eating with each other. I glanced at her from time to time, observing her dainty mannerisms. When she caught me looking at her, she straightened her posture and cleared her throat.

"Um, I'd wanted to talk to you about the consultation with the surgeon later," she started, taking a sip of water from her glass.

"What about it?" I asked with a raised brow. "We're not having a discussion about whether or not you have to do it so—"

"It's not that," she interrupted, giving me a sheepish shrug when I frowned at her interruption. "Sorry."

"You will be if you do that again," I said firmly and took a sip of my whiskey. "What about the consultation?"

She shifted in her seat a little before pushing food around on her plate. "I wanted to ask if there was anything in particular that you wanted me to have? Like... did you have a certain way you wanted me to look or anything? I want to make sure I look attractive for you."

I chuckled and shook my head. "I don't care what you look like. I'm not looking to be attracted to you. I want to make sure you're not easily recognized; that's it. Concealing your identity is the whole point of this surgery."

She nibbled on her bottom lip for a few moments. "I mean...my looks will matter at some point," she said softly. "If you're planning to having a child with me, they're going to have half of my DNA, which means they can share features of mine that you don't like."

I had to admit she had me there. I didn't fully think about that aspect in the grand scheme of things. Now that the idea was brought to the surface, it brought many different scenarios to the table as well. Despite owning casinos, I wasn't much of a gambling man when it came to odds that were too high or too unpredictable to try to beat. I couldn't risk the 50/50 chance of my kid coming out looking like a fucking gremlin because his mother was far from physically attractive..

After a few moments, I shrugged as I twirled some pasta onto my fork. "Having a baby with you doesn't require me to have to use one of your eggs," I finally said.

She frowned at me, folding her arms across her chest. "Then why not get a surrogate instead of just planting someone else's fertilized egg inside of me?" she asked. I smirked at her when I noticed the rejection that weaved itself throughout her words, but annoyance quickly replaced my amusement when she continued. "That probably would've been a lot less expensive and less of a headache than having to marry someone to have a kid."

"Because I do things the way I want to do them," I snapped. "How I decide to have my heir is my decision. You'll fall in line either way."

Silence filled the dining room once again, giving me a moment to process what she'd said. The more I thought on it, the more a new idea brewed. A smile slowly spread across my lips but I remained quiet as I finished my dinner. When Angelo came back to take away the plates, I leaned back in my chair with my gaze fixated on her.

"You know what? I think you're right," I said.

Her brows furrowed as she regarded me. "About what?"

"About the surrogate. That would actually make more sense like you said."

"Oh." She blinked for a few moments, surprise and what seemed like hope blooming in her gaze. "Yeah. That would probably be the best thing for you and your life with what you're trying to do."

"Yep. You were right."

She nibbled on her bottom lip again as she seemed to ponder her next words. "So...does that mean you're canceling the wedding and sending me back to prison then?"

I tilted my head back and release a laugh that filled the dining room. Bursting her bubble was going to damn near orgasmic. "Why the fuck would I do that?" I asked, still chuckling.

She frowned. "Well, if you're using a surrogate, you wouldn't have a need for me," she said. "You'd said I was only here to be your public wife and to give you an heir. You don't need a wife if you can just use a surrogate."

I shook my head as I stood, grinning at her. "Nothing about our arrangement would change if I used a surrogate," I said, my grin turning into a full smile. "It would only mean I wouldn't have to take a nine-month break from fucking you up. So yeah, your surrogate idea is a much better one. Thanks for that, dollface."

Watching her face blanch at my words caused me to

laugh once more. It was always so much fun watching the hope drain from someone. She'd thought she had the upper hand for a fleeting moment, only to find out she'd added to her own destruction.

She could've had nine months free from abuse had she not opened her mouth. But a woman like that couldn't control herself, which only made this so much more fun for me. I always loved when people wrote checks their asses couldn't cash when it was time to pay out.

———————

The surgeon was right on time as expected. Alyssa sat on her bed in a paper gown as Dr. Wynn drew lines on her face and chest to decide how to do the things she'd chosen. When asked if she had any idea how she wanted to look or who she'd wanted to look like, she surprisingly said Marilyn Monroe.

I was actually a little shocked. I didn't take her as the type to know much about Marilyn Monroe aside from the little quotes here and there that some women used for aesthetic purposes. I definitely didn't mind having someone as beautiful as a Marilyn look-alike on my arm in public; maybe it would help me tolerate her a sliver more.

"So when are you looking to get this surgery scheduled?" Dr. Wynn asked after he finished writing his notes.

I stroked my chin as I examined the marks he'd made around her nose, lips, and her breasts. "Is all of this something you can get done at the same time? I mean, time is of the essence here," I said.

Dr. Wynn shrugged. "We could get the breast implants and her rhinoplasty out of the way in one go. I'd hold off on the lip fillers for a week after that. Since she'll have to be put under for the first two surgeries, I don't need her lips to be swollen prior to surgery. It'll make it harder to tube her, which could cause damage to her lips if we have to work too hard." He put his notepad in his pocket. "Swelling can be unpredictable, so I'd say to schedule the lip fillers a week after the bigger surgery, maybe even two weeks if you can. You just don't want to do too much to her face all at once or you won't get the desired results.

I nodded. "I can agree with that," I said. "So we can possibly do it next Wednesday then?"

"I'm all booked up on Wednesday, but I have an opening on Thursday morning if that's okay."

I waved my hand. "Fine. Do it Thursday."

"I'll put you down for Thursday morning." He pulled his phone out and took a picture of her face and the markings he'd made before doing the same to her breasts. "You'll need to bring her to the office on Wednesday for pre-op things, though. I can't do a home visit for that, as it has to be on the books."

"She'll be there," I said mindlessly. Dr. Wynn said his goodbyes and dismissed himself, leaving me alone with Alyssa. I looked down at her as she sat on the side of the bed, her gaze to her lap. "Go into the bathroom and get that washed off. The girls will be in here in a moment to get you ready for our activity for the night."

No sooner than the words fell out of my mouth, Valorie, Aimee, and Kora all walked into the room, bowing slightly when they saw I was still in the room.

"We're just here to get her ready, sir. Should we come back?" Aimee asked, her sweet voice almost making me cringe. I shook my head.

"No, I was just about to leave. You have an hour to get her ready. I'll be back in exactly an hour."

"Yes, sir," the three of them said in unison.

"Good." I looked to Alyssa. "Don't give them any trouble. I have no problem switching tonight's activity to something painful."

"I won't," she said, swallowing hard as she looked at me with wide eyes. After looking at each of them a final time, I stalked out of the bedroom, closing the door behind me. My phone vibrated in my pocket as I headed to my bedroom, Dr. Horton's name appearing in the text preview that popped up on my screen.

Horton: Everything came back clean so you're good to go with your activity tonight.

I blacked out my phone screen and tossed it on my bed once I'd reached my room. I figured she would've been fine, but it was better to be safe than sorry. I stripped down to my boxers and stretched out across my bed. A woman's pleasure was never my concern, but I figured it would be a nice reward for my future wife. She'd been behaving after all. Maryse was so adamant about not trusting Alyssa, probably thinking Alyssa would turn on me the moment she got a chance to.

I grinned to myself as I closed my eyes for a moment. Maryse might've been right, but she underestimated another trait from my captive. While she probably felt helpless and defeated, there was something that broke through the surface during our office hours last night. Having me praise her and verbally show her that she was doing a good job gave me info beyond her having a praise kink.

She was a woman desperate to be loved by someone.

I was a pro at manipulating anyone to my will, especially women. She may have endured physical abuse from multiple men in her life while growing up in foster care, so physical pain would only get me so far. Now it was time to switch gears.

A woman in love was a woman less likely betray me. Scars from physical pain would heal but nothing lasted longer than emotional and mental scars. She could try to think of ways to escape her luxurious prison, but little did she know, she was already caught in my web.

'Til death do us part, right? I wasn't capable of falling in love, but I was a master at pretending. And tonight would be a night for her to remember. By the time I was done with her, I'd bet my left nutsack that any plans of wanting to get away or turn on me would be gone in a flash.

I chuckled to myself as I put my hands behind my head, staring up at the ceiling. "Let the fucking games begin."

CHAPTER ELEVEN
LIA

"Please take a quick shower to get the ink off of you," Aimee said with a gentle smile. "We don't have much time and we have a lot to get done."

I nodded and mindlessly headed to the bathroom, shedding the paper gown and the rest of my clothes. My reflection gave me pause as my eyes wandered over the multiple lines drawn on my body. I sighed softly. Next week, I wouldn't look like this. It would be a bit bizarre to look in the mirror and not recognize the person that looked back at me.

Next week, my nose would be different and my breasts would be a little bigger. I palmed my current breasts. I actually was glad to get a size or two bigger. My small breasts were one of my biggest insecurities, so it was something I'd willingly changed.

Movement in the bedroom reminded me I was on a time crunch. I wasn't sure what Silas had planned, but it required getting ready. Since I hadn't had my surgery yet, I already knew I wasn't leaving the house, but it was still both nerve wracking and exciting to think about what he could have up his sleeve.

I jumped in the shower and quickly scrubbed my face and chest to get the ink off before lathering up my body. The orchid scent of the shower gel clung to the steam of the shower as I bathed, a knock on the door prompting me to hurry up and rinse off. I rushed to turned the water off and dried my body as I went back into the bedroom, surprised to see makeup and hair things arranged on the bed.

"Am I going somewhere?" I asked as I sat on a stool Aimee gestured to.

She shook her head. "Mr. Arnett just requested this for the night."

"Oh." Aimee combed through my wet hair while Valorie primed my face with some kind of cream. "Do you know what he has planned then?"

"No," Valorie said, her words clipped.

I took that as a sign to not ask anymore questions, allowing them to work in silence. Aimee blow dried and curled my hair while Valorie worked on my makeup. When they were finished, Kora gave me a lacy nightgown to put on and spritzed my skin with a flowery perfume that smelled expensive. A timer went off and Aimee breathed a sigh of relief before she giggled.

"We beat the clock!" she exclaimed, clasping her hands together.

Valorie looked at me before adjusting my hair. "Mr. Arnett would like you to sit on the floor in a kneeling position and wait for him to give you further instruction," she said.

"Am I able to go look in the—"

A solid knock stopped the rest of my sentence as I quickly got on the floor in the desired position. My heart raced in my chest and my nerves got the best of me. I had no idea how I looked, and could only hope they did a good enough job to please Silas.

Kora moved over to the door and cracked it open before revealing Silas standing there in a pair of silk pajama pants. I looked up at him nervously, trying to see if I could read his expression to figure out what he thought of my look, but there was nothing there.

He was so hard to read, his face usually blank of expression majority of the time. The only time you really knew he was angry was if it filtered through his voice, but even then it was hard to tell when he would mask it.

"Thank you, ladies," he said with a nod as he stepped into the bedroom. "You're dismissed for the night."

"Thank you, sir," they said in unison. They quickly gathered their supplies and left the room, closing the door softly behind them.

Silence cloaked the room as Silas only stared at me. I fought the urge to fidget as I silently waited for him to give me some kind of direction. His dick print was visible in his pants, the sight of it making my mouth pool with saliva at the thought of sucking him off again. For some odd reason, it turned me on to know that I made him feel good, that I made a billionaire feel good. I hoped to have the chance to do so again tonight, because if he was too busy feeling good, maybe he'd be too preoccupied to want to hurt me.

"I had a very stressful day, Alyssa," he started, tilting his head to the side as he regarded me. "I think I want to relieve a little stress with you."

My stomach dropped to my asshole as my breath hitched in my throat. I swallowed the bubbling anxiety threatening to spill forth and forced myself to answer.

"What would you like me to do, sir?" I asked softly, still not moving from my position.

He took a couple of steps forward until he was in front of me. He untied the drawstring on his pants. "You can start by using your mouth," he said, his voice husky and deep.

This time I didn't hesitate with his order. I grabbed the

waistband of his pants and pulled it down enough to free his thickening cock. I took it into my hands and stroked it, relishing in how heavy and thick he already was. He hissed when I took him into my mouth, his eyes sliding shut as I worked my mouth and hands.

His hips flexed slightly, his hand in my hair urging me to take more of him. I watched his expression—the only real time I could read his face—and used it to guide me. Every groan that slipped from his lips sent a buzz straight to my clit, causing me to whimper around his cock as I grew wet between my thighs. I switched to stroking him with one hand while moving the other between my legs, circling my clit as I sucked him off a little faster. I was already so wet and needy, praying to God that he'd fuck me just to relieve the growing ache inside of me.

His eyes zeroed in on my hand and he frowned, letting go of my head before stepping back from me completely. I looked up at him with wide eyes, hoping I hadn't just fucked up the moment by doing something I shouldn't have. A surprised squeak left my mouth when he grabbed me by the throat and yanked me to my feet, bringing our faces inches from each other.

"You don't touch yourself unless I give you permission," he said, his eyes blazing heated passion and annoyance. "Do you understand?"

I nodded, licking my lips. The taste of lipstick suddenly

coated my tongue, replacing the subtle taste of the precum Silas dripped on my tongue moments before.

"Yes, sir," I whispered.

He stared at me for so long, almost as if he were fighting with himself on whether to hurt me or let me continue. His hard cock pressed against my stomach and my pussy practically pulsed with need to have him fill me. Before I could blink, his lips were against mine, displaying his dominance and pulling a needy moan from me.

Every muscle in my body wanted to reach up and touch him, but I didn't want to do anything out of turn. My body buzzed when he dipped a hand between my thighs, growling down my throat as his fingers glided up and down my slick slit.

"Already so fucking wet," he murmured against my lips. "What a needy little whore you are."

I whimpered in response, allowing him to force me backwards with every step he took forward. I spilled back onto the bed, watching him as he pulled his pajama pants all the way off and stalked toward me. Goosebumps rose along my skin as he lifted the thin nightgown up, forcing me to sit up in order to fully take it off. He took a moment to look over my body, his eyes filled with something that I couldn't quite place.

He snapped out of whatever he was in when I squirmed under his intense gaze, hovering over me to kiss me once more. The way he'd handled my body was a complete 360 from how he'd handled me just two days ago. It was almost as if I was with someone else entirely instead of the psycho I knew him to be.

My hands fisted the comforter on my bed, scared that I'd break this soft trance he was in if I dared to touch him. I closed my eyes as pleasure consumed me, relishing in the feeling of his warm lips and tongue pampering each nipple before his kisses trailed down further.

My breath caught in my throat the moment he sucked my clit into his mouth, my back arching. My moan filled the space around us, the pleasure growing more intense when his flickering tongue tickled my sensitive clit.

"Silas," I moaned, rolling my hips against his mouth.

Out of all the men I'd been with, he was the second guy to have gone down on me. The first guy was terrible at it, almost to the point to were I didn't trust anyone with teeth to be anywhere near my clit. But Silas was so skilled, so precise in his tongue action and the amount of pressure he sucked my bundle of nerves with.

When he slipped two fingers inside of me, tapping the sweet spot that made my eyes roll into the back of my head, my body unraveled for him, shaking and convulsing as incoherent words and moans spilled from my mouth.

He didn't say a word, only continuing his task through my orgasm. When the pressure became too much, I tried to squirm away, but he held me still, continuing his torturous assault on my clit until I came a second time, my juices trickling onto the comforter beneath me.

He finally released my clit from the delicious suction he'd created with his mouth, flickering the tip of it with his tongue as I jumped and trembled. He stood and looked down at me, the bottom half of his face glistening with his rightfully earned bounty as he stroked his hard cock.

I moved to sit up, wanting to return the favor but he tightly shook his head.

"Don't fucking move," he growled.

I swallowed and flattened myself back on the bed, waiting for his next move. After a few quiet beats, he took a step forward and pulled me to the edge of the bed. A shiver rolled down my spine when he rubbed the head of his bare cock up and down my pussy, every stroke over my clit sending chills along my nerve endings.

We both moaned when he sank into me, pausing for a moment. He planted a hand around my throat while the other squeezed my thigh in his hand, and then he began to pound into me. Unlike the first time around, the pain was mixed with pleasure as my pussy stretched to accommodate his girth.

The moans that fell from my mouth were loud and almost sounded inhumane. Silas clamped a hand over my mouth as he grip on my throat tightened, which both terrified the fuck out of me while heightening my pleasure.

"Oh fuck," he moaned, his hips slapping against mine. "The way this pussy squeezes my cock is fucking amazing."

He moved his hands from my mouth and throat and lowered himself even further until we were chest to chest. Without missing a beat, he hooked his arms behind my knees and brought them forward, opening me up to him to allow him even deeper inside of me.

"Oh—my—god," I moaned, my words choppy over his violent thrusts. Every thought of escape was rattled into nothing, the only thing consuming my mind being this man and the pleasure he brought.

"Look at you taking every inch of my cock," he murmured in my ear. "Feels good having my thick cock stretch this tight little pussy, doesn't it?"

"Yes!" I moaned.

"I love a woman who can take it rough," he panted, his cock damn near knocking against my cervix. "I'm going to have so much fucking fun with you because you're gonna love the way I fuck you."

"Fuck me," I moaned, unable to stop myself from scratching his back. "Oh my god, Silas; fuck me!"

He buried his face in the crook of my neck, muffling the spine-tingling moans that spilled from him. Without warning, my entire body locked up as an orgasm crashed into me, robbing me of my voice as my juices spilled forth. He raised his head, his eyes rolling back as he thrust like a madman.

"Fuck," he choked out, his hips stuttering a bit before heat flooded inside of me. He gave me three more thrusts as he emptied himself inside of me before he paused, panting and slick with sweat.

Neither of us said anything for a while as we worked to catch our breath. There was that awkward moment of "what now" that I wasn't sure of how to handle. In the manual he'd said that we'd never share the same bed, but a part of me hoped that was a part of my reward tonight. As if hearing my mental question, he finally pulled out of me and staggered back a few steps, releasing a breath.

"You squirted on the comforter," he said as he grabbed his pajamas pants from the floor and pulled them on. "I'll have one of the girls come change it while you're in the shower."

Then he left me there alone, confused about the state of things between us but too exhausted to dwell on it.

The next morning, the sun seemed a lot brighter than it had since I'd been here. Birds chirped outside as I rolled onto my back and stretched, soreness spreading throughout the muscles of my lower body.

A sleepy smile graced my lips as I slowly sat up in bed. I couldn't even put last night into words. Silas could pretend all he wanted, but I knew passion when I felt it. Last night wasn't just sex between a captor and his captive; it felt as if it were more than that. He'd had a stressful day at work and came to me for comfort. I wasn't sure what this meant for us in the future, but it was nice to know that he was capable of being gentle.

Maybe that was the gateway to wiggle my way into his heart, I thought to myself with a grin.

I glanced up at the clock to see that it was almost seven, which meant that it was only a matter of time before one of the women came to wake me up. I forced myself out of bed to prepare for breakfast, reminding myself not to wear pajamas or whatever Silas deemed to be "workout clothes" to the dining room.

I couldn't wipe off the goofy grin on my face as I moved around my bathroom and bedroom to get ready. Even Maryse gave me a weird look to see that I was already awake and in a good mood. When I spotted the journal on the bookshelf, I grabbed it and sat on the bed, wanting to write a small entry before breakfast. And after last night? I had plenty of things I could write about.

I clicked the pen and let my thoughts fly.

. . .

Day 4 In Hell

After last night, I'm not even sure I can even call it hell. Now it feels like limbo, filling me with confusing shit that I'm still trying to process. When Silas said that pleasure would be a reward, I thought it would've been mediocre. When dealing with a psychopath, his version of "pleasure" simply could've been a punishment without pain.

But man, oh man was I wrong.

The things I felt last night were nothing like anything I'd ever felt. Every guy I'd been with—Ralph, Antonio, Caleb, and even Mario's stupid ass—never made me feel that way. Last night was the first night I'd had sex and MY pleasure was taken into consideration.

Maybe Silas has something in that heart of his after all. Maryse might've thought he was empty just because he never settled down, but she didn't feel the things I felt when he was between my legs. She didn't feel the fiery passion and lust that pulsed between us with every swipe of his tongue and every thrust of his cock.

. . .

I blushed and bit my bottom lip as memories of last night flooded my mind. My clit throbbed at the memory of Silas's mouth and tongue on me, his strong hands on me.

I closed my eyes for a moment, remembering the strong, violent thrusts he gave me and how he praised me for taking his cock. A shudder rolled through my body before I continued writing.

I know love at first sight exists, but is it possible to fall in love with someone's cock? The way he fucked me last night was addicting and exhilarating, something I'd want every night if he'd let me. I don't know what he has in store for me during tonight's open hours, but I'm going to be on my best behavior just in case he's in a generous mood.

Maybe being his wife won't be too bad after all. And if I can get him to open up more, maybe we can make this situation into a relationship that we both want forever.

signed,
    a hopeful fiancée

I closed the journal with a small smile. Silas wasn't a lost cause; he just needed the right person to love him. He was capable of feeling something, it was evident in the way he fucked me last night, the way he sought solace between my legs.

If I have nine years with this man, I needed to make the most of it. He had potential regardless of what anyone else said, and I was determined to bring out the man I knew he could be.

A soft knock sounded on the door before Aimee poked her head in. She slipped into the room and smiled at me.

"Good morning, Alyssa," she said. "Sleep well?"

"I did," I said with a nod.

"I'm glad to hear that." She gestured toward the hallway. "I'll escort you to breakfast."

I looked down at the journal in my hand. "Could I actually get a split second to put this in a safe place?" I asked. "No offense, but I'm not sure I can fully trust that someone won't try to read it."

Aimee looked out into the hallway before turning to face me. "Please be quick."

She stepped out of the room and closed the door a little, giving me enough cover to slip the journal under my mattress. I quickly rushed over to the door and smiled when Aimee opened the door fully again. She regarded me for a few moments before forcing a small smile of her own.

"Thank you. I'm ready now," I said.

She gave me a small nod and led me down the hall. As

we walked through the house, giddy butterflies filled my stomach as we got closer to the dining room. Things were left in an awkward state last night when he left abruptly.

I wasn't sure what I expected; he'd made it clear that we wouldn't sleep together, but I still thought it would've been different than...that. I wasn't expecting romance, but I thought he would've said something other than acknowledging I squirted on my comforter and getting someone to change it.

All of the butterflies fluttering around in my stomach ceased their flying and drowned in stomach acid when I reached the dining room, Silas nowhere to be found. I tightened my jaw as I took a seat.

It wasn't unusual for him not to be here for breakfast; in fact, I used to be glad to have a moment away from him. But I'd wanted to talk to him about his abrupt departure last night, wondering if I'd done something that put him off or if he'd snapped out of whatever trance he was in.

I made a mental note to talk to him about it during open hours, granted that we even got any talking done. My body tingled at the thought of him touching me once more, kissing me, fucking me—

"Here you are, ma'am. Enjoy," the chef's gruff voice said, snapping me out of my daydreaming. I blinked and looked up at him, giving him a small smile.

"Thank you," I said.

When he walked away, I looked down at the plate and winced. It wasn't the disgusting prison-like food they'd given me the first couple of days I was here, but this plant-based nonsense wasn't much better.

I'd never been a fan of veggies growing up, not that I had much access to them anyway. But being forced to eat nothing but fruits, veggies, and whatever this "meat" was made of was like a different kind of torture.

I ate the peanut butter and banana toast and something that looked like scrambled eggs with bell peppers but definitely didn't taste like eggs. I wouldn't complain, though; whatever Silas wanted was what I'd do.

The day went as it usually did. I did yoga in the backyard, which was well-needed for my sore muscles after Silas folded me like a pretzel last night. All I could do was pace my room after lunch, constantly watching the clock for when Silas would finally be home.

I tried to occupy my time with looking through wedding magazines, fantasizing about how beautiful I would be walking down the aisle, how handsome Silas would be standing there, waiting to receive me.

By the time open hours finally rolled around, I was so anxious that I could hardly stand still. Maryse appeared in my doorway holding a bathing suit.

"Mr. Arnett wants you to change into this for this evening's open hours," she said and placed it on the bed. I nodded, waiting until she closed the door behind her before I hopped off the bed.

I moved over to the window and looked out into the backyard. Silas was sitting on the side of the pool with a glass in one hand and his phone in the other. It made me slightly disappointed that sex was probably off the table, but it would give us the chance to talk.

I wasted no time stripping out of my clothes and slipping into the bikini Maryse had left for me, knocking on the door to alert whoever was on the other side that I was ready.

Maryse led me out into the backyard, the night air comfortably warm. Silas looked up when I approached him, putting his glass down as he regarded me. I wrapped my arms around myself, suddenly self conscious as he just stared at me without saying anything.

He nodded toward the pool. "I've heard that you spend a lot of time looking at the pool from your bedroom window," he said. "Why don't you take a swim?"

I looked back at the pool. While the water was inviting and I wanted nothing more than to jump into it, it almost seemed sinister to have him allow me to do so willingly. He continued watching me, his eyebrow raising when I only stood there. I forced a small smile on my lips and finally nodded.

"Thank you," I murmured.

His eyes heated my back as I sat on the edge of the pool and slid into the water. It'd been so long since I'd been a pool. The last time I'd been in one was during one summer at a camp my foster parents sent me and their bio daughter. That seemed like such a long time ago, a fleeting moment of a fun time, lost in a memory of the surrounding neglect and abuse.

I pushed the thoughts from my mind and swam around. For once, I felt free. For the second time in my life, I didn't have to worry about anything other than keeping myself from drowning.

I thought back to that summer camp my foster parents sent me to. We were only gone for two weeks, but it was two weeks of feeling normal, of having friends, of not having to worry about someone doing something to me. No one knew I was an orphan and for the first time in my life, I'd felt normal. I'd spent so much time in the pool that day, even to the point that one of the camp counselors said that I should look into swimming for sport.

But everything went to hell in a hand basket when I came back to the reality waiting for me outside of the camp.

Swimming over to the edge of the pool, I pulled myself halfway out of the water and looked to Silas in way I hoped was seductive.

"The water's nice," I said. When he only stared at me, I continued. "You should get in."

"I'm fine where I am."

I slipped my hands behind my back and untied my top, placing the wet top on the side of the pool before smirking at him. "Are you sure?"

After a few moments of hesitation, he finally stood and walked over to the side of the pool before sitting down. He slid down into the pool next to me, moving to stand directly behind me. I turned around to face at him, my breath catching in my throat. His cold blue gaze was intense as he stared at me, his body so close to mine that his body heat crashed into me in waves. I cleared my throat.

"I, um..." I nibbled on my bottom lip. "I want to get to know you a little."

"Why?"

His face was blank of any expression, making it hard to read him. I shrugged slightly. "I mean we're getting married in a few months. I just thought it would be a good idea to know who I'm marrying."

He was silent for a few moments before he shook his head. "Everything you need to know is in the manual. You don't have to know me in order to marry me."

I took a chance and ran a finger down the middle of his stomach under the water. "Wouldn't you want your wife to know you?" His hard stare remained on me as my hand moved down and rubbed his thick cock through his swim trunks. "Don't you want me to know how to fuck you just how you like it?"

He gripped my wrist tight and pulled it away from him. "How about we talk about the money you took from me instead?"

That one sentence was enough to douse any lustful fire burning within me. I swallowed hard, my heart beating a little faster as I looked up at him. I thought we were past this. I was already serving my punishment, he got the money back by selling the accountant's kids, and he already made it clear that he would punish me however he saw fit for the next nine years.

With the dangerous way he looked at me, being in this pool no longer seemed like a good idea. I thought back to my first morning here, remembering how he'd tried to drown me in the kitchen sink. Now, he had me pinned to the wall of the pool with no one else around, not that it mattered. No one helped me when I screamed for my life in the mudroom, when I was struggling to breathe after he held me underwater in the kitchen, and no one helped me when he left me bloody and broken after he used me. No one in this house had my best interest in mind, which made all of this that much scarier.

"Why'd you do it?" he asked.

I looked at him for a long moment before I sighed. "I just...I wanted something different, I guess," I murmured, dropping my eyes to the crystal clear water. "After living a life with hardly anything, I always thought money would make things better. I thought a life without having to worry about bills or where my next meal came from would've been a lot better than the life I was living." I shrugged. "I guess I just wanted to escape my miserable existence."

He scoffed. "And here you are, surrounded by the best that money can buy and yet you're still miserable," he tsked. "Money doesn't make problems go away. There's only so much shit you buy, places you can visit, and things you can do before this shit becomes old." He shook his head. "All you did was trade your miserable freedom with a luxurious prison. Doesn't seem very smart."

"Yeah, I've realized that," I said, my voice flat as I looked toward the house.

He was quiet for a few moments. "In the mudroom that night, you'd told me I couldn't hurt you worse than other people have." He frowned at me. "What did you mean by that?"

I looked at him with a raised brow before I giggled. His frown deepened as he regarded me, but he didn't say anything. After a few moments, my laughter died down on a sigh. "You can't seriously think you're the first person to rape me," I said with a bitter chuckle. "It happened so much that I was convinced that it was on the foster father checklist."

Nothing registered on his face. "I guess it makes sense why you didn't scream the way I wanted you to."

I rolled my eyes. "Right, because men like you love to get one off to the soundtrack of someone else's pain," I said sarcastically.

"You catch on quick." He backed away from me and I frowned. This conversation was going in the opposite direction of where I wanted it to be. I wanted to go back to the Silas that was in my bedroom last night, not the cold, insensitive bastard in the pool with me. "Anyway, tell me about the shit you went through in the system."

"Why do you even care?" I mumbled.

"I don't. Just curious."

I snatched my bikini top from the side of the pool and put it back on, memories threatening to drown me. "I don't want to talk about it."

"You don't have a choice."

I stared at him for a long moment, watching him lower himself further into the pool until his eyes and the top of his head were the only thing above water. He looked like the predator he truly was as he stalked toward me, finally standing to his full height to tower over me.

I tore my gaze away from him as tears burned my eyes,

angry and ashamed that he wanted me to cut myself open and bleed for him when he wouldn't even give me the same courtesy.

"I was lucky to have been picked by a foster family since I was a teenager, which is rare," I started, swallowing the knot of trauma that lodged itself in my throat. "This family was really well off, so I thought I was having my own Daddy Warbucks like Annie the orphan did in the movie. I thought I could convince them to fully adopt me if I could get them to love me." A single tear rolled down my cheek after a failed attempt at blinking them away. "But Daddy seemed to love me a little too much, and Mommy wasn't approving of the way he loved me."

"How long did he do it?"

"Six months," I said and sniffled. "When his wife caught us one night, she only focused on me and said that I ruined her family. She didn't even bat an eye at the fact that her husband was fucking a teenager."

"Did they send you back for that?"

I scoffed. "Yeah, after she beat me and let him rape me for the last time for a few hours. They took me back to the group home and left me on the doorstep in the middle of the night, bruised and bloody." Fresh tears slipped from my eyes as I looked down at the water. "They did that and no one cared. No one cared when one of the teen orphan boys raped me. No one cared when male staff members at the group home took turns with me. No one ever cared."

I didn't even know why I was telling him all of this. Why the hell would a psychopath care about someone else's pain? He probably got off on hearing how other people hurt me.

"I see," he finally said. "Are they the only ones who hurt you?"

I shook my head. "I seem to attract broken men who love to hurt women." I sighed and met his intense gaze again. "I only took your money because I thought I could buy my way out of my shitty life. I figured if I had a better life, I could finally attract what I wanted and be happy for once."

"And that is?"

I shrugged, dropping my gaze. "To be wanted and loved by someone," I murmured.

It was what I'd searched for my entire life, but I always looked for it in the wrong places. It always came in the form of a closed fist, a punishing cock, or harsh words. The soft love I wanted never materialized for me, doing nothing but further solidifying my beliefs that I wasn't worthy of that kind of love.

"Love is a social construct," he said dismissively. "Movies and television make you think love can only be one way, but it isn't true. People have different ways of loving."

"Love is never supposed to hurt," I countered.

He shrugged. "Love can be whatever it's perceived to be by the people in it. A useless emotion, really."

"You can literally have any woman you want. Why did you choose me for this plan for yours?" I asked with a frown.

"I'm sure you've picked up on the fact that I'm not a good man," he started.

"I'm sure you could be; you just choose not to."

"You're delusional if you think that." He regarded me for a few moments. "The woman I'm with should have just as much to lose as I do."

"Why go through the trouble of that, though?" I asked. "What do you have to hide to settle for someone like me? There are plenty of women who'd accept a huge payoff to be quiet about something—"

"All it takes is a scorned woman opening her mouth to cause my empire to fall," he interrupted.

I rolled my eyes. "I think you're being paranoid and dramatic."

"Do you remember what happened to Maxwell and his family the night you arrived here?" he asked, cocking his head to the side.

I shivered at the thought, remembering their

screaming, the smell of their blood in the night air. "The only reason why you're still alive instead of in the ground for witnessing that is because there's no one for you to tell." He smiled, the action chilling me down to the bone. "There's no one out there looking for you. There's no one wondering where you are. Society thinks you're rightfully rotting away in prison right now instead of being trapped in my house as my own living sex doll. You're literally the perfect captive."

My jaw dropped as I watched him get out of the pool. I always hated how men could be so callous and mean. I didn't need any reminders about how lonely I was in life and that I had no one worried about me.

"Wow," I murmured, still trying to wrap my mind around his words.

He flopped down on the poolside lounge chair and grabbed his whiskey glass, finishing it off. "Get over here and suck my cock like the used up whore you are."

And just like that, the lust and excitement I'd felt prior to open hours disappeared into nothing. Shame burned my cheeks as I made my way out of the pool and walked over to him. I fought the urge to cry as I sucked and stroked his cock, his moans no longer filling me with lust or making me slick between my thighs. He'd forced me to talk about my traumatic past only to throw it in my face, making sure I knew I was nothing but a used up whore to him.

Apparently, that was all I was to anyone. Every man I'd been with always had time for me when they were horny, but were never available when I needed someone. I didn't know what the fuck I was thinking when I assumed last night was some kind of breakthrough for us.

I was so desperate for affection, for something, that I was willing to live in a delusion that did nothing but set me up for hurt and devastation.

And I fucking hated myself for it.

Silas quickly pulled out of my mouth and shot his load all over my face and chest, panting as he cursed under his breath. And just like last night, he simply fixed his swim trunks and moved away from me.

"You can head back to your room now. I'm done with you for the night," he said and walked away, leaving me feeling used, empty, and worthless.

I grabbed the towel he left behind with shaky hands and wiped my face, unable to stop the tears that fell. The darkness beyond the pool was so tempting to run into, wanting to take my chances with the wilderness beyond the tree line than to spend another night in this hellhole.

"It's time to go to your room," Maryse said, suddenly appearing next to me.

I sighed softly and stood, following her back into the

house as I continued wiping myself off. She left me alone in my room, locking the door behind her and leaving me with silence.

I made my way to the bathroom and looked at myself in the mirror. Tears glistened in my eyes as I took in my reflection. There were still traces of Silas's cum on my skin, a blaring reminder of what he perceived my worth to be.

"I'm just his living sex doll," I whispered to my reflection.

A living sex doll with no worth other than to be used and tossed back into the dark.

Alone.

CHAPTER TWELVE
SILAS

Marriage was a fucking joke.

I forced a smile on my face as I used every brain cell I had to keep up this act in front of other people. I had no idea why people got married. I'd only had Alyssa for two and half months and I was already fucking bored with her. I hadn't even been able to touch her for a few weeks while she recovered from her surgeries.

With the time quickly winding down for planning this wedding, she and I were finally sitting face to face with Jerry in his wedding planning boutique. I was nervous as fuck about having her out in the open, but I couldn't do every single thing in my house. I also couldn't keep my so-called fiancée locked away from the world. The media would get a picture of us being here and pretending to be in love and all that bullshit, and that would stop them from hounding me about her in the meantime.

"Ah, Mr. Arnett!" Jerry's voice called when we walked into the building. I looked around and finally saw him approaching us from the side, his tailored pink suit standing out in all the white decor. He looked to Alyssa and smiled. "And you must be the lovely Alyssa." She started to shake her head but she glanced at me, swallowing hard when I glared at her.

I was already on edge having her out in public for the first time. Her surgery was a success and did its job. She didn't look exactly like Marilyn Monroe obviously, but she didn't look as she used to. Her previous honey blonde hair was now much lighter and curled, so she could've passed for a cheap knock off of Monroe.

She was definitely prettier than she was, but it didn't make me anymore attracted to her. In fact, I didn't feel shit. I was just glad to have that part of my plan done.

She finally turned her attention back to Jerry and extended her hand, nodding. He took her hand into his and kissed the back of it. She let out a nervous giggle but didn't respond, quickly pulling her hand back. *Good.*

"I apologize we're putting all this on you at the last minute," I said, wrapping an arm around Alyssa's waist when Jerry motioned for us to follow him. "Things have been pretty insane lately between work and our personal lives. She had to have surgery after a skiing accident, so we were solely focused on her healing."

"Oh, those slopes can be unforgiving," Jerry tsked. "I'm glad to see you're feeling better. It almost looks like nothing happened at all. If only I could look as beautiful as you after having an accident."

Alyssa laughed but it was awkward and forced. I cleared my throat.

"I appreciate you being able to squeeze us in. I'm sure you're a very busy man," I said, noting all the other couples in the boutique.

Jerry waved his hand dismissively. "It's quite fine, Mr. Arnett. You're here now, so we can get this process moving along." He gestured to the binder Alyssa held. "I'm assuming this has what you'd like for your wedding?"

She glanced at me and I subtly nodded. She cleared her throat, dropping her gaze to the front of her binder. Though the contents were the wedding section that was in her manual, I'd put it in a separate binder for her to bring here.

"Yes. While I was, um, recovering, I spent a lot of time putting together some things that I wanted."

"May I?" Jerry asked, holding out his hand. Alyssa placed the binder in his hands. I frowned as her eyes nervously looked around the bridal store. I followed her gaze, which was a shit idea when I was already paranoid. It seemed as if she were clocking exits to find a means of escape if she thought I wasn't paying attention.

As if on cue, our security moved closer to potential exits, her shoulders deflating a little. Satisfaction filled me as I relaxed a little. The sooner I got this bullshit over, the sooner I could lock her away again.

"Is there a budget for this wedding?" Jerry asked, though his attention remained on the binder as he continued to flip the pages.

"No. She can have whatever she wants," I said.

Jerry looked up at me with wide eyes. "There's nothing I love more than a generous groom!" he exclaimed.

I kissed Alyssa's temple, the action making my stomach flop in disgust. "My future wife will always have what she wants," I murmured, locking with her bewildered gaze.

I fought the urge to clench my teeth as well as the urge to fucking choke her. I'd given her a pep talk before we'd even stepped out of the car to prepare her for this appointment. She only had one rule: go along with anything I did or said.

The fact that I was fighting for my life to make my affection seem real, I would've assumed she'd have no problem falling in line considering how fucking needy she was for my touch and affection at home. Now, she was acting as if I'd suddenly grown two heads, which caused Jerry to raise an eyebrow at us.

"Uh oh," he said, closing the binder and looking between us. "Are we sure there's no budget? I'm not getting happy vibes from the happy couple."

"I'm sure," I said before Alyssa had the chance to speak. "She may still be a little upset with me about a disagreement we had prior to coming here."

"Well, that's all a part of love and marriage," Jerry said with a chuckle. "Anyway, these are all great ideas to start with and we can definitely arrange all of this. You're going for a glamorous wedding theme, right?"

She finally pulled away from my gaze and turned her attention to Jerry. "Yes," she murmured.

"I can definitely see why; you're marrying a billionaire, you lucky woman," Jerry said with a wink. I rolled my eyes. If for whatever reason I had to remarry, I definitely wasn't doing this wedding shit again.

A few women approached us, one of them pushing a cart with cake slices. Jerry went on a spiel about each slice and Alyssa tried them all, offering a piece to me from time to time but I declined. I stood and paced the open space behind the couch she sat on as they went on and on about flowers arrangements and establishing the wedding colors.

Donovan smirked at me, probably thinking "I told you

so" after he'd told me a million times that I didn't need a wife to have a baby. Now, I'd wished I would've listened and went the surrogate route anyway. Had I known the headache of this wedding planning shit as well as molding an unwilling woman into the perfect wife, I would've ditched this plan the moment it popped into my head.

"Honey, could you come sit, please?" Alyssa asked, turning to look at me. The pet name was awkward coming out of her mouth. I couldn't pinpoint if it was because I'd never heard her call me anything other than my name when I fucked her, but it was something that made my fucking skin crawl. When I only stared at her, she waved me back over. "We need to pick the menu together. I don't want to hear you complaining about the food at the reception."

I ground my teeth and moved back to sit next to her. I wasn't interested in any of this shit, hence the reason why I'd told her she could pick everything. *This is usually the happiest time of a real couple's life, so act happy,* I mentally reminded myself, trying to give myself a mental pep talk to get my head in the game. That was all this was, a game that had a bigger purpose. I had to see this through.

Alyssa was so engrossed in her planning that she actually smiled and laughed. The appointment shifted from awkward tension to something comfortable and exciting —at least for her. She was sitting closer to me, her hand appearing on my thigh at some points. I took her cues and acted accordingly, kissing her neck as she spoke.

She giggled and shrugged me off. "Will you concentrate, please?"

"I am concentrating," I said, kissing her bare shoulder before moving my lips to the shell of her ear. "I'd concentrate better if those red lips were wrapped around my cock."

She swatted me with the menu she held, smirking at me as I laughed. "Silas, please," she said with a giggle.

"Okay, okay." I scanned the menu. "There needs to be plant-based options, as Alyssa doesn't eat meat." She tensed next to me, but I ignored it. "My parents prefer fish over beef, so I'd like dishes with lobster and scallops."

"On the same plate or different dishes?" Jerry asked, looking up from his iPad screen.

"Different. So, a lobster and shrimp entree and one with scallops."

"Lovely," he said before tapping the info in. "Do you have another meat in mind or is that all you'd like?"

"Lamb chops and beef Wellingtons."

Alyssa went quiet, pretty much letting me choose the dinner menu. She didn't speak again until Jerry asked about desserts. Aside from my request in making our wedding cake plant-based, she chose the other things she wanted, concluding our menu.

"I just want to say that I want an invitation to this reception of yours," Jerry joked. "Just looking at this menu is making my mouth water."

I chuckled. "You know you're more than welcome to come," I said.

He put the iPad down on the end table next to his chair. "So, have you finalized your guest list yet?"

"I have a few RSVPs I'm waiting on, but it should be finalized before the month is out," I answered.

Jerry looked around before he leaned forward, lowering his voice. "Are you wanting to hire bridesmaids and groomsmen?"

I nodded. "I'll definitely need to hire some for her. I have the men I need."

"And how many men do you have?"

"Nine," I answered.

"Perfect," Jerry said with a nod. "I'm going to email you a form to fill out. This is what we'll send to the bridesmaids so that they know how to interact with the bride. It'll allow them to practice the stories that you'll give them for how they know Alyssa to say at the reception or if anyone asks them anything."

"Sounds good to me," I said, a slight grin on my lips. "I didn't even know hiring bridesmaids were a thing."

"Anything is possible, Mr. Arnett," Jerry said with a chuckle.

"I need to use the bathroom," Alyssa said.

My body immediately tensed at her request. The only person who knew what was actually going on between us was Jerry. It would've been suspicious to deny her the basic human right of going to the bathroom when she needed to, so I forced a smile.

"Sure, go ahead," I said. One of the female employees approached with a soft smile.

"I'll show you where they are," she said, leading Alyssa away. I looked to Donovan, who nodded and followed behind them.

"You seem to have hit the jackpot with that one," Jerry said, sitting on the edge of his seat.

I shrugged. "She'll do for what I need to get done."

"Has she met your parents?"

"Unfortunately, that's in two days," I said, my sigh mixed with a groan.

Jerry chuckled. "You know, it's not a bad thing to settle down, Silas. Maybe she'll bring something out of you that's been hidden all these years."

"There's nothing hidden. I've never been in love, Jerry. You know that."

"I think you just haven't found the right person," he mused.

I rolled my eyes, growing irritated. "The person who stole over half a million dollars from me definitely isn't the right person," I said through gritted teeth, immediately realizing I'd fucked up by saying too much.

"Ah, now it makes sense," he said. He studied me for a few moments. "So, the ski trip accident is just a cover up?"

"What are you talking about?" I snapped.

"The woman you brought here isn't the woman whose face was all over the news when word got out about what she did. Looks like she got a whole new makeover."

I shook my head. "I wouldn't reward a bitch who stole from me with a makeover," I said. "She broke her nose and it healed terribly so she needed a nose job. There was no fucking way I could bring her out in public looking like that."

"I see," he said, nodding. While he knew that I planned on finding a woman to marry by force, he hadn't known that it was a woman that was supposed to be in prison before my verbal slip up.

The plan had always been to find a suitable woman off the street, which was probably what I should've stuck with. I'd forgotten that her crime was plastered over the news when she was arrested at the office.

I looked at my watch and looked around the boutique, my nerves and paranoia getting the best of me. "What the fuck is taking her so long?" I mumbled.

The fact that Donovan hadn't come back to get me or sent an SOS via text should've helped me remain calm, but it didn't. I didn't like not being in control, and I damn sure didn't like having no control in public spaces.

It was too easy to make a wrong step in public and end up on the front page of the newspaper by the morning. I had no fucking idea how to navigate situations like this. I couldn't fully trust that she wouldn't run away. I'd ditched the plan to have her fall in love with me because she was too clingy and fucking annoying. I had to hope that the punishments she'd endured was enough to keep her in line as it had while she was at home.

I flagged down one of the employees and stood up. She walked over to me with a bright smile.

"What can I do for you, Mr. Arnett?" she asked.

"Could you check on my fiancée, please?" I asked, returning her smile. "She's been in the bathroom for a little while and I just want to make sure she's okay."

"Oh, of course," she said and headed that way. I followed behind her, my heart racing as my irritation mounted.

"Do you mind if I come in with you in case someone's wrong?" I asked as we approached the bathrooms. "She wasn't feeling well this morning and I don't want to give her the opportunity to lie to me if she's still sick."

"Um, I don't know..."

"It'll be quick, I swear. I just need to have my eyes on her for a moment just to make sure she's okay," I said.

"It's really no problem, Julia," Jerry said as he appeared behind me, clapping me on the shoulder. "As long as it's quick."

"It will be," I said, my voice low as I stalked to the bathroom.

I didn't even wait for Julia to enter first before I pushed the door open. I walked further into the bathroom, my body tightening when my gaze fell on Alyssa. She and another woman stood near the sink, an iPhone in Alyssa's hand.

She looked up and her face immediately paled. The phone dropped from her hand and hit the floor, the woman next to her shrieking before she bent down to retrieve it.

"Lia! My phone!" she said, letting out an annoyed huff. "Great. My screen is cracked to hell."

"I apologize about your phone, ma'am," I said, forcing the tightness out of my voice as I reached into my pocket and pulled out my wallet. The woman snapped her eyes to me before they widened, her cheeks turning pink when she recognized me.

"Mr. Arnett! It's so nice to finally meet you," she gushed. "I wrote that story about you in the paper a few years ago. We only spoke through email and your team members, but it's nice to meet you face-to-face."

I pulled out the two thousand dollars I had in cash and

held it out to her. "Hopefully this is enough to fix your phone. I apologize again." I looked to Alyssa, who still stood there like a deer in headlights. Though my blood boiled beneath my skin, I forced myself to remain calm as I gestured toward the bathroom door. "We should get going, honey. We have another appointment to get to."

Alyssa swallowed hard and timidly walked toward me, speed walking past me as if she expected me to reach out and grab her. Every muscle in my body fought the urge to lash out at her. I gave the woman a small wave before leaving the bathroom.

Jerry looked at me in confusion as I headed for the door. "Did something happen? Why are you leaving?"

"My apologies, but we're late for another appointment," I lied. I needed to get her the fuck out of here and figure out what she told the newspaper bitch. It was as if my worst fears were materializing right in front of me, and I needed to do damage control quick. "I'll call you this evening to schedule another appointment."

I rushed Alyssa outside, halting the two outside security guards when they moved with me. "What's wrong, boss?" Dylan asked.

"Stay where you are. I'm about to call you with instructions," I growled before nearly shoving Alyssa into the car. I quickly pulled out my phone and dialed Dylan's number, watching out the window as he answered.

"Yeah?"

"There's a woman in there that writes for the paper," I seethed. "She's wearing a bright yellow one piece or whatever the fuck it is. Alyssa had her phone for whatever reason and the woman called her by her real name, so I can't trust that she doesn't know what's going on. Follow her, kill her, and bring her phone to me."

"What?!" Alyssa shrieked, resulting in me slapping her across the face.

"Shut the fuck up. I'll deal with you in a second," I growled.

"You got it, boss. It seems like she's leaving now."

"Then get to it." I watched the woman dash toward the parking lot like a bat out of hell, which further triggered my anxiety. Maybe she was on her way back to her office to write a story on whatever the bitch next to me said to her. "And when you kill her, get back the money I gave her. She can't spend it in hell."

Dylan chuckled. "You got it," he said and hung up.

"She didn't do anything!" Alyssa protested.

"What did you say to her?" I asked, my voice calm and even.

"Nothing!"

"Then how does she know your real name?"

I met her terrified gaze, waiting for her to answer. Her mouth opened and closed a few times before she cleared her throat. "It was an accident that slipped," she said, her voice thick with tears. "I didn't even realize I'd said it."

I scoffed and shook my head. "It slipped, huh? Did you suddenly forget your name from the time we left the car earlier until that point?"

She frowned at me. "Well, it's not my fault that you think you can just assign me a new name and think I'm supposed to just forget who I am," she snapped. She shrunk away from me, pressing her back to the door when I glared at her. I waited for her to correct herself, but she didn't, which only made me more upset.

I pinched the bridge of my nose and blew out a breath. "Fine then," I finally said. "If you want to be Lia, then be Lia."

"What?" she said, but I didn't repeat myself. If she wanted to be Lia, I'd make sure she got what she wanted.

———

Watching *Lia* walk on egg shells around me for the next two days was actually comical. Every single time she saw me, she'd apologize profusely, trying to blame her words and actions on the pain medication she'd been taking after her surgery.

Her apologies went in one ear and out the other. She'd been off those pain pills for weeks; I'd made sure of that.

Either way, I agreed with her. Who the hell was I to strip her of her name and identity? If she wanted to keep her name, I simply had to respect her wishes.

Since I was off today, I was having lunch with her at home. We ate in silence but I could feel her eyes on me. After a long while, she cleared her throat and put her fork down.

"Why haven't you punished me?" she asked.

I paused mid bite, narrowing my eyes at her before I bit into my sandwich. "The fuck kind of question is that?" I asked, my mouth full.

"You apparently had the woman that works at the newspaper killed, but you haven't done anything to me," she said. When I only stared at her, she wrapped her arms around herself. "I saw it on the news while I was working out."

"Well, the woman isn't a threat anymore, so what do I care?" I asked with a shrug. I looked down at my watch. "I have a quick meeting to get to. We'll be going to my parents' house at six, so please be ready."

"Sure."

"And be sure to look pretty. I have a surprise for you when we get back tonight."

Her eyes widened as she regarded me, nibbling her bottom lip. "A...surprise?"

"That's what I said, right?" I pretended to scroll on my

phone. "I'll have to confirm to make sure it'll be delivered on time, but we'll prepare for it anyway." Her eyes burned a hole in the side of my head as I continued messing on my phone. "Yep, it'll be delivered as scheduled, so dress nice. You won't have time to change afterwards and I don't want fucked up pictures."

The fear and terror that once blazed in her eyes relaxed as a soft smile settled on her lips. I almost wanted to laugh in her fucking face. She had no fucking idea what her surprise was, and I knew for a fact she wouldn't be smiling when she saw what it was.

"I will," she murmured.

"Good. I'll be back in a couple of hours," I said and left her in the dining room alone.

———

Donovan pulled up to the Donahugh Law Firm and parked. I looked through the information on my phone one last time, making sure I had everything correct. After *Lia's* fuckery at the boutique, I knew I wanted this punishment to mean something. Ever since she came into my possession, I'd called her by her new name so she could get adjusted to it. Here we were nearly three months later and she was still using her previous name when I'd clearly told her not to.

She'd cut it way too close with that fucking writer in the bathroom. I still had no fucking idea what she said to the woman. It was a good thing that her phone screen was completely shattered, otherwise, the woman could've sent something to someone else before I could stop her. Since she wanted to be Lia so fucking bad, I'd give her a little surprise to make her wish her previous life never existed.

I texted my contact, letting him know I was outside. I looked out the window, grinning to myself as I watched a man dart out of the entrance, nervously looking around as he approached my car. He quickly opened the door and slid into the backseat next to me.

"I know I'm a little behind on my casino debts but—"

I held up a hand to stop him. "That's not what this meeting is about."

"It's not?" He pulled out a handkerchief and dabbed at his sweaty forehead. "Then...what is it?"

"I need a favor from you," I started. "My fiancée isn't doing what she's supposed to and is acting very ungrateful for the new life I'm trying to give her. So I need you to help me teach her a little lesson."

"What kind of lesson?"

I smirked at him. "Oh, I think you know what I'm talking about." I opened my phone and showed him a picture, grinning when his face went pale.

"How did you—"

"The how isn't important," I interrupted. "But I need you to do this for me."

He shook his head. "I'm not that kind of man anymore, Arnett," he stammered.

"This isn't up for debate," I said and shrugged. "A car will be parked in this very spot at eight this evening to bring you to my house."

"I can't—"

"Either you do it or I'll put a bullet between your eyes since I still don't have my money you owe me," I said nonchalantly.

"If I do this, will you and I be good?"

"Sure."

He dabbed his forehead again before he nodded. "Okay, fine. I'll do it."

I smiled, putting my phone in my pocket. "I knew you'd come around, buddy," I said, clapping his shoulder. "Even though Lia isn't yours anymore, I'm sure she'll be so happy to see you."

"I guess," he mumbled.

"So, that settles it then. You'll be picked up at eight so don't be late."

"I won't."

"Good. Now get the fuck out of my car."

He scrambled out of the backseat so hastily that he nearly fell out when he opened the door. I chuckled when

Donovan pulled off.

"Who's he?" he asked.

I shook my head and looked out of the window. "Doesn't matter," I said and left the conversation at that. It didn't matter if no one else knew who he was, but Lia damn sure would know.

And I couldn't fucking wait for her reaction when she saw him.

CHAPTER THIRTEEN
LIA

"And here comes the beautiful couple!" a boisterous voice boomed once we got out of the car.

I turned around to see a much older version of Silas walking out of the front door, a big smile on his face as he watched us. Silas got out of the car and lifted his hand in a wave before turning to me.

"Don't forget what I said," he growled between his teeth. "If you fuck up here, you can forget about the surprise and prepare to spend the entire night in the mudroom with me."

His threat was enough to burn any lingering thoughts of trying to get help, though I was sure this was the last place I'd ever get real help from. This was his parents' house, for fuck's sake. Why the hell would they help me escape from their son? If they knew what I'd done to end up in this position, they probably would've turned my torture session into a family affair. Dealing with one psycho was enough; I wasn't stupid enough to try to take my chances with an entire family of them.

"I won't," I murmured.

Silas's stern, hard gaze moved away from me before his cold demeanor broke into a beautiful smile as he led me up the stairs. The house was so grand, way too grand for just two people to live in. I never understood why rich people bought these massive houses with seven or eight bedrooms when it was only them or just them and their spouse.

Their home wasn't as big as Silas's, but it was just as beautiful on the outside. It had a beautiful slate gray paneling with white accents, large windows that probably filled the place with beautiful natural light during the day. The turrets on the home almost made it looks like a castle, the large bay window on the nearest turret revealing a woman who just stared down at us with a cold gaze.

I swallowed hard and tore my gaze away from the window. It was unnerving to meet the people who raised the man set on ruining my life. His father seemed so jolly and inviting, waving us in and chattering about something that I could barely hear over my anxiety.

Meanwhile, his mother seemed distant and cold, a lot

like how Silas was whenever he wasn't pretending for other people. Being here scared the shit out of me, but maybe it would help me figure out the man I was going to marry.

"You must be the lovely Alyssa," his father said when we stepped into the house and stopped in the foyer. His father quickly closed the door and moved over to me, taking my hand into his. "It's so nice to meet you."

"Likewise, Mr. Arnett," I said softly with a small smile, shaking his hand.

He laughed and waved me off. "Mr. Arnett was my father. Please, call me Greg. You can even call me Dad if you'd like."

"Dad, please," Silas mumbled, wrapping an arm around my waist and pulling me back from Greg.

Greg held his hands up with a grin. "Just saying. I'm just excited that you both are here." He wagged his finger at Silas. "I thought you were full of it when you said you were engaged, but I guess you made a believer out of me!"

I watched as he grabbed my hand and admired the large diamond ring Silas had put on my finger. I wasn't sure whose ring it was or where he'd gotten it from, but tonight was the first time I'd seen it. He hadn't given it to me when we went to see the wedding planner, but I guess he wanted it to be more real for his parents.

"Mary Anne, get in here! Silas and his lovely fiancée

are here!" he called out before looking to Silas. "Beautiful ring, Silas. You did a great job, son."

"Thanks," Silas mumbled, shuffling next to me uncomfortably.

Ever since the incident at the wedding boutique, he seemed on edge about taking me outside the house. I hadn't meant to tell the woman my real name. Lia had been my name for the twenty-six years I'd been alive, so it was an honest mistake. I didn't even know she was a writer for the newspaper, which now made sense.

A part of me wondered if she'd seen me with Silas when we walked in and followed me into the bathroom, wanting to question me about our relationship. I'd asked her if I could use her phone, thinking maybe there was someone I could message if I could get into my Facebook profile. The moment the phone was in my hand, I'd had second thoughts, knowing I'd suffer a brutal punishment if I failed.

Before I could even make a decision, Silas burst through the door and that poor woman lost her life because of me.

Clicking heels stopped Greg's excited chatter, everyone turning in the direction of the sound. A tall, slender woman strolled toward us, her posture straight and poised. She wore a sleeveless lavender dress that stopped at her knees, her black stilettos clicking along the marble floor with each step.

Her stone expression was unmoving as she regarded us, which was strange as fuck. I always thought mothers were happy to see their adult children, even more so when their adult children brought someone home. But she didn't seem very excited to meet me; she didn't even seem happy to see her own son.

"It's been a while since we've seen you, Silas," she said. There was a slight foreign accent to her voice, which made me curious to know more about her and where she was from.

Silas nodded. "Things have been busy with work and planning a wedding and all," he said with a shrug before looking to me. "Honey, this is my mother, Mary Anne. Mom, this is my fiancée, Alyssa."

She looked down at me with a slight frown on her thin lips. I gave her a small smile and awkwardly held my hand out. "It's so nice to finally meet you. I've heard so much about you," I said. I'd never been in a serious enough relationship to meet someone's parents, so I had no idea what the fuck was appropriate to say in this moment.

An amused grin lifted her lips. "Like what?" she asked.

The question was simple enough but it was enough to stump me. Now I knew why Silas did all the talking while we were out in public.

Silas sighed and pushed my hand down. "She's trying to be polite, Mom, which is what you should try to do," he snapped.

She slid her cold gaze to her son. "I don't think lying is polite," she said. "Lying people can't be trusted."

Greg chuckled nervously before steering his wife further into the house. "How about we head to the dining room? I'm sure everything is ready for dinner by now," he said.

"Yeah, that's a good idea," Silas muttered. As his parents walked ahead of us, Silas roughly gripped the back of my neck. It took everything in me not to make a sound at the slight pain that came with his grip as he lowered his mouth to my ear.

"Don't say another fucking word. I'll do the talking if they ask questions," he growled in a deep whisper. "Do you understand?"

I nodded, releasing the breath I hadn't realized I'd been holding when he let go of me. He suddenly pressed his lips against mine, one hand cupping my cheek while the other one rested on my hips. It was such a violent flip of emotions that it nearly gave me whiplash. Greg chuckle a few feet away from us, which quickly gave me context for Silas's actions.

"Alright, love birds. Not in the foyer, will ya?" he said.

Silas slowly back away from me, a warning in his eyes

and a smirk on his lips before he looked to his father. "Sorry. Sometimes I can't help myself," he said. "Let's go, honey."

Emotions and wanting to be loved came easy to me, but the pretending that I knew Silas was doing made me feel like shit. I thought I might've been able to see something different within him as I spent more time in his possession, especially when I had my surgeries.

The entire time I recovered, I only saw him if he was home for a meal, but otherwise he was nowhere to be found. Every single day he showed me I was nothing but property, his "living sex doll" as he'd told me by the pool two months ago. So when he pretended to be what I wished he was, it left a sticky trail of sadness and rejection that was hard to clean off when I was alone again.

Silas pulled out a chair for me when we got to the dining table, and I gave him a small smile before I sat. Greg and Mary Anne watched us like a hawk as a woman came out of nowhere and poured red wine into our glasses before disappearing again.

"So, how did this happen?" Mary Anne asked, looking at me.

I raised an eyebrow and glanced at Silas, who glared at his mother. I shifted in my seat. "I'm sorry?" I finally said. I fought the urge wince as Silas gripped my thigh under the table and squeezed tight, the pain making me grab his wrist to keep myself from crying out.

"I've never seen Silas with a woman longer than a week in his entire thirty-five years of being alive, so how did this happen?" Mary Anne clarified. "You want us to believe that you two have been together long enough to want to get married and the media didn't know until you announced an engagement?"

Greg sighed and pinched the bridge of his nose. "Mary Anne—"

"Because I know how to keep my personal life out of the media," Silas said with a nonchalant shrug. "Do you think my relationship would last with everyone in my fucking business?"

I picked my glass up with a shaky hand and took a few gulps of wine. Being drunk through this dinner would be better than listening to them fight.

"So, tell me how the two of you met?" Greg asked, changing the conversation.

"I'd like to hear the answer from the young lady," Mary Anne stated when Silas opened his mouth. I glanced at him, torn on what to do. Greg and Mary Anne looked at me expectantly, so I giggled nervously before leaning toward Silas, rubbing his arm.

"He actually tells the story better than I do," I said, smiling at him.

"I'm sure he does, but I'm interested in hearing it from you," Mary Anne said as she picked up her glass and took a sip of wine.

Silas patted my knee lightly, so I cleared my throat and acted my ass off. "It's actually quite silly, but we met at the Saki Moto sushi restaurant," I started and looked at Silas. Annoyance and confusion colored his gaze but he didn't say anything. The muscle in his jaw ticked but he forced a small smile. I pulled my eyes away from his hard gaze and focused on his mother. "I was there with a few of my friends and he was a few tables away having a meeting, I think."

"I was talking with Jason Leon about a partnership," Silas stated.

His words gave me confidence. "It was my friend who had a crush on him and another one was teasing her about it when we noticed him," I continued. "I jokingly sent him a drink and blew kisses at him like an idiot—it was silly, really—but then he came over to our table and fussed at us about interrupting his meeting and made me go on a date with him for being an inconvenience."

"And somehow she managed to thaw the ice block that I thought was my heart," Silas concluded, looking at me with a small smile. I couldn't quite read whether or not he was upset. He didn't look as upset as he did earlier and he hadn't squeezed my thigh again in warning, so I wasn't sure if he was angrily plotting my punishment or temporarily pleased with my quick thinking. After a long, tense moment, Greg finally laughed.

"That definitely sounds like Silas. Someone simply breathing is an inconvenience to him," he said, still chuckling. Mary Anne's expression hadn't changed, her suspicious eyes bouncing between me and Silas. She was highly perceptive, and a part of me hoped she'd realize something was wrong and dig into it. I wasn't sure if she'd do anything if she knew the truth since Silas was her son, but it didn't stop me from hoping that she might be able to help me.

Dinner was disappointingly quiet. I'd always imagined family dinners to be like the ones I saw on TV, full of laughter, conversation, and family bonding. They'd had those kinds of dinners when I lived with my foster family, but I was hardly a part of the conversation back then. Silas's family was cold and empty aside from Greg's jolly demeanor. This was nowhere near the family of my dreams.

Mary Anne's cold stare made me uneasy all throughout dinner, so much so that I couldn't wait to leave. I spent the majority of the time brainstorming ways to get Silas to take me home just so I could defrost from the ice she consistently threw at me from across the table. It was bad enough that everyone else had juicy pot roast with mashed potatoes, fresh string beans, and buttered rolls while I was stuck with some bullshit salad. Now I had to get a silent third degree stare down while starving to death.

When Silas phone rang, he frowned when he looked at the screen and quickly excused himself to answer it. The silence that filled the room in his wake was damn near deafening. Mary Anne watched Silas retreat before she turned her sights back on me.

"You shouldn't marry him," she said, her voice firm. My eyes widened in faux surprise. *No shit, lady.* Instead, I cleared my throat and forced a confused frown on my face.

"I'm sorry?"

"Marrying my son would be a mistake," she said. "I'm sure you're blinded by his money and the glamorous life you think is waiting for you on the other side of the wedding broom, but none of that will cover up the horrible things he's capable of."

I shook my head. "Silas hasn't done anything to me that makes me feel like I'm in danger," I said. The lie tasted like motor oil and acid as it spilled from my mouth, burning my tongue and teeth as the words slipped past. "He's given me no reason to fear him."

"How did you really meet?" she asked, clasping her hands and tucking it under her chin and she leaned forward.

"We met at the sushi restaurant as I said," I stated with a frown, hoping I was believable enough. "I don't have a reason to lie about anything." *Unless I don't value my life.*

"I'm completely sure that's a lie," she snapped. "Silas doesn't date. Even if you met him at a restaurant, you would've been a one-time thing before he discarded you, just like he's done with all the others before you."

"People can change—"

"Silas is a clinically diagnosed sociopath," she interrupted. "He doesn't experience emotions like everyone else. He's probably advanced to a full on psychopath at this point!"

"Dear, please. You're scaring her," Greg murmured, patting her arm.

"She should be scared, scared enough to walk away while she still can," she said and sighed. She took a moment to gather her thoughts. "Silas is very skilled at manipulating the people around him, pretending to be a good guy for however long it takes until he gets what he wants. He preys on the weakness of others and will use it to torture them later. Once you marry him, you're trapped in his web and you may not be able to get back out."

I fought the tears that threatened to burn my eyes. Everything she'd said were things I'd already experienced or witnessed. Where the fuck was this warning before I made the decision to steal from him? Why didn't they get him whatever help he needed to help him manage the fucked up parts of himself? I wanted to be angry at them for failing him, but I didn't know the first thing about raising psychopaths or sociopaths as children, so I had no room to judge.

I gave her a small smile. "Silas has taken very good care of me and has been there for me in my darkest moments," I said, my voice trembling a little. I blew out a breath to steady myself. "I give everyone the benefit of the doubt before condemning them, and Silas has shown me that he's capable of feeling things, of loving me. He hasn't shown me anything else."

She released a humorless chuckle and shook her head. "You know, I used to think like you," she started and took a sip from her wine glass. "Silas was my precious little boy, my only child after failing so many times to get pregnant. I used to think he was such an angel until he wasn't." She paused for a long moment. "I thought he was just going through a phase as boys do, but then he started to break things when he didn't get his way. He'd punch holes in the wall." Her bottom lip trembled and Greg reached over to rub her back.

"You don't have to talk about this, Mary Anne," he murmured to her, but she straightened her posture and regained her composure.

"Then it upgraded to him threatening to kill me, drowning the family dog, and then he broke my arm because I told him he couldn't go to a party with a kid I knew was a bad influence." She dabbed her eyes with the napkin in her lap. "Those kind of people don't change; they only get worse. I don't know how long you've been together, but I'd assume long enough if you're engaged. Marriage is his way of trapping you, and you need to get away from him before he actually kills you."

I swallowed hard. What the fuck was I supposed to say to that? My current life was nothing but walking on egg shells around him, wanting to make sure I was doing the right things to avoid punishment. All it would take was one wrong decision to land me in the mudroom, and one bad decision and an angry Silas to land me in a grave. Had I been a normal woman, this information definitely would've sent me running for the hills. No sane woman would stick around to wait and see if a man would abuse her if the information came from his own mother.

But she didn't know I was already trapped. She didn't know I wasn't necessarily his fiancée, but his property. She didn't know he changed my identity, forced me to get surgery, used me, raped me, and abused me whenever he felt like it.

She didn't know I was already lost.

"I think what she's trying to say is that you should be mindful," Greg said, to which Mary Anne scoffed.

"No, I'm saying she should get out while she's able to," she said.

Silas reappeared before I could say anything else, frowning down at his phone. "I'm sorry to cut this short, but we have to get going," he said. "Something just came up that I have to handle immediately."

"Aw, it feels like you two just got here," Greg said on a sigh as he stood. "I'll walk you to the door."

Mary Anne got up and walked away without a word to either of us, leaving Silas shaking his head as he looked to me. "Let's go."

I got out of my chair and walked with Silas and Greg to the front door. Greg hugged me tight before smiling at me.

"It was very nice to finally meet you," he said. "I apologize for Mary Anne. She's—"

"A bitch," Silas interrupted, glaring in the direction his mother disappeared in.

Greg sighed. "Hopefully the next meeting will be better than this one. Please don't let anything she said get to you."

"I won't," I said with a small smile, but the damage had already been done. Even though I'd called Silas a psycho, I hadn't realized I'd been dead on about him. That realization made it seem even more scary than it was before.

"Well, I won't hold you two up," Greg said as he opened the front door. "Get home safely."

"Thanks, Dad. We'll come by again soon," Silas said, wrapping an arm around my waist and leading me out of the house.

Neither of us said anything as we made our way to the car. I nearly held my breath once I was settled into the backseat, expecting him to tear into me the moment we pulled out of the circular driveway. He replied to a text message thread for the first five minutes of the drive before putting his phone to sleep and stuffing it in his pocket.

"What did my mother say to you?" he asked, his deep voice breaking the tense silence around us.

My first instinct was to lie, as I didn't want him to think I'd initiated the conversation about him. But I also didn't know how far away he was or whether he'd heard what she'd said himself. I dropped my gaze to my hands that sat in my lap.

"She basically—"

"I don't want to know what she 'basically' said; I asked you what she said to you."

I pursed my lips and swallowed down the sigh that

threatened to come out. "She said you were a sociopath and that I shouldn't marry you."

I wasn't sure how I expected him to react, but laughing was nowhere on the radar. His laughter bubbled and swelled until it filled the back of the car. It would've been a pleasant sound had he been laughing at something else, not at the fact that his mother called him a sociopath.

"What else did she say?" he asked when he pulled himself together.

"That you killed your dog, broke her arm, and you'd trap me in a marriage so you can hurt me," I said with a frown. "She said if I didn't leave you, you were bound to kill me."

He chuckled and shrugged. "That's not something you didn't know already," he said. Terror slid through my veins like icicles, chilling me to the bone. "But she's accurate about the other shit. I mean, I think I'm well past sociopath status at this point, but hey, who really cares about the difference really?"

A knot formed in my throat as I looked at him. Wanting a family of my own wasn't worth feeling as if I were walking on a battlefield for the rest of the nine years I had to serve. To know that his abusive ways dated back to much a younger age than now was concerning. What if that diagnosis was genetic and passed down to our children?

An involuntary shudder rolled through me at the thought. I couldn't imagine bringing a child into the world only for them to inflict the same kind of pain and misery their father did to me. The idea of giving birth to another maniac was terrifying, almost comparable to having the Anti-Christ.

I jumped when Silas was suddenly next to me, kissing my neck. "I gotta say, you surprised me," he murmured, his hand resting on my thigh. I remained as still as a statue, unable to gauge if he was serious or trying to lure me into a false sense of security.

"W-what do you mean?"

He paused in his actions and pulled back to look at me. "Everything that happened tonight." He stared at me for a moment. "Why'd you change the story? I already had one in the manual."

I shrugged. "Everyone that works at the headquarters know that you don't attend charity events yourself; you only donate on behalf of the company. Then she would've asked me what I did for a living to get an invite to such charity events, and you didn't have an answer prepped for that. I just figured it would be more believable meeting in a random restaurant than a charity event where everyone knows everyone."

His lips were pulled into a slight frown as he regarded me, mulling over my words. "I see," he finally said and began kissing my neck again. "Well, it was a good shift of plan. Good girl."

I hated myself and the way my stomach fluttered when he called me a good girl. Anytime he said it, it meant pleasure was on the horizon. Though the moments were rare, it was always nice to have some kind of "romance" attached to his actions. If lying to his parents or the public would get me that, I'd do whatever I had to do just to feel his passion again.

"Mmm," I sighed when his hand disappeared under my dress. My thighs spread for him automatically, as if his hand were a key to unlock my body. His lips left goose-bumps pebbling my skin as he placed light kisses on my neck and shoulders.

"Seeing how you didn't cave and tell them the truth makes it easier to trust you," he whispered. "Your loyalty makes my dick hard."

I tightened my jaw, the lust that'd started to bloom within me quickly fizzling out. He'd said that as if I had a choice in the matter. It was either lie for him and have a chance to survive or tell the truth and be killed.

Tears threatened to form but I quickly blinked them away. Now wasn't the time to dwell on how truly fucked up my situation was. It wouldn't change anything and there wasn't much I could do about it right now.

"Oh," I moaned when his fingers pushed my panties to

the side and circled my clit. He turned my head toward his and devoured my mouth, filling me with passion and lust that suffocated my worry and apprehension. My hips rocked against his hand until his fingers were slick with my juices, my moans disappearing into his mouth.

"Can't wait to get you home and show you your surprise," he murmured against my lips. "And then I'm going to have this tight little pussy stuffed with my cock."

"I want it so bad," I moaned when he slid two fingers into me. I lifted my leg to give him more access, my walls squeezing his fingers as they stroked that sweet spot inside of me. I squeezed his forearm and whimpered, pulling a deep chuckle from him.

"Ready to come so soon? I was just getting warmed up," he said, taking my earlobe into his mouth.

"Silas, wait," I moaned, but it was too late. His fingers pumped quicker, zips of electric ecstasy pulsing over my nerve endings. I squeezed his bicep tighter as my back arched. "Fuck, I'm gonna come!"

"You better hurry because we're almost home," he said. I glanced ahead and saw that the house was quickly approaching in the distance. His thumb went to work on my clit, quickly pushing me over the edge. My orgasm tightened every muscle in my body, my breath catching in my throat as pleasure consumed me.

My moans filled the back of the car, settling down

around me like warm dust that reabsorbed back through my skin to get me ready for what he had waiting for me inside.

He kissed my temple. "Come on. Let's get you to the bedroom," he murmured. I nodded, my entire body buzzing as I followed him out of the car. Silas pulled his tie off and covered my eyes with it. "I don't want you peeking before I'm ready for you to."

I smiled and allowed him to lead me into the house. "Can I get a hint on what it is?" I asked.

"Nope. You just have to be a good girl and wait until I'm ready to show you," he said. My smile grew even wider as excitement tingled my skin. I had no idea what he could've ordered for me that would require him to cover my eyes, but I was so anxious to see it. I'd been thinking about this surprise since he'd first told me about it. When we got inside, I was relieved when we walked past the mudroom, so I knew I wasn't in trouble at least. I shook off the rest of my lingering worry and followed his lead.

"Everything is ready as you've asked," Maryse said as we passed her.

"Perfect," he said. We kept walking and finally stopped in front of what I assumed was my bedroom door. "Are you ready to see what I got for you?"

"If it means I'll have your cock inside me soon after, then yes," I purred, causing him to chuckle.

"Then let me not waste anymore time," he said and opened the door. He held my shoulders as he urged me further. The moment I walked into the room, I froze. Nausea suddenly overwhelmed me as the familiar cologne hit my nose and anxiety warnings fired off on all cylinders.

"Silas?" I asked with a nervous chuckle.

"I'm right here, darling," he said, rubbing my arms. "Okay, take a few steps forward and hold your hands out."

I swallowed the ball of nerves that threatened to choke me. *Relax, Lia. It's probably just a coincidence since it's a common cologne,* I thought as I complied with his command. Rough hands tightly clasped around mine just as Silas pulled the blindfold off. My eyes widened when I saw who held my hands. I tried to jerk away from him, only for him to tighten his grip and smile at me.

"It's been a long time, Princess," he said.

So many different words screamed to be let out but my mouth was too shocked to move. How the fuck did Silas even know who my foster father was? I'd told him about the abuse I'd suffered the week before my surgery, never thinking he'd bring my abuser back to punish me.

"Enjoy your night with her, Raymond," Silas said as he backed away toward the door. "For safety reasons, we have to keep this door locked. Wouldn't want my little captive trying to escape."

I looked at him in horror. "Don't leave me here with

him!" I shrieked, roughly snatching away from my foster father to rush to Silas but he fisted my hair and yanked me back against him.

"Thank you, Mr. Arnett. I'll use my time wisely," Raymond said.

The scent of his cheap cologne made me want to throw up, even more so now that he was pressing his body against the back of mine. When Silas closed and locked the door, Raymond wasted no time pulling and tugging at my dress to get it off.

"You have no idea how long you've been on my mind, Princess," he murmured in my ear, his hand under my dress frantically trying to pull my panties down. I tried to pry his arm away from the base of my throat, tears burning my eyes.

Mary Anne was right. Silas took sensitive information I'd told him and exploited it to fill his own sick needs. The betrayal I felt was devastating, but I shouldn't have been surprised. He wasn't loyal to me. He didn't care about me. I was stupid enough to tell him the truth, giving him the benefit of the doubt of possibly taking it easier on me if he knew the rough life I already had.

I threw my head back and head butted Raymond, scrambling away from him as curse words flew from his mouth.

"You fucking bitch!" he seethed, holding his nose. I

rushed over to my closed bathroom door and tried to open it, only to find it locked.

"No," I whispered to myself as I jerked the handle, praying the door would magically open. I turned and pressed my back against the door, looking for places I could escape to.

Raymond checked his hand for blood, relief flooding his face when he didn't see any. I looked to the closet, thinking that was my best choice. No sooner than I made the mad dash to the bed to cross over it, he grabbed me by the hair again, landing a punch right at my temple.

My vision went fuzzy as I fell to the ground, my ears ringing as the pain settled. I forced myself to my knees and tried to crawl away from him, shrieking when he kicked me in my ribcage.

"I didn't want to hurt you tonight, Lia," he panted, kicking me again. I coughed and held my ribs, groaning when he grabbed me by the back of the neck. "You know I never wanted to hurt you."

"But you did, you sick fuck!" I snapped, spitting in his face.

He wiped a shocked hand down the side of his face before punching me again, disorienting me. The bedroom door seemed so close but also so far, tears burning my eyes at the realization that I was trapped in here with a monster I thought I'd left in my past.

He dragged me over to the bench at the foot of the bed and bent me over it. He pinned me down to the bench by tightly pressing down on the back on my neck, forcing me to remain bent over. His other hand flipped my dress up and roughly pulled at my panties until the threads ripped, the fabric hurting me in the process.

"Please don't," I cried, trying my hardest to lift my head but he kept me pinned down. My head and jaw hurt, the lights in the room making me feel nauseous to the point that I didn't want to keep my eyes open anymore. His disgusting cologne suffocated my senses until all I could smell was him. He was all I could see, all I could feel. He scoffed in disgust when he touched me between my legs.

"I hate the fact that that asshole gets to touch you when you should've been mine," he growled. Silent tears leaked out of my eyes as he quickly used my ripped panties to wipe away the traces of my previous orgasm. "You know your pussy feels better when you're not dripping wet like this."

"Wait," I quickly said when that familiar sound of his belt buckle hit my ears. "I'll do it willingly. I won't fight you. Just let me go, please."

He paused in his actions, my heart beating so loud as I waited for his response. He sighed. "Princess, it hasn't been that long has it?" he murmured. "Having you fight me was the best part."

A scream left my lips as he roughly thrust into me, the friction between us sending a sliver a pain throughout my lower body. He kept me pinned to the bench as he pounded into me, his moans falling over me like thick slime attempting to drown me in despair. I kicked my legs, which only earned me a punch in the side that took my breath away.

"This sweet pussy is just how Daddy remembers," he moaned, practically lying on top of my back as he sawed into me. "That's a good little girl. Squeeze my cock just how I like it."

"Get off of me!" I cried when I finally caught my breath. The rage and shame that pulsed throughout my spirit held me in a tight chokehold. My mind flipped back and forth between between the past and the present, so much so that I had a hard time discerning which one I was in.

"Please get off of me! I don't belong to you anymore!" I wailed, fighting against him. He pinned my arm behind my back so tight that my forearm throbbed with pain.

"You always belonged to be, Lia," he panted, his hips slapping against my ass with each stroke. "Always. Always. Fucking always."

My sobs were broken with each violent thrust he put

inside of me, my arm burning the longer he held it. I no longer felt like an adult; instead, I felt like helpless, 16-year-old Lia who wanted love from a parent but only got abuse and trauma instead.

"Daddy, please, don't."

"Shh, Princess. It'll hurt at first, but I promise Daddy will make it feel good soon. Be a good girl and take the love that Daddy wants to give to you."

"You always took my cock so good," he moaned. "So fucking tight after all these years. I missed you so much."

I couldn't do anything but sob. I cried for everything the 16-year-old me lost back then. I mourned the last shred of dignity I had. When my eyes fell on the red dot directly across from me, I realized it was a camera for Silas to take pleasure in watching my assault.

And there was nothing I wanted more in that moment than death.

CHAPTER FOURTEEN
SILAS

"That's it; scream, you fucking bitch," I growled through clenched teeth as I quickly stroked my cock.

Her terrified face filled the screen of my iPad and her panic-laced voice flowed from my noise-cancelling headphones. Raymond's only rule was that he started on the bench where I'd put a camera. I wanted to see her fear, her pain, her helplessness as the tormentor from her past came back to give her another trauma memory.

When she'd revealed the abuse she'd suffered the night in the pool, the sadness, humiliation, and fear that swam in her eyes and body language nearly made me come in my trunks. I wanted to replicate that and record it so that I could keep it forever. It both gave me the perfect soundtrack to listen to when I needed to rub one out and it was the perfect punishment for her after what she'd done.

I watched them fight, tingles skating my skin with each blow he delivered to her body. Something sick and twisted inside of me loved the sight of someone else's demise. There was nothing more satisfying than watching the bitch who wronged me get what was coming to her.

She stole money from me and she suffered. She tried to out me and now she was suffering even more. It had to be a new kind of torture to already be in one Hell, only for your previous Hell to show up within it.

A slow smile creeped across my face as I continued stroking my cock. She wanted to be Lia, so I brought Lia back to her as she asked. Maybe now she'd be ready to drop her fucking identity for good.

"*Please don't!*" she wailed as he wrestled her onto the bench. Her despair pulled a groan from my lips as I sank further into my bed, my hand tightening just a little more as I pumped my cock. The motion-sensored camera panned out until Raymond was also in the frame, his hand between her legs.

"*I hate the fact that asshole gets to touch you when you should've been mine,*" he grunted and I grinned.

Too fucking bad, dickhead. I get to destroy her tight pussy for the next nine years, I thought.

I tapped Alyssa's face on my screen to pan the camera

back on her. Tears leaked from her eyes as she bit her lip and squeezed her eyes shut. Raymond tossed the torn fabric to the side as he panted. *"You know your pussy feels better when you're not dripping wet like this."*

Had I been a normal man, I probably would've been disgusted. Knowing that he used to fuck her when she was a teenage girl made it obvious that he got off on hurting her. Had she been as wet as she was when I'd had her, he could've made it feel good for the both of them.

I couldn't blame him, though. I'd been deep inside of her when she wasn't wet and it was a feeling that still made my toes curl if I even just thought about it.

"Wait," she pleaded, her eyes wide with panic as her nostrils flared. *"I-I'll do it willingly. I won't fight you. Just let me go, please."*

It was almost like watching a movie in which I didn't know the characters. "She's full of shit, Ray. Don't listen to her," I murmured, shaking my head as my hand slowed on my cock. Nothing happened for a few moments but Alyssa didn't move. Hell, even I stopped stroking my cock in anticipation for what he would say.

He finally sighed. *"Princess, it hasn't been that long has it? Having you fight me was the best part."*

"Atta boy," I murmured when she screamed. She squirmed against him, tears spilling from her eyes as her face twisted in pain. I put the iPad down for a moment and closed my eyes, quickly stroking my cock as her pain-filled voice filled my ears. The rapid slapping in the background as Ray violently pumped into her and her broken sobs was like refreshing water on a blooming flower, pleasure growing and rooting itself throughout my body.

"Fuck," I groaned when she released a sound I'd never heard from her. It was a mixture of pain, fear, and humiliation strung together in a long whimper that broke off into another sob, the sound raising goosebumps on my arms. I picked the iPad up, needing to see her face. "I bet you don't want to be Lia anymore, do you, slut?"

I'd looked on just in time to see Raymond punch her in the side, her mouth falling open as she struggled to catch her breath. She gasped and squirmed, her head still firmly pressed onto the bench.

"*This sweet pussy is just how Daddy remembers,*" Raymond groaned. "*That's a good little girl. Squeeze my cock just how you know I like it.*"

A shudder ripped through me when I thought of the way she squeezed me the first night I'd raped her. She was so fucking tight around my cock already, but her tightening around me even more was enough to make me spill into her then. Just the thought of it threatened to make me come.

But I had to pace myself. I was waiting for a particular moment that I knew would eventually come. I just had to be patient a little while longer to get the orgasm I was after.

"*Get off of me!*" she shrieked, bucking to try to get him off of her but it only made him moan in ecstasy. Multiple emotions quickly passed over her face as desperate, frustrated tears rolled down the side of her face. "*Please get off of me! I don't belong to you anymore!*"

"You will as long as you decide to be Lia," I said out loud, slowly stroking my cock.

"*You always belonged to me, Lia. Always. Always. Fucking always.*"

I watched as her face morphed into something I hadn't seen from her. In that moment, she looked like a frightened child, biting her lip and squeezing her eyes shut as if it would help make things go away faster. She cried even harder when she opened her eyes again, begging Raymond to stop but unable to free herself from the hold he had on her.

"*You always took my cock so good,*" Raymond moaned. "*So fucking tight after all these years. I missed you so much.*"

"Enjoy it while it lasts, asshole," I growled, tuning him out and focusing solely on Alyssa. Her eyes fell on the camera, growing wide when she noticed it. I stroked my cock quicker. "There it is. There's the money shot."

Everything happened in delicious succession. Her mouth fell open as her skin paled, her eyes glued on the camera as silent tears spilled from her eyes and soaked the bench.

She exhaled a breath in defeat, her gaze going blank as she broke for him, as she broke for me. Her fight was gone, her fire was out, and witnessing the demise of Lia was the sexiest thing I'd ever seen in my fucking life.

A choked moan forced it way out of my throat as I came, rope after rope of cum spilling from the tip of my cock and all over my hand and the towel across my lap. I closed my eyes as ripples of pleasurable aftershock snapped through me as I slowly stroked my cock, panting slightly. Alyssa's whimpers and Raymond's moans still sounded in my headphones, so I pulled them off and tossed them on my bed next to me.

After making sure the camera was still recording, I put the iPad to sleep before forcing myself out of bed to get cleaned up. A grin settled on my face as I was I made my way to my ensuite bathroom.

I bet she'll learn her lesson now, I thought to myself. I had to give it to myself; this was the best thing I could've ever thought of to hurt her.

The next three and a half months would be easy sailing now.

———

I fought the urge to laugh at her when she finally appeared in the dining room for breakfast the next morning. As agreed, Raymond had her all night before he left as scheduled at five this morning. I'd gotten up multiple times through the night to check on them on the iPad, seeing that he was still raping her at one, three, and four-thirty in the morning.

He definitely took advantage of the hours he had, not that I blamed him. He wouldn't be touching her again, but I was grateful for the work he put in on my behalf.

She limped into the dining room and took her seat at the opposite end of the table, wincing as she sat down. She didn't speak or look at me, keeping her gaze at the wooden table. Her hair was pulled back into a low ponytail, displaying the bruises on her face and neck. When she walked in, I noticed that her right forearm was bruised and swollen.

"Looks like someone enjoyed their surprise last night," I taunted, taking a sip of orange juice. She didn't respond or react, continuing to keep her gaze down. "So, who are you today? Are you still Lia or are you ready to be Alyssa?"

"Alyssa," she said, her voice hoarse.

"Are you sure?" I mused. "You seemed dead set on being Lia, so I was trying to give you what you wanted. So if you want to be Lia, I can have your old boyfriend Raymond come and spend the night with you."

She winced as she repositioned herself in her seat. "I'm sure."

I watched her as she ate breakfast, noticing that she was using her left hand instead of her right like she usually did. She was having avocado toast with an açaí fruit bowl but with the way she winced in pain every time she had to chew something, one would think she was biting into fucking barbed wire. I didn't say anything, though. I could only imagine the pain and discomfort she was in after being raped multiple times last night, but I didn't feel sorry for her. She'd brought it on herself.

"I have something to do at work for a few hours, so I'll be gone most of the day. We'll be taking engagement photos for a magazine in two days, so you need to prepare yourself for that," I said as I cut into my omelet. "You need to soak in an ice bath for the next two nights to help with the bruises and swelling."

"Okay."

"Open hours will continue as usual tonight as well."

"Okay."

I frowned at her. I wasn't sure what I expected, but her pathetic state pissed me off. She was more pale than she usually was, her eyes puffy and still red. Dark circles made a home beneath her eyes, a telltale sign for the lack of sleep she probably got the night before. When she finished her breakfast, she only stared at the wall behind me without a word until Aimee walked in.

"May I be excused?" Alyssa asked, her voice cracking on her words.

I looked to Aimee. "Put her in an ice bath and work on covering the bruises she has," I said and waved a dismissive hand at the both of them.

"Yes, sir," Aimee said softly before helping Alyssa to her feet. When Aimee grabbed Alyssa's right arm to help stabilize her, Alyssa cried out, clutching her arm to her chest. I frowned, wondering if she was just bruised or if Raymond managed to break something.

There wasn't much time to dwell on it once Maryse came into the dining room, frowning at Alyssa's state as Aimee led her away. Once they were far enough away, Maryse walked a little closer and frowned down at me.

"Don't you think that punishment was a little too far?" she asked, keeping her voice down.

"You know me better than that, Maryse. I'm almost offended," I chuckled, but she wasn't amused.

"Considering that I'm the one that had to clean her up this morning and make her presentable enough to come to breakfast, I think I know what too far looks like," she said, her voice firm. "That woman needs a doctor and possibly an x-ray. Her arm doesn't look good."

"So call a doctor and get an x-ray," I shrugged, taking a few gulps of orange juice. "Problem solved."

She shook her head. "Why would you do that days before you're due to take these photos? You do remember they're going to be published in a magazine for the whole country to see, right? These bruises aren't going to go away overnight."

"One, because I fucking can. Two, of course I remember. They're fucking photos; Photoshop exists."

"That was still unnecessary—"

"Let me stop you there, Maryse," I interrupted, growing irritated with her. "Alyssa is my property. I can fuck her, beat her, torture her, punish her, or use her any fucking way I see fit. If I wanted to give her a severe punishment for being caught with a reporter's phone in her fucking hand and talking to her about God knows what, then I will. So, don't tell me that I went too far. Too far would be shooting her and letting her old foster father fuck her as she bled to death. Too far would be slitting her throat and forcing him to fuck her corpse. So trust me; I haven't even scraped the fucking surface for how far I'm willing to actually take shit around here."

She pursed her lips together, unfazed by my words. "I'm simply trying to make sure you don't dig yourself into a hole you can't get out of," she said. "The route you're taking is a dangerous one."

I scoffed. "The route you're taking will be a dangerous one if you continue going straight." I stood from the table and frowned at her. "I'd advise you to turn left, as that's where your business is."

"Whatever you say, Silas," she said, her voice tight.

"Yeah, I know it's whatever I say," I muttered, grabbing my suit jacket from the back of the chair. "As I told Aimee, she needs to be prepared for the photoshoot. Soak her in an ice bath to see if it helps with the bruising and swelling or whatever. I'll be back after this auction."

"Sure."

I ignored the attitude she had and walked out of the house, meeting Donovan in the driveway as he talked to Corey, another security guard. Donovan looked at me, shielding his eyes from the sun.

"Ready to rock and roll?" he asked.

"Yeah. I can't afford to be late this time," I said, getting into the backseat when he opened the door.

As we made our way to the casino, Maryse's words replayed in my head. I wasn't sorry for any decision I'd made, but it probably wasn't the best idea to do that mere days before we were due to take pictures. Either way, it was a lesson that she had to learn. I couldn't afford anymore fuck ups from her. I had no idea what she'd told that woman in the bathroom or what she had time to do on that phone to risk it happening again.

My father always said it was best to be proactive instead of reactive, so I took a proactive approach to prevent her from doing it again. That time was only talking to a lowly reporter who was probably only trying to talk to her to get an inside scoop on our upcoming marriage, a sound bite that cost her life. Next time could be a potential escape or her running into someone I either didn't have in my pocket or knew people who weren't under my control that could bring me down.

That wasn't a risk I was willing to take for anyone.

"So, can you answer my question from last night?" Donovan asked from the driver's seat after a while.

I looked up from my phone screen, my brows furrowed in confusion. "What question?"

"I asked who that guy was last night," he said, glancing at me in the rearview mirror. "Apparently he means something to her if you let him stay with her all night unless you owed him a favor."

I shook my head and put my phone in my pocket. "He was her foster father at one point," I said on a sigh. "She told me a few months ago that he used to hurt her and shit, so I filed that information away for a rainy day. Last night was that rainy day."

"Cold blooded," Donovan said with a chuckle. "How did you know it was him, though?"

The information was definitely a pain in the ass to get.

CPS records were confidential, and since Alyssa was now an adult and was supposed to be in jail, I couldn't request them on her behalf. I had to go through legal means under the guise of seeing if she was legally adopted to be able to sue her family for the money she'd taken.

My lawyer fought tooth and nail for an entire month, asking for concrete proof in order for us to drop that part of our claim and they finally gave us the information I wanted. Seeing that her previous tormentor was a man already on my shit list for owing me money was icing on the cake, one that I tucked away to use if I needed a severe punishment.

"It took some digging to find him," I said. "But it was necessary for the lesson I needed to teach her."

"You think she'll shape up?"

I looked out the window at the passing trees, the morning sun rising higher in the sky. "She doesn't have a choice. The next time she pulls a stunt like that, I'll just kill her and be done with it."

"That'll just make you have to start your search all over again."

I shrugged. "At this point, I'd ditch the plan entirely and go the surrogate route," I said. "If for any reason she doesn't survive her prison term with me, I won't bother with another woman."

"Probably best anyway," Donovan said.

The rest of the ride was quiet, leaving me to immerse myself into my thoughts. The wedding would be here before we knew it and there were still things to do. She still needed to pick bridesmaid dresses along with her wedding dress and I needed to do the same for my tuxedos for myself and the guys. The whole process was tedious and annoying, and a part of me didn't even want to bother with the ceremony.

I sighed deeply. Because of my status in the community and bachelor reputation, it was a pretty big deal that I was getting married. Everyone expected the billionaire to have a Hollywood-like fairytale wedding even though I had no love story to go along with it.

All Alyssa and I were doing was putting a beautiful white bow on a steaming pile of shit and selling it as a happily ever after when it was nothing like that. Even though I was good at pretending, Alyssa wasn't.

I already knew that her shutting down would be obvious to outsiders as we prepared for this wedding. This was supposed to be the happiest moment of our lives if we were a normal couple, but I knew she was anything but happy.

And if I weren't careful, the public would know that, too.

"Fuck," I muttered, pinching the bridge of my nose.

"What's up?" Donovan asked, looking at me from the rearview mirror.

I blew out a breath and shook my head. "It's nothing. I'll fix it when I get home," I lied and clenched my teeth together to keep from saying anything else. With every punishment I'd dished out, it was becoming more and more apparent that fear alone wasn't enough to keep her in line. It would only send her into survival mode, and those kind of people were dangerous. As someone who'd been through a lot throughout her life, pain was something she'd always known. All I was doing now was filling her with resentment and desperation, which would come back to bite me in the ass soon enough.

Pretending to be in love was hard to do, especially when the person I was with craved it. It was the whole reason I'd deviated from my previous plan of having her fall in love with me. She was clingy as fuck, whiny, and annoying to where I didn't want to be around her for too long. But a hurt, angry woman was a plotting woman, and I couldn't have that either.

Not when I had so much to lose.

"You wanna watch the auction from the car or something?" Donovan asked, snapping me out of my thoughts. I looked around to see that we were outside of the casino already.

"Must've spaced out. Didn't even realize we'd made it here that fast," I said.

He chuckled as he got out and walked around the car to open the door. "I wouldn't say it wasn't fast. You were just in your head for a while."

I shook the remnants of the thoughts away as I got out. "I'll call you when the auction is coming to a close."

"Alrighty then," he said with a nod and walked around the car to get in.

My mood shifted the moment I stepped inside the casino. It was always my favorite place to be. The air was always charged with excitement, hope, and a sprinkle of luck that people always came in with before they gambled away their life savings, paychecks, or bill money. While it brought joy to people who managed to win, it ruined lives more often when people lost everything they had. There was nothing that made my dick harder than someone's misery, and this casino always supplied it in spades.

"No! Fucking cheating ass machine!" a man yelled as he slapped the side of a slot machine.

A smirk formed on lips as I passed him, watching him tightly grip his hair in frustration as he stared at the machine, waiting for it to change its mind about taking his money. Being in the casino was like walking through a money vault, knowing that all the money people had in their pockets would eventually become mine.

Despite the cigar smoke and the smell of nervous sweat, all my brain processed was the crisp scent of money this place would rake in, especially with our promotion of free food and drinks for those playing table games.

I walked past most customers unnoticed as I headed toward the other side of the casino to access the secret entry to the bottom level. A couple of employees greeted me in passing but I continued moving without bringing too much attention to myself.

I checked my watch, seeing that I was still making good time. Considering that Harold hadn't texted me yet to see where I was meant that he either wasn't here yet or I wasn't late enough by his standards just yet.

The dinging from machines and music from the casino dissolved the moment I stepped through the door that led to the offices. Everything was dark and quiet aside from the lights in the hallway. I continued on, reaching the keypad on what looked like a dead end wall. I punched in my code and the wall slid back, revealing the steel door and the security guard outside of the door.

He stood when he saw me. "Hi, Mr. Arnett," he said with a nod of his head.

"How are you, John?"

"Well as always, sir. Enjoy the auction," he said as he unlocked and opened the heavy door.

Smooth jazz music surrounded me as I made my way

down the spiral staircase. Many familiar faces came into view when I stepped off the last stair, noticing my three best friends already gathered at the bar. Leeland was the first person to notice me, holding his hand up to wave me over. Harold and Charlie turned to face me right when I reached them.

"It's about time you made it, you asshole. You're always the last one here," Leeland said, shaking my hand.

I rolled my eyes as I chuckled. "Because I'm the only one out of the four of us who doesn't live within the city limits. If you missed me, Leeland, you could've just said that."

"I bet you'd like that, wouldn't you?" he snickered.

"I love all attention," I joked before looking to Harold and Charlie. "How long have you all been here?"

"I mean, technically, we all just got here," Harold said just as a bartender slid a glass of bourbon toward him. "And these two idiots just got here, too. So, it's not really a big deal that you're the last one here. It's not like you're late."

Charlie gave Harold a playful shove. "Way to go being a snitch. Let me know if you want me and Leeland to step away long enough for you to suck Silas's dick while you're at it," Charlie retorted, sending the rest of us into a laughing fit.

The bartender paused and looked at me. "Whatcha drinking, Mr. Arnett?"

"You know I like a good whiskey, Sam," I said. He nodded and patted the bar counter.

"You got it!"

I pulled myself together and shook my head, turning my attention back to my friends. "I'm flattered, boys, but I'm already taken. You'll have to please each other now."

Leeland snorted, taking his glass from the counter when the bartender placed it down on a napkin. "Speaking of taken," he said and took a sip of his Jack and coke that he always ordered no matter where we were.

"I'm listening," I said, taking my drink from the bartender with a nod of thanks.

"What punishment did you end up giving the girl for what she did at the wedding planning appointment? I've been thinking about this ever since you mentioned it a few days ago," he said.

"Yeah, I'm interested to know about this, too," Harold said.

I smirked and gave them the run down of last night, relishing in their wide-eyed expressions and slack jaws as I recounted the pain and torture Raymond put Alyssa through on my behalf. They weren't new to my brutality, but it was probably a new low for me to stoop as low as getting her abusive foster father who traumatized her once before to do it all over again.

Even as I told the story, I couldn't believe I'd actually pulled it off. It was so extreme that it didn't feel real, but it was. I couldn't help but feel both impressed and proud of myself for coming up with such a plan.

Once I concluded my story, Charlie let out a low whistle and shook his head before downing his drink. "Jesus Christ, you're diabolical, man. You constantly remind me why I'm both grateful and relieved to be your best friend and not your enemy," he said, still shaking his head as he tapped his glass on the bar top for a refill.

"And I thought I was fucked up," Harold chuckled. "I'm actually kind of jealous, I'm not gonna lie. That's some serious brutality, brother. I fucking love it."

Leeland clasped my shoulder and gave me a little shake. "My man! I, too, am jealous. That kind of violent thinking is enough to give a man a boner. Too bad you're not my type," he teased.

I gave him a playful shove and smirked. "Yeah, yeah. It was a fucking sight. I swear, the minute she looked at the camera and realized I was watching her was a fucking masterpiece. Witnessing the exact moment she broke made me come so fucking hard. It was beautiful."

"You lucky fuck," Leeland fussed, taking a gulp from his glass. "I swear, you have all the fun."

"Well, you know I'm always willing to share with my brothers," I said with a wicked grin. "Lucky for you desperate bastards, I recorded it to rewatch later. If you don't annoy me tonight, I might be nice enough to send it to you."

"Definitely send it to me. It'll be my entertainment since Michelle has me in the doghouse again," Harold muttered into his glass.

"Your wife is an uptight bitch who should be happy she's not with one of us," Charlie said.

"Agreed," Leeland and I said in unison.

Even though Michelle was a fucking cunt ninety-three percent of the time, we didn't have to worry about her exposing anything within the business. Her father, Joseph Wilder, worked with us closely and did a good bit of investing in our earlier years of setting up. Even though he wasn't physically active within the business, he still earned a shit ton from his investments. Anytime Michelle thought she could get out of control or try to cause problems for Harold, Joseph quickly stepped in to put his bitch of a daughter back in her place.

"Anyway," Charlie continued before pointing at me. "You better tread lightly, my friend. Too much abuse can create a monster."

Harold, Leeland, and I exchanged looks before bursting into a fit a laughter. "Her? A monster?" I laughed some more and wiped my eyes. "Sometimes I wonder why you never went into stand-up comedy."

He rolled his eyes. "You assholes are laughing now, but you're missing the point," he stated, sipping his drink.

"And what point is that, Dr. Phil?" Leeland teased.

"Because all you're doing is filling her with resentment. And a woman who grows to hate you will stop at nothing to hurt you."

"She's literally locked away all day until she's brought out for me to use her like the worthless slut she is," I said with a shrug, tilting my drink to my lips.

"Okay, okay, hold on," Harold said, holding up a finger. "You guys know I hate to agree with Charlie, but he's actually right now that I think about it."

"Yeah, thanks for the half-ass cosign, fucker," Charlie mused with a smirk.

Harold waved him off. "Yeah, yeah, you're actually not talking out your ass for once," he said with a grin, resulting in a shove from Charlie. "But yeah, Silas, you may want to pace yourself in all this brutality if you want this to be a long-term thing."

"Why the fuck would I do that?" I asked.

"Like Charlie said, a woman who hates you can be dangerous. If she gets to a point to where she feels like the only thing she has to choose between is dealing with you or death, I'm positive she'll choose death. And if she does that, she'll make sure to take you down with her."

My grip on my glass tightened as I took another sip, the whiskey now tasting like sludge. That was one of the many things that plagued my mind on the way here, even more so after witnessing her lose her fire and seeing how dead she was inside at breakfast this morning.

I knew she'd become a liability and a danger to keep her around the more I hurt her, but it was addicting at this point. Being able to inflict pain on her during open hours was something I looked forward to during the day, so it wasn't going to be easy to just...stop.

Besides, if I gave her the benefit of the doubt to think she was smarter than she probably was, I'd assume she wasn't stupid enough to fall for my nice guy act after everything I'd done to her. In fact, it would probably bite me in the ass if she caught on to me playing with her emotions. But I was running out of time and options on how to whip her into shape, and I was running out of patience.

She needed to get with the program fast before she walked down the aisle. Once we were married, I wouldn't be able to just keep her locked up in the house. Otherwise, it would seem too suspicious if the only time she was out was if we were together.

Sometimes being in the public eye fucking sucked.

"Yeah, I know. I'll figure something out," I finally said, polishing off the rest of my drink before tapping the bar top with my glass for a refill.

"Women who grew up like her look for love in all the wrong places, you know," Leeland said, pointing at me. "All you have to do is be nice to her sometimes. There are plenty of women who stay in toxic ass relationships all because they think their abusive boyfriends love them."

I shrugged. "She knows I'm fully incapable of love."

"Unless you give her the illusion that you're not," Harold said, also pointing at me. I frowned.

"And how the fuck am I supposed to do that?" I asked, genuinely curious.

"It's all about what you say, psycho," Charlie teased with a chuckle. "You have to say shit like, 'You're making me feel things I thought I'd never feel,' or sappy shit like that."

"Oh, oh, I got one." Harold put his drink on the bar top and walked up to me, so close that we were nearly chest to chest. I raised an eyebrow as I watched him, leaning back and swatting his hand away when he reached for my face.

"The fuck are you doing?" I asked.

He rolled his eyes and grinned. "I have to actually show you so that you know how to do it, Hollow Man." I smirked at him and forced myself to be still for him to demonstrate what he thought I should do. He cupped my face and looked into my eyes, and it took everything in me not to laugh at him. "You know, I was always told that I didn't experience emotions like normal people. But you...you make me feel things I didn't know I existed. I feel...alive with you, finally feeling something other than numbness."

After a few awkward beats of silence, Leeland started a slow clap. "And scene! You two can be boyfriends elsewhere," he teased. I chuckled and pushed him, making him spill his drink. "Hey!"

"That's for being an asshole," I said before looking to Harold and chuckling. "But uh, thanks for the demonstration, I guess."

"I am the king of romance," Harold boasted, puffing up his chest.

"Well, I'll figure this shit out," I said with a shrug. "She has a punishment tonight, so maybe I'll use it to get my abuse out of my system for a little bit."

"Solid plan," Charlie nodded. "Kind of like a bachelor party before you get married to your 'nice guy' role."

The lights around us grew dim before I could respond, signaling that the auction was about to start. The other men and women around us moved away from the bars and headed to their tables to prepare. I grabbed my refilled glass from the bar top and took a sip.

"Looks like we're about to start. We'd better head to our seats," I said.

The four of us walked over to our designated section and took our seats, grabbing our bidding buttons attached to our chairs. I watched as our usual host, Geoff, took the stage and did his usual introduction.

"Ladies and gentleman, welcome to another AE Underground auction!" his booming voice exclaimed. "We have many woman and men up for auction, so get those checkbooks ready and your bidding fingers warmed up. Good luck and happy bidding!"

The women my companies were bidding off were usually first, so there wasn't much to pay attention to just yet. I didn't really choose the girls through auction, the guys usually did that. I didn't care as long as they were able to bring in money and was worth taking a risk on.

I took a sip of my drink to settle my growing nerves. Though my body was present, my mind was a million miles away. I needed to do some serious damage control within the next three and a half months to convince my fiancée to be loyal to me. The guys were right; why the fuck would she be loyal to someone who caused her pain when it would be easier for her to push me far enough to kill her?

It was so easy to get caught up in just wanting to hurt her when I saw her as nothing but property. From the first time she stepped foot into my home, she was simply a woman I'd bought and planned to punish for stealing from me. But the public didn't see her that way.

They didn't know of her crime and how she came to be in my possession. They simply thought she was the woman that finally managed to make me fall in love and want to spend the rest of my life with her. To them, she wasn't the bitch that stole over a half million dollars from me. They definitely didn't know that she was supposed to be in prison, not preparing to walk down the aisle to me.

I ground my teeth. There was so much the public didn't know or understand. They were so easily fooled into believing anything unless someone gave them a reason not to. They thought a supposed inmate was my future wife and thought I was a stand-up guy.

They were so fucking wrong.

I shook the lingering thoughts from my mind and focused on the auctions, bidding alongside my brothers just to give me something to focus on in the meantime. I'd give the guys' advice a fair shot, just to say that I tried if shit went wrong. My life wasn't the only one at stake if Alyssa turned on me; my friends' lives hung in the balance as well. I'd make the sacrifice for them and would deal with the discomfort that came from pretending with this woman. But tonight, I'd make sure I got all my aggression out before trying to change.

———

By the time I got home, the sun had disappeared over the horizon. The auction had been a success, making us triple the amount of money we'd estimated. I thought we'd do good to clear two million, but we'd cleared a little over six. I hadn't expected to be at the casino all day, but there was so much shit that had to be handled after buying all the women we did.

After spending hours counting money, signing over ownership papers, and receiving papers on the girls we bought, we had to deal with the tedious tasks of assigning girls to their brothels and arranging pickup. I rolled my shoulders once I got out of the car and walked toward the house. At least I had open hours available to be able to unwind.

Maryse gave me a tight nod when I passed her instead of speaking, probably still pissed about our conversation this morning. I didn't have time to worry about that. Other people's emotions weren't my problem. Had she minded her business, there wouldn't have been a problem to begin with.

"Bring Alyssa to the theater room and bring a disposable floor pad," I ordered as I continued walking. "She shouldn't have anything on but a robe."

"Yes, sir," she responded, her voice clip.

"And use the time it takes to get her ready to lose the attitude," I said over my shoulder. "I'm not in the mood for your shit tonight."

I rounded the corner before she could respond, strolling past doors until I got to the big double doors on the opposite side of the house. I pushed them open and walked into the theater room, flipping on the lights. I walked over to the projector at the back of the room and turned it on, hooking my phone up to it. After scrolling through my videos and finding the one I wanted to play, I selected it before strolling over to the front row of seats, sitting in the middle of it.

The silence enveloped me, giving me a moment to breath. My mind was tired and running a thousand miles a minute at the same time. I was still dreading having to limit my brutality when just the sight of her made me want to slap her around.

I opened my eyes when the door opened, shuffling feet moving toward me. I looked over to see Maryse and Alyssa and frowned, noticing that Alyssa's face looked worse than it did before I left this morning.

"What the fuck is going on with her face?" I asked Maryse.

"Swelling, Mr. Arnett. That's what happens when someone is injured," she said, her voice clipped as she placed the pad on the chair next to me.

I pinched the bridge of my nose and blew out a breath. "Get the fuck out of my face before I hurt you, Maryse," I growled. "And if you talk to me like that again, you won't get a warning."

"You asked me a question and I answered it, sir."

"GET THE FUCK OUT!" I bellowed, my chest heaving as rage and annoyance burned through me. She wasted no time scurrying her ass out of the theater room, quickly closing the door behind her.

My gaze fell back to Alyssa with a scowl. "Well, I guess a blow job is out," I muttered. "Take that robe off and get over here."

She hesitated for a moment before she shuffled over to me, her mouth tight in discomfort. I unfolded the paper pad and put it on the floor in front of me, pointing it. She sighed inwardly, still holding her right arm closer to her body. The bruising along it seemed worse, which did nothing but piss me off. Maryse had so much shit to say about her injuries, but it was obvious that the doctor wasn't called. There was no way she'd be ready for these pictures in a couple of days, which meant I'd have to reschedule it for next week.

She got on her knees and reached for my pants, but I swatted her hand away and shook my head.

"Turn and face the screen and bend over," I said as I unfastened my belt.

Her eyes widened as she slowly shook her head. "Please," she croaked, tears already glittering in her eyes. "I'm still really sore from—"

"I don't remember asking you how you felt." I pulled my cock out and stroked it in my hand. "Turn around and bend over."

"I'm literally begging you," she pleaded. I stared at her for a long moment, watching as her tears spilled down her swollen cheeks.

"Don't make me ask you a third time, Alyssa," I ground out.

A sob shook her body as she slowly turned around on her knees, getting into position. She hadn't put her right hand down, instead holding that arm against her body. I grabbed the remote and turned the screen on, the still from the video appearing. Because Alyssa had her head down, she hadn't seen what we were about to watch, but she'd know soon enough.

"Please," she sobbed. "I learned my lesson, I swear! I'm already hurting so much."

I moved onto the floor behind her, rolling on the condom I retrieved from my wallet. "Maybe you'll remember these punishments when you think of doing something stupid," I said. She was so red and bruised from the waist down. Raymond certainly left no part of her untouched. I pressed play and her head snapped up once the video started playing.

"No," she whispered, immediately dropping her head.

"Oh no you fucking don't," I growled, grabbing her hair and yanking her head up.

"Please, I can't—"

A blood curdling scream clawed out of her throat as I forced myself between her walls, groaning when they squeezed me out of reflex. Her entire body went rigid, the pain probably shocking her system. I fisted her hair in a tight grip to keep her head up, forcing her to relive her night with Raymond while I planted a new violent core memory now. It was beautiful the way her screams harmonized with the screams that came from the video.

The way her swollen, sore walls massaged my cock with each punishing stroke I gave her was powerful enough to make me throw this good guy shit out the window. Even though I had on the thinnest condom I could buy, I wanted to feel her without one. The angry heat that flooded her pussy and the friction increased my desperation to feel how slick her blood made her walls. But no matter how bad I wanted to be skin to skin with her, I wasn't stupid enough to be bare inside of her when blood was involved.

I lost myself in the pleasure consuming me, her hoarse screaming and broken sobs spurring me on.

"Oh fuck, I love it when you scream," I moaned, tilting my head back with my eyes closed.

"I'm sorry!" she cried. "Please, Silas, I'm sorry!"

Her words only forced me to let go of her hair and grab her hips just to have the leverage to truly pound into her.

"Fuck your sorry," I growled.

She was now laying on her chest, unable to keep herself up with one arm. The moment her knees slid apart, opening her legs widen, her screams turning into something like a choking gasp, the pain rendering her silent. Thankfully, her screams from the video kept me going.

"The guys told me I had to stop hurting you before you started to hate me. I want you to hate me," I continued, a moan spilling from my lips when her walls rippled along my cock. "You're nothing but a useless bitch that's only good for making my dick wet. You have no fucking idea how hard I came last night watching him rip you apart, and I'm going to do the same tonight after destroying you, you fucking bitch."

She continued gasping, her body seeming to grow limp as the seconds went by. I leaned forward and wrapped my hand around the front of her throat, feeling myself coming to my end. Her hand weakly clawed at my throat when I squeezed, every muscle in her body tightening in panic.

"You fucking bitch," I growled, choking her as I sawed

into her. "I refuse to pretend to be something I'm not for you. You're getting exactly what you fucking deserve." My entire body tingled, almost to the point of overwhelming me. I ground my teeth as I delivered what I knew would be my last strokes before I met my end. "Fuck. You. Fuck. You. Fuck. YOU!"

My orgasm slammed into me, tightening my entire body and robbing me of my breath as I flooded the condom. My vision swam as aftershocks left me trembling over her back as my hips moved involuntarily. Pleasure zipped through my dick with every jerk, my balls emptying into her and leaving me a panting, exhausted heap.

I dropped my hand from her throat and forced myself to take deep breaths. "Fuck," I murmured, my cock still twitching inside of her. I looked down to see her completely unresponsive beneath me as her screaming continued on screen. I frowned as I pressed two fingers to her pulse point, slightly relieved that she still had one. It was thready and probably weaker than it should be, but it still left me with a few minutes.

My cock was still rock hard when I pulled out of her, the condom tinted with her blood. Against my better judgment, I hoisted her up and turned her around, propping her upper body onto the theater chair. I rolled the condom off and dropped it on the disposable pad, repositioning myself before sliding back into her.

She didn't scream, she didn't move, she didn't react. I bent over her, my chest to her back and my cheek resting on the back of her head as I slowly pumped into her, her walls sending streaks of pleasure through my dick that warmed my entire body.

"It feels so fucking good to hurt you," I whispered, kissing her cool shoulder. "This pussy is so tight...so bruised...so perfect for me to break. You make me lose all self control when I'm inside you." My arms circled around her, one hand resting on her stomach as the other moved down to softly stroke her clit. "I'm addicted to how you scream for me, how you bleed for me. I can't let that go." I closed my eyes, pumping my hips a little faster. There was no way I'd be able to do what the guys wanted me to. I was obsessed with the sensations I got from hurting her.

I placed soft kisses on the exposed side of her swollen cheek as I quickly rubbed her clit. She was still unresponsive but breathing, her pussy twitching and contracting around my girth.

"That's it, baby. This sweet pussy knows how to squeeze me even when you're not here to participate," I whispered, groaning into the crook of her neck. It was too bad that she wasn't awake to witness the tender way I handled her now.

It was so much easier to say stupid shit when she was unconscious, as I wouldn't have to deal with the blowback later. I pushed her knees apart a little further, my eyes rolling back as I sank deeper into her. A few more rapid strokes of her clit and her pussy sent me over the edge one more. Squeezing and pulling, squeezing and pulling until I exploded deep inside her with a moan that rattled my soul.

I remained glued to her back with my eyes closed, my fingers still circling her clit. My dick jerked each time she squeezed me, residual pleasure skating over me. I came to terms with how fucked up I was to have this sick desire to brutally hurt this woman.

After spending majority of my life being numb to everything, causing her pain seemed to bring something to life inside of me. I also came to terms that if I didn't find a way to control myself and my addiction to her pain, I was bound to kill her before we had a chance to get married. How the fuck did you find the thin line between what was enough and what was too much with shit like this?

She was so warm against me, so silent, so broken. Her bruised skin was like a piece of art I wanted to admire forever. Once my dick became too sensitive for her pulsing walls, I reluctantly slipped out of her warmth but continued to hold her. I simply allowed myself to relax against her, my eyes closed as I continued stroking her clit while moving my other hand from her stomach to palm one of her breasts, still needing to touch her.

Harold was on to something. It wasn't love that made me feel alive; it was her misery and tormented spirit. I knew I could lose everything behind her, but I wasn't ready to let go of something so addicting.

The true beast had been awaken, and I'd follow this feeling until death.

Even if my empire burned in the flames with me.

CHAPTER FIFTEEN
LIA

There was something comforting about the inky blackness of nothing.

It was like a blanket fresh out of the dryer when you were cold, or a lover's embrace when you had a bad day. It was that space between life and death, where you weren't dead yet but you were barely grasping to life.

The silent darkness was a safe space, a time to give my spirit a moment to breath without pain. And as you waited in limbo, you crossed every finger and toe in hopes that the door to the other side would open for you, taking you away permanently.

But some of us never got that lucky.

Embezzlement was a serious crime, but I never imagined it would be worth a death sentence. At this point, I whole heartedly believed that Silas had no intention of walking down the aisle with me. If he kept doing what he was doing, there was no way I'd survive the month, never mind the next three and a half months.

Time passed by in flashes, almost as if I were time jumping within my own life. The last thing I remembered before passing out was the intricate gold threaded pattern on the thin carpet of the theater floor, Silas's angry words breaking each time he tore into me.

Fuck. You. Fuck. You. Fuck. You.

I remembered being in the back of a car alone, my body wrapped in a scratchy blanket as I laid across the backseat. Anytime I opened my eyes, my vision swam and I became nauseous, but I remembered streetlights sweeping over my face in a warm orange glow when I would look up.

I remembered the bright lights of unfamiliar room, low voices talking about things I couldn't get my mind to process. There was something said about my arm. Something about stitches. Something about treatment. Everything faded in and out, Silas's frowning face looking down at me being the last thing I saw before I passed out completely from pain and exhaustion.

When I jumped awake again, I was back in my bed, fire licking up my spine and spreading through my body at the sudden movement. I opened my mouth to scream but nothing came out, my throat raw and achy. Tears burned my eyes as I squeezed them shut.

How much do I have to take before I can leave this hell for good? I was angry about being alive. Being alive meant more opportunities to be hurt and used. I didn't want to be anyone's property anymore. I didn't want to get married, I didn't want a family with him, I didn't want to be here anymore. I just wanted him to kill me already, but there was no end in sight.

An IV machine beeped softly next to the bed. Everything on my body hurt, even turning my head to look at the machine. I was nauseous, tired, and weak. Tears leaked from my eyes as I took in the lavender cast on my right forearm. My face was still tight and painful, my eyes feeling as if they'd been rubbed raw with glass. A bag of saline and a smaller bag of what I assumed was medicine dripped through the IV slowly, leading to the IV in my left arm.

The door opened and Maryse walked in, a sympathetic look on her face when we locked eyes. I hated all of them. I hated her and the other women. I hated the security guards. And I definitely hated Silas Arnett with every fiber of my being. How fucking sick was it to listen to a woman scream and do nothing?

How fucked up was it to see a woman with bruises and injuries and not help them? It was baffling that the women who worked for him seemed unbothered by his brutality. Turning a blind eye to someone's atrocities was always easy when you weren't on the receiving end. And from the women in this house, it was a betrayal, a slap in the face to ignore the suffering of another woman.

"You're awake," Maryse said with a small sigh, closing the door behind her. She walked over with a small pouch clutched in her hands. "Are you in any pain?"

Angry tears burned my eyes as I continued staring at the ceiling. I didn't know why she cared. She didn't care when my old foster father raped me for hours. She didn't care when Silas violated me the following night. I didn't need her faux concern or care when it wouldn't do shit for me now. She sighed.

"I'm so sorry this happened to you," she said softly. "I told him he was going too far before but this...this was extreme."

Silent tears rolled down the side of my face. "There's no crime you could've possible done to deserve what you went through the other night," she continued. "You don't belong here."

I finally forced myself to meet her gaze, noticing the tears glittering in hers. My throat hurt when I swallowed, my lips cracked and dry as I licked them to try to speak.

"You have to help me," I said, my voice barely a whisper. Each word felt like a razor slicing away at the soft flesh of my throat. "If I don't find a way to get out of here, Silas will kill me like his mother said he would."

Maryse sat on the side of the bed with a sniffle, bowing her head. "He was always a troubled kid," she started, her voice low. "I used to think I was safe. He liked me enough to want to bring me with him when he moved out of his parents' home, so I figured he'd keep me around." She quickly swiped at her eyes and shook her head. "But I've realized that Silas doesn't care about anyone. Everyone is disposable to him."

"Then help me," I croaked. "His mother told me to leave before it was too late. I don't think I'll survive something like this again."

She shook her head. "It's too dangerous. If we fail, he'll kill us both."

"He could kill us both anyway just to entertain himself if he wanted to," I said. "Please, Maryse."

"There's nowhere for you to even go. You're supposed to be in prison, remember?"

I winced as I tried to take in a deep breath. "I'd rather take my chances out there than to be a sitting duck, waiting to be slaughtered."

She was quiet for a long moment before patting my knee and standing back up. "I think you should focus on recovering right now," she said. "You're hurt pretty bad and that'll take time to heal. There's no need to put yourself in more danger just because you're scared and wanting to get away."

"Then what do you expect me to do? Heal until he's ready to break me again?"

"I don't know what to tell you, Alyssa. Regardless of what you want, you're too weak to do anything right now."

As frustrating as it was, I knew she was right. I was in no shape to try to do anything and I definitely couldn't withstand any kind of painful punishment right now. I blinked back the tears that threatened to form. If I couldn't escape physically, I could try to escape mentally. Wasn't that how manifesting worked?

"Can I have a pain pill or something?" I asked. "I just want to sleep and not exist for a while."

She held up the pouch she had. "The doctor left you with a little IV medicine to help you. I had to beg him for this when Silas wasn't around because I knew the pills wouldn't work as fast as this would."

"What is it?" I asked with a raised brow, but even doing that made my face hurt.

"It's morphine." She unzipped the pouch and pulled out a small glass bottle. "This is for the really bad pain. You'll still get pills when they're due so we can stay on top of your pain."

"Anything that allows me to be asleep," I mumbled.

I watched her as she placed the pouch on the bed and pulled out a syringe, skillfully prepping the medicine in silence. "Have you ever had morphine before?" she asked as she removed the needle and connected the syringe to my IV line.

"I can't remember." I watched her as she pushed the medicine through and grabbed another syringe with saline. My eyes fluttered closed as a warm feeling ebbed and flowed throughout my body until I was numb. "Are you also a nurse or something?"

"I used to be."

I let the medicine soothe me into a state of fuzzy peace, my body feeling as if it was bobbing along the tides of a calm ocean. I couldn't remember having medicine that made me feel like this, but it did wonders for the pain I'd felt not too long ago.

"Why'd you stop?"

"I...accidentally gave a patient the wrong medication and it killed them," she said. My eyes popped back open but she shook her head. "It wasn't intentional. I was just overworked, tired, and not paying close enough attention." She shrugged. "They didn't seem to care that a new nurse was struggling or that no one would relieve me to gather myself. So I lost my license and have had to live with that regret since then."

I fought through the fog to grab the right words. "How did you end up with Silas?"

"I just applied for the nanny position his parents had."

"And if you realized the kind of person he was back then, why did you stay?"

She zipped the pouch up, her lips pressed into a thin line. "Because I thought I could help him," she finally confessed. "He spent a lot of time alone because his parents were always out either working or being social. I thought he just needed someone to be there and care for him. His parents had all but thrown the towel in with him, leaving him with me majority of the time. I thought loving him would heal him." She shook her head. "But you can't heal people who don't have the ability to feel anything. Love means nothing if he can't receive and reciprocate it."

Her words swam around in my head. It was so funny how I thought I could do that very thing at the start of all this. I thought he'd change if someone was patient enough to love him, but all he'd do was drain the life out of them. It was hard to wrap my head around the fact that there were some people who couldn't feel the emotions that normal people did. I wondered if he ever felt happy, sad, or excited.

The only time I got a reaction out of him was when he was hurting me somehow or if it was lust-driven. Other-wise, he was cold and callous. He lacked empathy and the ability to connect with people. It was no wonder he'd been single for so long. Every woman on this planet was lucky that he hadn't chosen them to be with him.

"Anyway, enough about me," Maryse said with a sigh. "Get some rest. I'll be back in a few with a protein smoothie for you."

I tried to nod but my head felt like lead. She softly closed the door behind me, leaving me with silence and the quiet whirring of the IV pump as it continued pushing things in my veins. I closed my eyes. When I left foster care, I thought the worst of my life was behind me. I was so happy to be able to make my own decisions and have a choice in the people who came in and out of my life.

I thought I'd be safe from abuse from predatory assholes pretending to be saviors only to hurt me. I was so ready to get the life I thought I deserved, one I thought was never possible for me.

But all I did was put myself in a more fucked up situation than I'd already escaped.

In moments like this, when I was broken and defeated, I mentally tormented myself for the decisions I made that led me here. I'd spent way too many days and nights in this room, wondering how my life would've been different if I hadn't taken the money.

I wondered where I would've ended up in a couple of years from now had I gotten therapy to deal with my trauma and focused on bettering myself instead of thinking I needed a man's love to complete me. There were so many things I wished I'd done differently, so many decisions I wish I could change, but hoping and wishing didn't do anything in the end.

Everyone always said that money couldn't solve your problems, but I didn't believe them. I'd thought all of my problems were related to money, and if I had more of it, I could finally be happy. But it wasn't enough. Buying designer clothes, bags, and shoes didn't change the fact that I had no family. Eating at fancy restaurants and pretending to be more important than I was didn't change the mold-infested, run down studio apartment I lived in.

Every transaction just left me feeling more empty than the last. It didn't make me happy, it didn't help me keep my boyfriend, and it didn't make anyone love me. All it did was prove that money was truly the root of all evil, landing me in the clutches of a violent psychopath who was determined to make me pay for every penny I took from him. I wouldn't be surprised if the total payment owed to him was my life.

As I laid there, my body becoming heavy with sleep, I made up my mind that I was going to find a way to expose Silas. Even if we did get married, I knew he wasn't going to keep me alive for the entire nine years he'd have me. If I had to die, I was going to take him down with me. I couldn't bear to think of him putting another woman through this, especially an innocent woman.

Since being here, I'd learned that his original plan was to snatch a random woman off the street and make her his wife and mother of his heir. Tears burned my eyes as I thought of him ripping a woman away from her life, her family, and her friends just to play a sick game of house with him until he got tired of her. I knew he'd go out looking for another woman once he got rid of me, and it made me sick to my stomach to know the cycle would only continue. Men like him didn't deserve to live. Men like him didn't deserve to have the power he had, power he used to hurt innocent people.

I exhaled slowly, sleep settling over me like a weighted blanket. I had to be smart about this. I didn't want to do something obvious that had the sure chance of failing. I had plenty of time to think about it while I healed, but for now, I just needed to sleep...

———

A few days later, I was finally able to move around with just a little bit of pain. Silas was nowhere to be seen, not that I was complaining. I remained in my room, eating my meals there and declining workouts. Maryse seemed to be on the sympathy train for me, so she hadn't told Silas that

I refused to workout, which allowed me to continue with my plan.

Every day I was able to, I wrote in the journal. At first, I thought it would've been traumatizing to write down the things that happened to me, but then I realized that maybe this journal wasn't meant for me to re-read. This would be my proof to both get me out of here and to have Silas locked away for good. I'd written every single detail of things that'd happened to me and the things I witnessed from the moment I was arrested.

I wrote about the dirty cops who helped bring me here, the crooked judge who aided in my kidnapping and the sale of two children. I wrote about how Silas orchestrated the murder of the accountant and his wife. Every single thing Silas did to me went into this journal, and I spared no detail.

My plan was to fill this journal with my story until the night before the wedding and either give the journal to a media personnel covering the wedding or convince Maryse to send it to a large news outlet. I bit the inside of my cheek. I still wasn't sure if I could completely trust Maryse. Regardless of whatever remorse or sympathy she felt, she was still loyal to Silas at the end of the day. I'd have to keep an eye on her for a little while longer before I decided to bring her into the fold.

I didn't trust anyone in this house.

Pages and pages of the journal were filled with the horrors that went on in this house. Even as the days passed, there were new things to add. It'd now been two weeks and I hadn't seen Silas once, not even for office hours. I wasn't sure if he was doing his own plotting or just busy and didn't want to be bothered with me, but it was a nice break.

I continued my schedule as usual once I felt pretty normal. Even though I didn't physically see him, I definitely felt his presence through the house. There were plenty of times when I'd walk past his office and heard a woman moaning his name beyond the door. The first couple of times I'd heard it, I thought he was watching porn and jerking off.

But then I'd see the women doing their walk of shame while I was having breakfast, giving me looks as if they were proud to have fucked my supposed fiancé. I just had to play my part and stay out of trouble. As long as Silas wasn't suspicious or constantly watching me, there was a chance I could pull this off.

After the incident at the bridal boutique, Silas no longer allowed me to leave the house. Jerry had to bring racks and racks of dresses for me to try on before I finally found one I liked. It was hard pretending to be excited for something I didn't want. Every dress looked like a fancy prison uniform to me, but there was no way I could tell Jerry that.

"I think you look beautiful in it," Jerry said as he clipped a veil in my hair. "How does it feel to wear it?"

"It feels fine," I said, looking down at the blinged out bodice on the dress.

Jerry scoffed. "Just fine? You're getting married to a billionaire, for crying out loud. You'd think you'd have a little more enthusiasm when you're in a $25,000 dress."

I shrugged, taking the veil off. "I just have a lot on my mind right now that's making it hard to be excited about this." I sighed. "I do like the dress, though, and I think this is the one I'll go with."

He stared at me for a long moment before he threw his hands in the air. "Whatever you say," he said. He moved behind me to unlace the corset. "I just never met a bride who isn't over the moon about trying on dresses and imagining what they'd look like on their special day."

I swallowed the lump in my throat, choosing my words carefully. "It's hard to feel that way when you don't even know if you'll make it down the aisle," I muttered. It was a general statement. Couples having rough patches in their relationships wasn't too out of the ordinary. Either Jerry didn't care or he already knew what was going on and knew that I was trapped regardless.

"Planning a wedding can be stressful for everyone

involved. It's just a bump in the road," he said, just as he loosened the dress. He helped me out of it and put it on the hanger. "Once you're dressed, we can decide on your bridesmaid dresses."

Even as he went on and on about different dresses, my head was nowhere in the conversation. My body tensed when I heard Silas's voice nearby, my teeth on edge as I heard his dress shoes clicking against the floor. He walked past the living room as if I weren't there, talking to the main security guard before they disappeared down the hall.

After not seeing him for two weeks, it was pretty unnerving to see him now. I didn't know what he had up his sleeve or if he'd been planning something. If I were being honest, I was worried he'd spent all that time working on a new way to hurt me. He was able to orchestrate my punishment with my old foster father in only a couple of days; I was terrified at what he could've possibly put together in two weeks.

Once I finished up with Jerry, Maryse took me back to my room. I looked at her with a raised brow when she looked around before stepping inside, closing the door behind her. "I just wanted to give you a heads up that Mr. Arnett is requesting you for open hours this evening," she said.

Fear tightened my muscles as my throat went dry. "I

can't, Maryse," I whispered, backing away from her. "I literally just healed from his last session."

"I know, I know, but refusing him will only lead to being punished. That's the last thing you need right now."

"Then what the fuck am I supposed to do?" I asked, tears burning my eyes. "He hasn't said a word to me or checked on me in two weeks! I can't just sit here and wait around for him to be ready to hurt me. I have to get out of here!"

"Keep your voice down," she hissed, looking over her shoulder as if someone would burst through the door at any moment. "Just get through the night. I'll help you find a way out of here."

"Why?" I asked. I still wasn't sure if I could trust her. For all I knew, it was a set up created by Silas to give him a reason to break me all over again.

"Because I don't think you're safe anymore," she murmured with a sigh. "It seems as if his punishments are becoming more and more extreme, and I don't know how many chances you have before he eventually kills you."

"How do I know I can trust you?"

"You don't," she said without hesitation. "All you can do is give me the benefit of the doubt. I've watched enough women come through here and be hurt by him, never saying a word. Today, it'll be you. Tomorrow, it could be me or one of the other women who work for him, or a random woman who happened to cross paths with him. Something has to change. He needs help."

"I think he's far beyond help."

"Not if he's forced to."

I stared at her for a long moment, fighting with myself on whether or not I wanted to trust her. At this point, I didn't have anything to lose. While I didn't want to die, I wasn't afraid to if I managed to stop Silas in the process.

This entire plan was a suicide mission no matter how I tried to spin it, but I had to try. If I saved even one life by sacrificing mine, I'd be satisfied with that.

"Well, if you're serious, then I need your help with something," I finally said, my heart beating a little faster.

"What is it?"

I moved over to my bed and lifted the mattress a little, pulling the journal from it. "I've written down everything that's happened to me and others since I've been here," I started. "The murders, the abuse, the child trafficking, all of it is here. I need you to get this to someone that Silas doesn't have in his pocket."

"That's nearly everyone in the city," she said with a frown.

"There has to be at least one person who isn't crooked," I said.

She pursed her lips as she stared at the journal. "Perhaps we can send it out-of-state. Giving it to anyone locally leaves too many opportunities for it to get back to Mr. Arnett."

"You're right," I said, nodding. "Do you...know of any news stations you can mail it to?"

"I'll look it up." She narrowed her gaze at me. "You need to be positive that this is what you want to do. Once you open this can of worms, you won't be able to close it."

"I know," I said, releasing a shaky breath. "But it has to be done."

"I'm not just talking about Silas. Exposing him would expose you, too," she said. "Exposing him won't give you your freedom that you think is outside of this house. It'll only send you to prison with people Silas has control over."

The realization of that sent a chill down my spine, but I shook it off. "I'd fight the charge. Everything the police, judge, and Silas did was illegal, which would have the case thrown out. But we have to deal with him first; I'll worry about myself later."

She nodded. "Depending on what I find, I'll put it in the mail after Mr. Arnett leaves for work in the morning."

Hope simmered in my chest at the thought of this nightmare coming to an end. If we pulled this off, it would bring down the most powerful man in the city. I was so desperate to have my life back, so desperate to go back to my shitty apartment and my shitty life. I wanted to get out of this city and start over completely. I wanted to be Lia, the girl who'd gone through so much and rose from ashes that should've suffocated her. I had to see this through. My future as well as any other woman that crossed his path depended on it.

Maryse straightened her posture. "Well, it's best that you prepare yourself for open hours tonight. He wants you in a robe and bare underneath," she said, reminding me of the awaiting nightmare. "If it's any comfort, just think that this might be your last one if things go as planned."

I gave her a small smile and nodded. "Thanks," I murmured. She turned to walk away, leaving me with my mixed emotions.

Please don't let this fail, I mentally pleaded before heading to my closet to prepare myself for another night of pain.

———

I was completely surprised when Valorie brought me to Silas's bedroom. He'd never brought me here since I'd been in his home. While my bedroom was filled with soft pastel colors, his was dark and cold. Everything was a pitch black color with angry red accents. Seeing him stretched across his bed in black silk pajama pants made him look like the devil himself. He looked at me, a frown etched on his lips as he regarded me.

"We'll make this quick," he said as he slid off the bed and moved toward me. "Ditch the robe and get on your knees on the bed."

I swallowed the emotions threatening to choke me as I did what he asked with shaky hands. I still had stitches between my legs and the thought of him ripping them just to rape me again made me want to run for the hills. There was a bar on the foot of the bed with leather cuffs on them along with some kind of fabric that looked like a sack of some sort. I nervously got onto the bed, trembling when he positioned the bar between my legs and secured my ankles into the cuffs.

"Put your arms behind your back," he ordered.

I blew out a silent breath of anxiety and followed his command. He took the sack and put my arms into it sliding it up until it was in the middle of my bicep. He tightened a drawstring at the top, which pulled my shoulder blades together. The drawstring was tight, making it hard to move my arms and left me completely at his mercy.

The silence in the room was so loud that it hurt my ears. He moved around behind me before the bed dipped with his weight. I jumped when his hair tickled my inner thighs, looking down to see his head between my legs.

He didn't say a word as he took my clit into his mouth. My body was conflicted. While I was grateful that he wasn't hurting me, I was confused as to why he was rewarding me. He hadn't spoken to me or been around me for two weeks. I wasn't sure if maybe he'd felt guilt for what he'd done or if he was just horny and wanted to prep me before he hurt me, but it made it very hard to relax.

Even though his mouth felt amazing, I winced in discomfort each time the muscles within my pussy twitched. Soft whimpers and moans left my lips, but I was too paranoid to fully immerse myself into the pleasure he put on my body.

The moment he created a perfect suction on my clit and sucked and licked my tight bundle of nerves in a rhythmic pattern, my body took the reigns away from my brain. My hips rolled back and forth, electric heat pulsing through my nerve endings as I moaned.

Even though the sensation was so good on my clit, the pleasure was always cut through with a sharp instant of pain when my muscles contracted. It was as if he could tell each time a wave of pain hit me, his sucking and licking becoming stronger each time I wince.

"Wait, wait, wait," I gasped, my orgasm threatening to knock me over. I now knew what he was trying to do. This wasn't pleasure; this was another form of torture that would hurt like hell.

He hummed against my clit and sucked hard, sending stars bursting in my vision as my orgasm rocked my foundation. I screamed out in pain, my walls spasming hard and quickly. Every squeeze and pulse of my pussy sent throbbing pain throughout my insides, pain that far overpowered any kind of pleasure he'd originally given me. He moaned every time I scream, taking pleasure in the way I fought to get away from him.

It was hard to maneuver with my hands stuck behind my back and the bar was held in place since his head and neck pinned it to the bed. Even after I came, he didn't let go of my clit, only pushing me further. Tears spilled down my cheeks as I wailed, trying my hardest to lift myself up enough to break the suction he had on my clit, but it only caused him to pull it.

"Please stop!" I begged, my voice thick with tears.

When he'd had enough of my jerking around, he roughly slapped my ass, glaring up at me. I couldn't do anything but cry as he continued his punishment, groaning into my wet flesh as he stroked his hard cock. It was as if something was inside my womb, threatening to rip me open from the inside with the violent way my walls contracted. He brought me to another powerful orgasm that brought waves of pain that rendered me silent, my juices spilling from me and onto him. My sobs were suffocating as I begged him. I was tired of being in pain. I was tired of being used. I hated being treated like someone's personal sex toy to abuse and degrade anyway they saw fit. I wanted it all to stop.

"You're hurting me! Stop!" I screamed, bucking against him with all the force I could muster, even if it hurt me in the process.

I screamed when he sucked my clit hard, a muffled groan vibrating against my wet flesh when he finally came. When he finally released my clit from his mouth, I fell forward on my chest as I sobbed. Instead of him moving, he simply wiped his cum-covered hand with a towel before reaching up and parting my slick lips. And for the next hour, he took his slow sweet time edging me with the quick flicker of his tongue before leading me into another powerful, painful orgasm that made me scream myself hoarse.

I was a trembling, sobbing mess by the time he was done with me, my pussy cramping so badly that I couldn't even stand upright to make it to my room. He simply dismissed me without another word, leaving Maryse to take me back to my room. She gave me another pain pill and ran a hot bath for me without a word. There was nothing else to talk about. Tomorrow, the plan would be initiated and by the end of the week, I'd either be dead or free.

The pain pill kicked in as I sat in the bath, easing some

of the cramps. If Maryse failed, I needed a plan B that I could do on my own. If for some reason she changed her mind or if she was caught, I needed to be ready to take action. If either of those happened, my life was over. I'd rather commit suicide and end my own misery than to allow Silas to continue his sick methods until he eventually killed me.

I had nothing left to lose, and I was ready and willing to welcome death with open arms.

CHAPTER SIXTEEN
SILAS

No sooner than I walked back into my bedroom after taking a shower, a soft knock sounded on the door. I tightened my towel around my waist.

"Yeah?" I called out, taking another towel to dry my hair.

The door cracked open and Kora poked her head in with an apologetic smile. "Sorry, sir. I don't mean to disturb you, but I need to talk to you about something."

"You could've already said it instead of wasting your breath and my time with what you said instead," I mumbled, rolling my eyes.

She looked over her shoulder back into the hallway before turning back to me. "It's an emergency, sir. I think you'll want to hear this in private."

I paused in drying my hair and frowned, immediately on edge. "Then come in and close the door."

She stepped into my bedroom and closed the door behind her, taking a few steps forward. I sat on the side of my bed, my mind already conjuring up all the fuckery she could be preparing to tell me.

My gut told me this was something regarding Alyssa, but Kora wasn't responsible for her. Alyssa's care was the major responsibility of Maryse, Aimee, and Valorie. Kora's main job was cleaning and assisting the ladies with Alyssa if they needed help, but it wasn't her priority. The fact that she was in my bedroom about an emergency didn't sit right with me.

I narrowed my eyes at her, growing impatient. "Are you going to continue molesting me with your eyes or are you going to start talking?" I snapped.

She cleared her throat and dropped her gaze. "Um, sorry." She blew out a breath to steady herself. "I think Maryse and that woman are plotting against you, sir."

I let her words settle into my head for a few moments before I laughed. "What the fuck are you talking about?"

"I...was cleaning in the hall outside of your fiancée's bedroom and I overheard them talking," she said nervously.

I folded my arms across my chest, an amused grin on my lips. "And what were they talking about?"

"I didn't hear all of it, but I did hear Maryse saying something about mailing something out of town or out-of-state or something."

"And you don't know what she planned on mailing?"

She shook her head. "I couldn't hear the whole conversation. I didn't even hear them at first until the woman started getting loud and Maryse told her to keep her voice down. That was when I started listening."

My grin quickly turned into a frown again. Pieces of a conversation wasn't enough proof to think that Maryse was planning to betray me, but the pieces that were heard didn't sound good either. Why the fuck would my long-time employee talk to my prisoner about mailing something? And what the fuck was Alyssa trying to mail that Maryse was going to help her with? I tucked the information in the back of my mind before turning my attention back to Kora.

"And that's all you heard?" I asked.

"The last thing I was able to understand was that whatever they plan on doing, Maryse is waiting until you leave for work to do it. I'm not sure what 'it' is or if it's in regard to mailing the package, but they're planning for tomorrow."

"Is that right?" I mused, stroking my chin.

"I think whatever they have is crippling," Kora continued. "Before Maryse left the room, she told the woman that last night would be her last punishment. It's almost as if she expects the woman to be free soon."

Anger slowly bubbled under the surface but I kept my cool. There still wasn't a guarantee that Kora was telling the truth, but I couldn't risk it if there was a chance that she was right.

"I see," I said, standing back up. "Thank you for that, Kora. I appreciate your loyalty more than you know."

She bowed slightly with a small smile. "Of course, sir. Please let me know if you need anything through the night."

"I will, thanks," I mumbled. "Oh, and Kora?"

She paused, her hand on the doorknob. "Yes, sir?"

"Don't say anything to anyone else about this. Don't ask Maryse anything, don't say anything to Alyssa. Just keep quiet. I'll handle it."

She nodded and opened the door. "I won't, sir," she said before she slipped out of the bedroom. I quickly moved to my closet and grabbed a pair of boxers and pajama pants to pull on before going to search for Donovan. He was coming down the hall for his nightly rounds when I left my bedroom, looking at me with a raised brow as he regarded me.

"What's wrong with you?" he asked.

"Come with me," I said, my voice tight.

He followed me to my office, sitting in one of the

chairs as I paced the open floor. I couldn't wrap my head around Maryse betraying me. Sure, we'd hit a rough patch these last couple of weeks after Alyssa's punishment with Raymond, but she knew me. She knew how I was.

None of the shit I did was new to her. She'd taken care of me since I was twelve years old; I saw her as my mother more than I considered my own mother. For there to even be an inkling of a chance that she was planning to destroy me sent a violent wave of rage washing over me.

"Talk to me, man. You even have me on edge now," Donovan said after a few moments.

"Kora just came to me and said she believes Maryse and Alyssa are plotting against me," I started, causing Donovan to snort.

"Maryse? Seriously?" he chuckled. "If I didn't know that you're basically a son to her, I would've thought you had her on your dick at some point because of how loyal she is to you." He shook his head. "Maybe Kora was mistaken."

"That was my same reaction, but I don't know." I shook my head and continued pacing. "The shit Kora said doesn't make fucking sense but she's sure it was Maryse in the room with her. She saw Maryse come out after she heard what she heard."

"What did she hear exactly?"

I recounted everything Kora told me, growing more

angry as I spoke. Something like this would get Maryse killed, which meant I needed to tread lightly when dealing with this situation. Asking her outright was out of the question; all it would do was cause her to lie and put off the plan until they thought I forgot about it. I couldn't have people I didn't trust around me and my business dealings, so I needed to get ahead of it before it became a problem.

Independent brains could become a cancer to the others around them. If Alyssa could sink her talons into Maryse, there wouldn't be anything stopping her from doing the same to the other women in the house. Women were too fucking emotional, which would make them easy targets if Alyssa could make them pity her.

"That's some serious ass shit, Si," Donovan said with a low whistle. "You better get concrete proof before you go off the handle. This could be a ploy for Alyssa to make you get rid of your most loyal caretaker just so she can manipulate the other women."

I nodded, recognizing that as a valid thought. "That's also an idea," I said. "But Maryse isn't stupid and she's not easily swayed. I mean, she's dealt with me and my bullshit since I was a kid. She isn't easily manipulated."

"Wait, the security cameras," Donovan said, snapping his fingers. "Check the cameras."

I couldn't help the smile the crossed my lips. It'd been

so long since I watched her on the cameras that I forgot I'd put them in there. For the first couple of days, I used to watch her while I was work, which was how I knew she hadn't read the manual back then. I'd purposely ask her questions knowing she hadn't read certain sections, which usually made my day because I knew I had a punishment to dish out once I got home.

But I'd stopped watching it because it got boring after awhile, watching her do the same shit day in and day out. All she did was talk to herself about nothing, pace back and forth, nap, flip through magazines or books, or look out the window. But just because I stopped watching didn't mean the cameras stopped working, and I could only hope that Maryse had a slip of judgement and forgot about the cameras, too.

Moving over to my computer, I quickly turned it on and signed in. Excitement sped up my heart as I opened the application for the security system, clicking on the camera feed for her bedroom. She was currently in the bathtub, Maryse kneeling next to the tub. Though I could see Maryse's mouth moving, she was talking too low and the camera was on the opposite side of the bedroom, too far from the bathroom to pick up their voices.

I ground my teeth. Something was definitely going on. Before I even brought a woman home, my rule to the caretakers were to not spend more time than necessary with my victim. Getting too close to someone in a desperate state wouldn't end well for them, and I thought Maryse would've been the last person I had to worry about. But there she was, doting on the bitch that wanted to take me down.

I tore away from the current feed and moved to rewind the footage. I wasn't even sure when this conversation happened, forgetting to ask Kora about it but not wanting to bring her back to ask. I put the rewind button on a 3x speed and watched as everything moved backwards. I sped through the time the room was empty, which was when she was with me for open hours, before slowing it down again.

My muscles tightened when it got to the part of Maryse moving back into her room and Alyssa moving backwards from her closet, both of them walking backwards to her bed. They stood there, Alyssa's hands moving about and waving a journal for a few moments before she walked backwards toward the bed, the journal disappearing back under the mattress.

That must be what they plan to mail then, I thought to myself, continuing to rewind. When I got to a good enough place, I paused it, allowing myself to calm down enough to be able to receive the information I wasn't sure I was ready to see. Alyssa was the least of my concerns; I didn't put it past her to try anything to get out of here.

But I'd be lying if I said Maryse's involvement wasn't a blow to me. I would expect my own parents to betray me before Maryse did. I would expect Harold, Charlie, or Leeland to railroad me before I thought Maryse would.

"You find anything?" Donovan asked, grounding me back to my current predicament.

I swallowed hard and nodded. "I think I might've found something. I'm about to play it."

Donovan stood and moved closer to my desk and I turned my monitor so we could both watch it. I wrote down the time stamp on the video on a notepad so I could check the hallway feed after this to see if Kora was in the hall at the time of this particular interaction. I clicked the play button and braced myself as I lowered the volume on the computer, just in case Maryse—or anyone else for that matter—was outside the door.

"...*refusing him will only lead to being punished. That's the last thing you need right now.*"

"*Then what the fuck am I supposed to do! He hasn't said a word to me or checked on me in two weeks! I can't just sit here and wait around for him to be ready to hurt me. I have to get out of here!*"

"*Keep your voice down!*"

"That's what Kora said alerted her to the conversation," I said idly.

Donovan shook his head. "I wanted to give Maryse the

benefit of the doubt, but it's not looking too good," he said, his tone solemn.

"You and me both," I murmured, still staring at the screen.

The heat of betrayal slithered through me and gripped my ribcage as I watched Maryse look over her shoulder. *"Just get through the night. I'll help you find a way out of here."*

"Why?"

"Because I don't think you're safe anymore. It seems as if his punishments are becoming more and more extreme, and I don't know how many chances you have before he kills you."

"How do I know I can trust you?"

"You don't. All you can do is give me the benefit of the doubt. I've watched women come through here and be hurt by him, never saying a word. Today, it'll be you. Tomorrow, it could be me or one of the other women who work for him, or a random woman who happened to cross paths with him. Something has to change. He needs help."

"I think he's far beyond help."

"Not if he's forced to."

I paused the feed and pinched the bridge of my nose. Donovan thankfully didn't say anything, which was best because I wasn't sure I could keep my composure. All I could hear was my blood rushing in my ears and the ringing white-noise that came with unbridled rage.

My brain struggled to accept the truth in front of me,

trying to find a rational way to explain this shit as if my eyes and ears didn't understand the information it just took in. I literally saw the two of them on the screen. I physically heard them with my own ears.

There was no other logical explanation that explained the fact that a woman I paid to take care of the woman I captured was agreeing to help her escape. There were no excuses I could've given to justify the things Maryse said. She was well aware of what would happen if Alyssa were to escape. I wouldn't be the only person who'd fall; this was so much more bigger than me.

Everyone who worked for me, everyone who helped me, everyone who knew and did nothing would all come down if they went through with this plan. Maryse knew that, and she still decided to go on this suicide mission with a woman she hadn't even known for a year.

"I know it's hard to see this, but we have to keep watching to see what they actually plan to do," Donovan said.

I opened my eyes and exhaled deeply. I knew he was right, but I wasn't prepared. Along with my rage, something else simmered beyond that, something I wasn't sure I'd felt before. If I had to put a label on it, I would almost say that I was...hurt. I knew I wasn't sad, because both of them would get what they deserved, but it hurt me that Maryse turned out to be so fucking stupid.

It hurt me to know that she let some random bitch get into her head and lead her down a path she couldn't come back from. It hurt me to know I had to get rid of the only woman I truly respected, the only woman I thought of as my mother. And no matter how much it hurt, I had to get rid of anyone I couldn't trust, including her.

I pressed play and continued watching with a clenched jaw. Alyssa walked over to her bed and slightly lifted the mattress before straightening her posture and holding a journal.

"*I've written down everything that's happened to me and others since I've been here. The murders, the abuse, the child trafficking, all of it is here. I need you to get this to someone Silas doesn't have in his pocket.*"

"*That's nearly everyone in the city.*"

"*There has to be at least one person who isn't crooked.*"

"*Maybe we can send it out of state. Giving it to anyone locally leaves too many opportunities for it to get back to Mr. Arnett.*"

I listened as they talked about their ideas, finding it ironic how Maryse warned Alyssa about the consequences for her without worrying about her own consequences. I ground my teeth as I stared at the journal Alyssa held in her hand, a journal that would cause a massive shit storm if it ended up in the wrong hands.

I needed to get the journal myself, but I needed to play

this smart. A part of me wanted to believe that Maryse was agreeing with her to get Alyssa to trust her. Maybe she would give me the journal when Alyssa handed it over. I'd have to wait until the morning to find out for sure, but I didn't have faith in her anymore. As of tonight, she was nothing to me. And come tomorrow, she wouldn't be breathing.

I tuned back in just in time to hear the end of the conversation. "...*in the mail after Mr. Arnett leaves for work in the morning.*"

"Looks like Kora heard what she heard after all," I said with a sigh, running a frustrated hand down my face.

"*Well, it's best you prepare yourself for open hours tonight. He wants you in a robe and bare underneath. If it's any comfort, just think that this might be your last one if things go as planned.*"

"*Thanks.*"

Maryse headed out of her room while Alyssa disappeared into her closet. Donovan sighed and sat back in his seat across from my desk as I blankly stared at the screen. After a few moments, he clasped his hands and rested his elbows on his knees as he leaned forward.

"What do you wanna do?" he asked, his voice dark. "You just say the word and it's done."

"I'm killing them both tomorrow," I stated.

"Should I make sure Maryse doesn't leave the house?"

I shook my head. "No. I'm calling out from work tomorrow to deal with this." The plan quickly formulated in my head as my brain kicked into hyperdrive. "First, I need all keys for all the vehicles on the property except yours. Once you and I are done here, I need you to update the rest of the security and tell them that none of them are to leave the property until this is dealt with. In fact, go get the keys now."

"Aye, aye, captain," Donovan said as he stood up, strolling out of my office. I took a moment to center myself and take a deep breath. This situation was no different than any other obstacle I'd faced. This wasn't the first time I'd had to kill someone after they threatened to expose me or my company, and I was sure it wouldn't be the last. But I'd be lying if I said it wasn't hard when it was someone you considered family who was stabbing you in the back.

Donovan returned with all the keys and put them on my desk. "That's all of them with the exception of mine," he said, holding up his own set of car keys. I nodded and scooped the keys up, turning in my chair to open my safe. Once the keys were secured, I turned back to Donovan.

"You'll take me to work as you usually do—"

"You just said—"

"Just shut up and listen, Donny," I said on a sigh. "I'm not actually going to work but I need to make those two bitches think I am. As long as Maryse has worked for me, she knows how long it takes you to drive me to work and come back. So we'll leave, drive the same route we usually take, and then come back." I drummed my fingers along my desk. "I'm sure while you're gone, Maryse is ask one of the guys for a ride or try to find keys to drive herself. She'll probably ask you when you get back. I'll wait in the car for however long it takes."

"What if she doesn't ask?"

"Trust me, I'm sure she will," I said. "Let the guys know what's going on. If any of the guys tell you that she asked them about keys or a ride, then you go to her and ask if she still needs one while you're heading back to town. She probably won't tell you to take her to the post office, but she'll tell you to drop her off close to one."

"And then?"

"Well, once she's in the car, I can deal with her."

"What if she doesn't have the journal when she gets in the car?"

I raised an eyebrow. "Then she wouldn't have a reason to get in the car," I said.

"Okay then." He stood. "Should I go ahead and put things in the car to prepare?"

I thought for a while. "Just prepare a gas can and charge the power saw. You can put it in the trunk in the morning."

He nodded and left me alone. I turned my attention

back to the security feed, resetting it to the current footage. Alyssa was now out of the tub and Maryse was gone. I watched her pull out the journal again and write for a little while before she tucked it back its hiding place before turning off her lamp, casting the room in darkness.

"Yeah, sleep tight," I growled to myself. "Tomorrow you'll be sleeping in the ground."

———

When I got up the next morning, it took everything in me to try to act as normal as possible. Even if I hadn't known what was going on, Alyssa looked nervous and uneasy. Maryse was nowhere to be found, but I wasn't worried about it. I had a plan that I was sure would work, so I wouldn't allow myself to get worked up just yet.

I didn't say anything to Alyssa during breakfast, even when she tried to talk to me. I knew if I said something, I'd be tempted to go ahead and kill her because I wouldn't be able to control my rage. Instead, I simply ate and left the table, instructing Aimee to take her back to her room when she was finished.

Donovan was already outside when I walked out of the backdoor, closing the trunk before looking at me. "Ready to go?"

"Yep," I said. He opened the backdoor and I slid into

the backseat. My entire body buzzed with anxious energy. I couldn't relax until I knew the threat was officially over. Even as we drove into town and turned back around toward the house, I couldn't help but wonder what was happening at the house. If Maryse wanted to, she could've called a drive share company even though it was a rule that no one could give out my address for any reason.

By the time we pulled back into the driveway, I could barely sit still. The anticipation of the inevitable was going to be the death of me, as patience wasn't my strong suit. I frowned when I saw Maryse standing outside waving her arm to flag Donovan down, holding a brown mailing envelope in her other arm.

"Roll the partition up. I don't want her seeing me before I'm ready for her to," I told him. The black tinted glass rolled up as he slowed down once he reached the end of the driveway. I listened as Donovan got out of the car, Maryse voice making my skin prickle.

"Could I use your car really fast?" she asked. "No one knows where the other keys are and I really have to get this package in the mail today."

"Then put it in the mailbox for the mailman," Donovan said, walking past her.

"It needs postage, though."

"I'll take it when I go back into town—"

"This has a time limit. I promise I'll be fast," she said.

The fact that she was lying through her teeth and adamant about getting this package out made it clear that she was no longer on my side. The only comfort I got out of this situation was knowing that her death would be as personal as her betrayal was.

Donovan sighed. "You're gonna have to give me a few minutes. I need to piss. Go ahead and get in the car before I change my fucking mind," he snapped before walking away. Relieved gratitude spilled from her lips as she quickly opened the door and hopped in, closing the door behind her. She closed her eyes and released a breath.

"This will be over soon," she whispered to herself.

"I agree," I said.

A short scream filled the car as she jumped, looking over at me with wide eyes. "Silas! I-I thought you were already at work," she stammered.

"I got all the way there and realized I forgot something I needed for a meeting and had to circle back." I gestured toward the package in her hand. "Where are you headed?"

She nervously licked her lips and clutched the package a little tighter. "Oh, um, I just need to drop this off at the post office. My niece's birthday is coming up and—"

"Out of all the people I put trust in, I never thought you'd be the one to betray me, Maryse," I interrupted her, unable to deal with her lying babbling anymore. "We've worked together for a long time. I even thought of you like a mom."

"Silas—"

"When Kora first brought your betrayal to my attention, I thought she was lying," I continued, shaking my head. "Not Maryse plotting with my captive to expose me. She'd never do that." I leveled my gaze with her widened eyes. "Looks like never actually has a date."

She quickly shook her head. "You don't understand—"

"What don't I understand?" I asked. "That you agreed to help her? That the reason you're in this car right now is to mail the journal she gave you to..." I scanned the front of the package, "CNN?" I let out a low whistle. "That's a good choice if you want the news to go far and wide to take me down."

Tears filled her eyes, which did nothing but piss me off. Apologies spilled from her lips, but we were past that point. Terror filled her voice when I opened my briefcase and pulled out the cord I'd cut from a jump rope.

"Please! It was a lapse of judgment and—"

"And I can't afford to have people around me and my dealings who have these kinds of lapses, Maryse. You know that," I said on a sigh.

She pulled on the door handle to try to open the door but because the child safety lock was activated, it wouldn't open. I took the split second she was turned to wrap the cord around her neck, tightening it as she fought against me. My chest burned as she flailed around.

I usually got a thrill when killing someone with my bare hands, but not this time. Maryse wasn't someone I thought I'd ever have to harm like this. I hated this shit, I hated it for her, but I couldn't save everyone from their own fucked up decisions. She'd fucked up in a way that couldn't be forgiven, and having to do this hurt me just as much as it would hurt her.

I didn't say anything as I strangled her. It was good that she wasn't facing me, as I didn't want to watch the life leave her eyes. The car rocked with her flailing movements, her thrashing and gasping growing weaker until she went limp in my arms. Even when she stopped moving, I didn't release her. My body trembled with anger and grief when her pulse ceased.

"I didn't want to do this, Maryse," I said as my throat burned. "But you left me no choice."

Donovan got in the car and rolled the partition down. "Ready to keep moving?"

I swallowed the grief that tried to choke me before pushing Maryse's lifeless body away from me. "Yeah. Drive around to the pit in the woods."

And as he cut through my property to get to the woods, an untamed hatred grew inside of me. Tonight would be Alyssa's last open hours session with me, and I'd make sure she suffered until she was dead.

CHAPTER SEVENTEEN
LIA

I'd been on pins and needles from the moment I'd given Maryse the journal.

I wanted to be optimistic that she had good intentions, but I couldn't be completely sure. I knew one of two things would happen today. On one hand, she could honestly want to help me and would be able to get the package in the mail so that it could land in the right hands.

But on the other hand, she could either betray me and give the journal to Silas or get caught and killed, which would result in my death as well. The latter outcome scared the hell out of me, but I knew that death would be better than dealing with the abuse ahead of me otherwise.

Maryse had come into my room to wake me up as she usually did, taking the journal from me and slipping it into the deep pocket of her apron. When I didn't see her at breakfast, I figured she was preparing it to be shipped. She'd stopped by my room before she left, giving me one last chance to change my mind.

"Are you sure you want to do this?" she'd asked.

Even though I was scared shitless, I nodded anyway. "Are you sure you want to help me? If you get caught—"

"I can handle Silas," she interrupted. "And he's not here right now." She'd gripped my shoulders and gave me a small smile. "Just continue the day as normal so that no one is suspicious. I'll let you know when I'm back."

But that'd been hours ago.

I did yoga, constantly looking around to see if she'd walk past one of the windows in the house as she cleaned. I'd asked the girls if they knew where she was, but they only told me she was running errands. As the day wound down, I became more and more anxious about where she was, where the journal was, and whether or not she'd fucked me over.

It was a special kind of torture waiting to see if something you knew was wrong actually worked. I wasn't even sure if Maryse had actually left the house, as I had to go back to my room after breakfast and I didn't see her since earlier this morning.

I spent hours pacing in my bedroom, chastising myself for giving her the journal. I should've stuck with original plan of waiting until the wedding so I could give the journal to someone myself. It was always dangerous having other people do things for you, especially when the person worked for the man who put me in this position.

An hour before dinner time, Valorie came to my room. "What would you like for dinner tonight?" she asked.

I stared at her, a bit stunned. In the months I'd been here, I'd never had a choice in what I ate. That alone was a red flag. Maryse had been missing all day and now they were giving me the choice to pick my own food?

"Silas doesn't usually give me a choice," I said with a frown. "Who's asking?"

"The chef, who else?"

I shrugged. "I don't want to get in trouble, so I'll eat whatever Silas told him to make."

"That's the problem; there's nothing on the menu, so the chef doesn't know what to give you. Since Silas is working late and no one can reach him right now, he wanted to ask you."

Though I was wary, I definitely wouldn't pass up the opportunity to finally eat something that I actually wanted. "Well, then I guess I'll have a cheese pizza then," I finally answered.

"I'll let him know."

"Hey, has Maryse returned from her errands yet?" I

asked right before she walked out the door. "I mean, she's been gone all day at this point."

"Why are you so concerned about where Maryse is?"

I swallowed my anxiety. It wasn't like I could tell her that I'd given Maryse my ticket to freedom this morning and she turned into a fucking ghost since then. "It was just a question. She's usually always here and suddenly she's not. Just thought it was strange."

"Maryse's whereabouts aren't your business. One of us will be back to get you when it's time for dinner," she said and left.

I rolled my eyes once she closed the door. "No need to be a fucking bitch about it," I mumbled, flopping down on my bed.

Time dragged by painfully slow, and I was so worked up by the time dinner came around that I couldn't even enjoy the cheesy goodness of the pizza. Silas walked in while I was eating, pausing to look at me.

He held an orange cooler in one hand and a briefcase in the other as he frowned at me. "What the hell are you eating?" he asked.

I stopped chewing and looked toward the kitchen. "They...they asked me what I wanted to eat, so I thought it was fine," I said.

He shook his head. "Whatever. Donovan, come with

me, please," he said and continued on. "And where the hell is Maryse?"

I was actually relieved to hear that he didn't know where she was. This whole time I thought she'd been caught or just hiding from me, but maybe she'd make it after all. Hope and excitement filled my gut as I continued eating. If she had been gone this long, maybe she was taking it somewhere out of town herself, just to make sure it got in the right hands.

Tears of joy threatened to burn my eyes but I had to keep my composure. I didn't want to bring unnecessary attention to myself or make Silas think something was going on if he wasn't already on to me. But I couldn't fight the small grin that rooted itself onto my lips.

I couldn't wait to witness that bastard's life fall apart.

When I finished dinner, Aimee came to take me back to my room. I looked at her in confusion when we walked past it. Open hours wasn't for another hour, and Silas never requested to have me before 8 p.m. I grew nervous as we walked toward the theater room.

"Is he having open hours early tonight?" I asked, my voice wavering with the nerves that bounced around inside of me.

"Oh no, he wants us all to meet him here. I think he wants to figure out where Maryse is or something."

"Does he usually do this?"

"No one has ever gone missing for him to have to do this. It's probably not a big deal, but I hope Maryse is okay wherever she is," she said, pushing open the door to the theater room.

A few security guards were already seated inside, Kora and Valorie sitting in the front row. Silas and Donovan stood at the front of the room in front of the screen, Donovan now holding the orange cooler Silas brought into the house. Aimee led me to the front row and we took our seats, looking to Silas. There was a disposable pad on the floor in front of Silas, which both terrified me and gave me flashbacks of the last time he and I were in here.

"I'm sorry to pull everyone from their duties for this, but this meeting is an important one to have," Silas started. "I want to reiterate that working for me requires confidentiality and loyalty, both of which I take very seriously. Last night, I learned something very unfortunate, something I'm not happy about. Everyone that works for me knows everything I have at stake if certain things were to get out."

It was as if time slowed. My mind raced trying to piece together what he was insinuating, praying that he wasn't referring to me and Maryse. If he knew about us last night, he probably would've killed us both then. But I survived the night and so did Maryse, so did someone else do something to warrant this dramatic speech from him?

"I only let people I trust inside my home, but I'm afraid I trusted the wrong person," Silas continued with a light sigh. "And because of that, I've had to deal with them to eliminate the threat to myself and my business partners."

We all watched as Silas slipped on a pair of gloves and turned to face the cooler, opening it. The girls screamed when he removed Maryse's head, her dead eyes pointed straight ahead. I couldn't even get my mouth to work in order to scream.

"I'm extremely grateful to Kora, who happened to overhear a conversation between Maryse and the conniving bitch I was stupid enough to try to marry," Silas continued, his voice hard as he glared at me. "Once it was brought to my attention, I went back and watched the security footage from your room to witness it myself."

My blood ran cold. How the fuck did I not notice security cameras? They'd never said anything about being able to watch me or anything, so I never bothered looking. The fact that he'd seen it meant there was no way to spin it. If he killed Maryse, someone who'd been with him for years, then I knew I was next. My brain screamed for me to run, but there was nowhere to go. I wouldn't even make it to the door before one of them would shoot me.

"How could you, Kora?!" Valorie screamed, slapping her across the face. Silas moved quicker than lightening, his fist slamming into the side of Valorie's face so hard that the click of her teeth hitting together was audible.

"The better fucking question would be how could *Maryse* do that!" he snapped, standing over her as she sobbed on the floor. "How the fuck could someone I called my mother do that?" He stared at her for a moment, fuming before he took a few steps back. Silas put the head back in the cooler and snatched the gloves off. He reached into the pocket on the inside of his jacket and pulled out my journal. "This is what cost Maryse her life."

"What is that?" one of the men asked from the back of the room.

Silas looked to me. "Why don't you tell them what this is since it's yours?" I willed my body to move, to do something but I was paralyzed with fear. "Don't worry about it, I'll tell them." He opened the journal. "This is a journal Ms. Lia here filled with everything that's happened since she's been here. She wrote about her kidnapping from the precinct, what happened with Maxwell and his family, the abuse she suffered. She sent Maryse on a suicide mission to mail this journal to a major news network to 'expose' me. Isn't that right, Lia?"

The fact that he'd called me by my actual name solidified the fact that I was as good as dead. He'd always called me Alyssa from the moment I was relinquished to him, only calling me Lia before having Raymond punish me.

The evil look in his eyes chilled me to my core, and it was in that moment that I realized I'd made a big fucking mistake. I should've listened to Maryse when she told me I was opening a can of worms I wouldn't be able to close, and now she was dead because of me. From the looks of it, the journal didn't even make it off the property, which meant our plan had failed before she even had a chance to do anything.

The sinking feeling of defeat settled into my stomach as I finally released the breath I didn't realize I was holding. Not only did I fail miserably, but I was also going to die. The journal was now in his possession and would probably be destroyed or locked away, leaving him to continue the cycle long after he got rid of me.

I took a risk and gambled my life and freedom in hopes of making a difference, but I lost. Instead of preventing another woman from going through the same things I had, I'd only given him a reason to make room for another victim.

"Let this be a lesson to all of you," Silas said. "No one is above my rules. Everyone knew how long Maryse had been in my life and that I thought of her as family. If I can do this to her for betraying me, then know that none of you are exempt from my wrath either."

He snapped his fingers to someone in the back of the room. "Take her to the mudroom, please. I want her stripped with her hands tied. Hook her to the chain in the ceiling."

Before I could even react, two men each grabbed an arm and yanked me out of my seat. I fought against them, trying to use their poor grip on my cast to my advantage but it only earned me a solid punch to the gut that knocked the wind of me. They dragged me out of the room as I fought to catch my breath.

Tears leaked from my eyes as we moved closer to the mudroom. I thought about everything that'd happened in my life, always wondering what I'd done to deserve such a painful existence. I survived through so much and fought so hard to make it through my past circumstances, determined to become someone someday. I wanted to look at my success one day and be proud of everything I overcame, wanting to make little Lia proud.

I never thought I went through all of that just for it to end like this.

The men were rough as they stripped me of my clothes and bound my hands together with heavy duty duct tape since I was in a cast. There was no point in fighting anymore. There was nowhere to run, and there was a strong possibility that there were already people outside waiting in the event that I did. I simply stood there and allowed them to secure a chain around the middle of the tape that held my arms above my head. They bound my ankles together with zip ties before leaving me alone in the room. My heart raced in my chest as I closed my eyes, silently sobbing.

All I'd wanted was a different life. I wanted to see if there was really more out there than abuse, pain, and loneliness. I thought stealing money would give me the financial means to get that kind of life. I made so many fucked up decisions chasing something that probably didn't really exist. Happily ever afters were dead and true happiness wasn't real. I spent my entire life chasing behind these things with my hopeful butterfly net, hoping to catch that one butterfly that was the prettiest of all— the butterfly representing love and being wanted.

But once I caught it, the only thing in my net were sharp, tiny shards of colored glass representing shattered hope. I was born and left to face the world alone, and now I'd die alone. If reincarnation was real, maybe I'd get a better shot at doing things right. And if it wasn't, then I'd gladly get off the ride for this part of my life.

Silas stalked into the room, holding some kind of tool in his hand. He stood across from me without a word for a few moments, his expression hard as he regarded me.

"I have to give it to you," he said with a sigh. "Had Kora not come to me last night with what she'd heard, you and Maryse would've gotten away with your little plan."

His words brought fresh tears to my eyes. To know we

were so close and could've survived this if we'd been more careful was devastating to hear. I almost wanted to break free long enough to kill Kora myself, the fucking snitch.

"I'll also say that you're the first woman who has managed to make me feel things," he said. "I spent most of my life feeling numb to a lot of things before you came around, but you brought a few things to life for me."

"Then you shouldn't get rid of me," I suggested. "There are so many things out there for you to feel and—"

"You made me realize how addicted I was to causing you pain," he said, lifting his arm. I gasped as pain filled my thigh when the machine went off. I looked down to see the head of a nail protruding from my skin. Blood rolled down my leg from the wound as I looked back to him with wide eyes. "You made me realize that it's not the act of sex I actually enjoy, but the pain I cause during it." He shot me again, higher up on the same thigh. My scream filled the room as my thigh burned. He fired two more shots that hit my arm, one of the nails going through my cast and right into my arm.

"Please!" I begged, but it was as if I were talking to a brick wall. His expression was blank as he moved closer to me, the nail gun still pointing at me.

"Because of you, I've had to kill the only person I knew who genuinely loved and cared for me. All because she let you get into her fucking head." A choked scream left my lips when he fired a nail into my stomach. "I have no idea why I thought you were the solution to my problem. I should've put a bullet in your head the minute you arrived."

Pain blinded me as he released four more nails that hit various places on my body, my vision swimming as nausea overwhelmed me. His voice seemed as if it were moving far away as the room spun around me. Had it not been for the chain holding me upright, I was sure I'd have fallen on the ground.

As he continued piercing my skin with more nails, I thought back to everything that'd happened in my life. Regardless of what anyone said, I knew I did my best with what I had. I didn't have a perfect life, but I never gave up when there were plenty of times I wanted to.

I closed my eyes as I mentally apologized to myself. I deserved so much better but never gave myself a chance. I put myself in fucked up relationships when I knew they weren't right for me. I made fucked up decisions when I knew they weren't good for me. I'd failed myself time and time again, my life ending before I truly had a chance to live it.

I'm sorry I never reached my full potential. I'm sorry I failed.

And then the world around me faded to black.

I was finally free.

CHAPTER EIGHTEEN
SILAS

I stared at Lia's lifeless body as she continued hanging from the chain.

She was filled with nails, the kill shot being five nails through her heart. I stood unmoving long after Donovan came in and confirmed she no longer had a pulse, long after a few of the men took her down and wrapped her up in the plastic she stood on. None of this felt real. It was as if I were having a fucked up out-of-body experience now that the adrenaline of everything had worn off.

It wasn't until Donovan clasped my shoulder and shook me slightly. "You still here, man?" he asked, concern etching his features. I blinked, turning to face him as I nodded.

"Yeah, I'm good," I said with a sigh.

"Well, Ansley's here," he said, just as the police chief walked into the mudroom. He looked down at the plastic-wrapped body on the floor and frowned.

"What the hell happened here, Arnett?" he asked.

"I eliminated a major threat," I muttered. I gave him the run down of the events that lead up to this, showing him the journal as well. Even as I recounted what happened, it still didn't feel real. A part of me thought I'd leave the mudroom to see Maryse somewhere else in the house, but I couldn't allow myself to live in delusion. I knew she was dead. It hurt that she was, but I knew it was necessary.

Chief Ansley looked down at the body with a sigh. "We'll get this cleaned up for you," he said. "I'll let the warden at the prison know of her status so that he can update her record there."

"Thanks," I said idly.

He patted my shoulder before he and a couple of officers grabbed the body and left the room, leaving me with Donovan. He moved to stand closer to me.

"You know you did the right thing, Si. You can't beat yourself up about it."

"I'm not." I put my hands in my pockets. "It's just unfortunate about Maryse."

"It is, but it's just a lesson that anyone can turn on you

at any point. You can never get too comfortable with people."

"Yeah, I know."

As I made my way back to my office, I passed the girls, who sat on the couch. Valorie and Aimee were inconsolable, Kora sitting in another chair alone crying softly. It was already weird without Maryse being here, but after her betrayal, I wasn't even sure if I wanted the other women here.

Women were too easily swayed with their emotions, which led to Maryse's demise. If this situation taught me anything, it was the fact that I didn't want to get married after all. None of this shit was worth the headache it caused in the end. I'd spent all that money on this woman just to have it go to waste. But I couldn't risk her manipulating someone else to do her bidding. As bad as I wanted to keep her around just to torture her for the rest of her days, I couldn't risk her trying something like that again.

I sat at my desk and opened the journal. I read through the entries, cringing at the detail she used to describe some things. Had this gotten to its destination, I would've been ruined. To see how close I was to destruction was sickening. Now I had to deal with the public talking about my failed engagement and what went wrong.

Pulling out my phone, I sent Jerry a quick text.

Silas: You can cancel all arrangements for this wedding. It's no longer happening.

His reply was swift.

**J. Kingston: Oh no! Should we just move the date?
Silas: No. I no longer have a bride.**

I put my phone on silent just as he called me, sending him to voicemail as I closed my eyes with a sigh. I gave her six months to become the perfect wife for me, but she failed. I gave her every tool she needed to be successful, but she still failed. At one point, I thought she had promise and would actually make it, but she barely made it four months. Now I was back to square one, but I was no longer in the mood to deal with whipping another woman in shape for marriage.

Donovan knocked on my door before stepping in. "Ansley and his crew just left with the body. Do you want one of the guys to take Maryse's head to the fire pit with the rest of her body?"

I nodded. "Might as well."

"So, where do you go from here?" he asked. "Are you starting the search again or giving up on the plan entirely?"

I sighed deeply. "I'm not bothering with this marriage

shit. Going through it with Lia just made me realize it was a bad decision in the first place. I can only pretend for so long, and I don't want a repeat of what happened tonight."

"I'm sure there's someone you can pay to give you a kid," he said with a shrug.

"Of course there is." I ran a hand down my face. "But at the moment, I need to lay low for a bit. I can't just announce I'm having a baby via surrogate when my engagement just fell apart."

"True."

I opened the journal and began ripping the pages out, pushing them through the paper shredder. For now, I'd bide my time and do damage control to fix the fuck up I allowed to happen. This time, I needed to be smart. I got lucky this time, but it wasn't a guarantee that I'd be this lucky again.

And as I shredded away the evidence Lia left behind, I shook off the negative shit that plagued my mind and prepared myself for the new journey ahead. The road to marriage might've crumbled away, but I'd get the male heir I was ultimately after.

"Get Jalen and Tommy on the phone. I have a job for them," I said after I'd shredded the last entry.

Donovan looked at me with a raised brow. "For another wife?"

"No, a potential surrogate," I said. "I won't be ready for her for a few months, but considering their track record when I was in search of a wife, I feel like they need a head start."

He chuckled and nodded. "I'll let them know," he said before he disappeared.

I tossed the empty journal into the trash can next to my desk. Now it was time to prepare for round two.

Let the search begin.

ABOUT THE AUTHOR

Tori Sullivan is an erotic horror author writing dark stories where happily ever afters come to die and the villains always wins. When she's not writing, you can find her listening to true crime podcasts, reading, and avoiding social situations.

———

Be sure to visit the new home of Ember Michaels and Tori Sullivan at Tainted Halo Press!

ALSO BY TORI SULLIVAN

Made in the USA
Monee, IL
16 May 2025

17575517R00249